The Devil's Concubine

Jill Braden

WAYZGOOSE PRESS

Publisher of quality genre fiction and literary non-fiction

THE DEVIL'S CONCUBINE

Copyright © 2013 by Jill Braden

Published in the United States by Wayzgoose Press.
Edited by Dorothy E. Zemach.
Maps by Will Mitchell.
Cover design by DJ Rogers.

Printed in the United States

ISBN-10: 1938757076

ISBN-13: 978-1-938757-07-5

This is a work of fiction. Names, characters, places, brands, media, and incidents are either the product of the author's imagination or are used fictitiously.

TABLE OF CONTENTS

THE SEA OF ERYKOLI

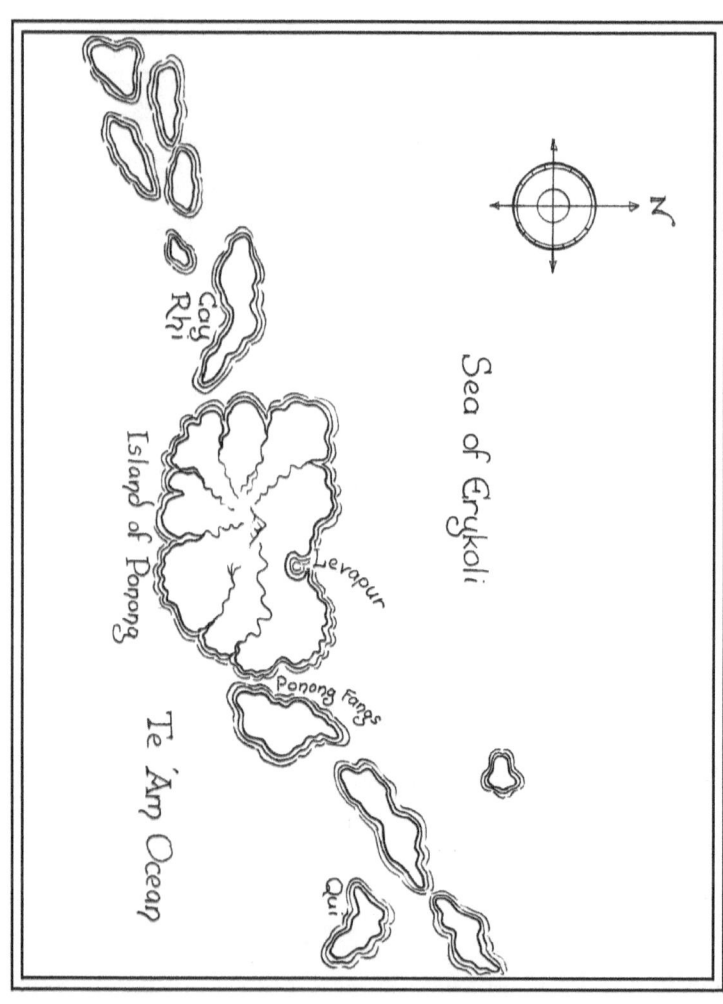

THE ISLAND OF PONONG

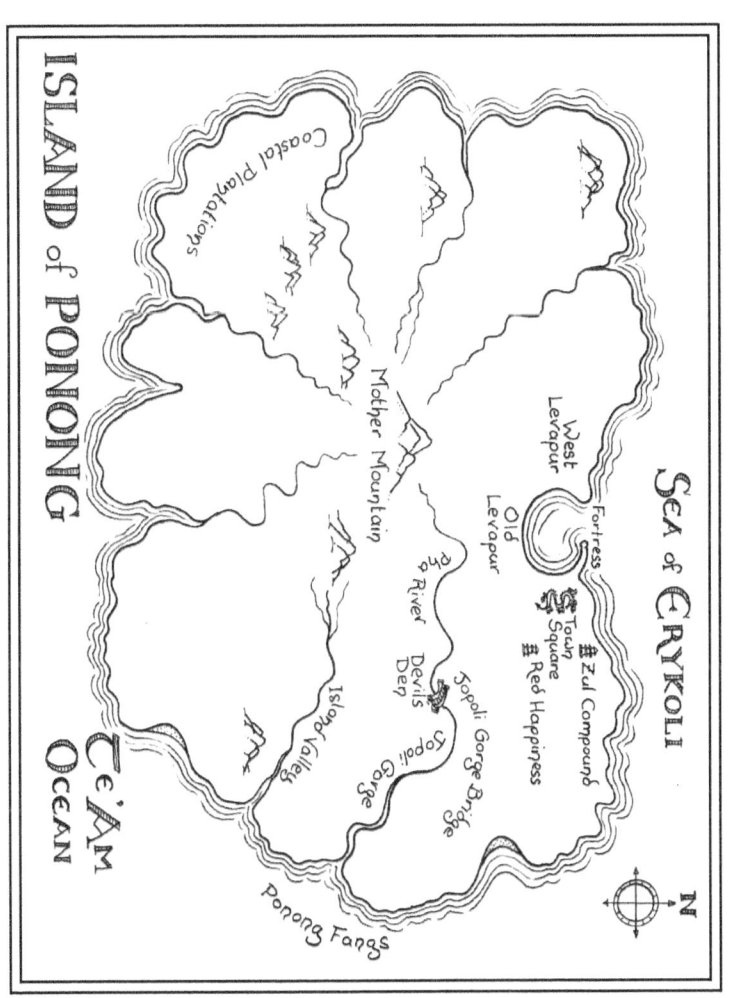

CHAPTER I: QUITAI

*L*ike a school of jewel-toned tropical fish on the reef, the crowd in the marketplace suddenly veered away as QuiTai stepped off the veranda of the sunset-pink building into the town square. They cringed back as she sauntered through the stalls, as if instead of her bright green sarong she were clothed in poison. She'd decided long ago it was their guilt that made them unable to meet her gaze, not judgment. The Devil's concubine had nothing to be ashamed of.

Further inland, the remains of Typhoon DirAmat still hung heavily in the air, but here the cooling breeze off the Sea of Erykoli tousled the prayer flags strung over of the market stalls. The sing-song voices of Ponongese women who balanced wide baskets of wares on their head rose above the din in a familiar chorus of "Mangos! Roasted jikal roots!" The scent of hot oil wafting from a tamtuk stand made QuiTai's stomach growl.

A big hand clamped onto QuiTai's shoulder. She knew from the chipped fingernails and hairy knuckles it was Casmir. Her nose wrinkled. She tried to shove his hand away, but his fingers dug into her collar bone.

"The Devil wants you," Casmir said.

She turned her head to look up at him. She glanced at his hand and then raised her gaze slowly to his face again. He let go of her.

Casmir could have been chipped from the granite Alps of his homeland by a sculptor inspired by the mythic heroes. Like his face, his voice seemed to have been cut from rock. Most of the werewolves in the Devil's pack had a brooding, wild man allure, but few had Casmir's extra spark of malevolence. His homespun shirt pulled tight over his muscles. Sweat stains darkened his collar. Hairy barbarians from the northernmost realm of the continent, the werewolves had never adapted to the humid heat of Ponong.

Ivitch, a taller, younger man with sparse facial hair and no chin, slunk into QuiTai's sight. When Ivitch had come to the island with the Devil, the bloom of youth had still been on his cheeks. Now he was old enough to have the beginnings of a moustache, but the wisps did not cover his mouth, which often hung open. Even with his facial hair filled in like the rest of the Devil's werewolves, QuiTai didn't think he'd look any smarter. The stupidity reached all the way up to his eyes. She had to keep reminding herself that even stupid people could cause a hell of a lot of trouble when they wanted to, and Ivitch always did.

Although they were Rujicks, in Levapur the Devil's men were known only as werewolves. While few people on Ponong could point to Rujick on a map of the continent, they knew exactly what a werewolf was and why it should be feared. That suited the Devil just fine.

The hairs on QuiTai's arms rose as a low growl rumbled from Ivitch's chest. She scanned the crowd around them for signs of trouble, but saw nothing that might have angered him.

"Snake eyes make my skin crawl," Ivitch muttered.

The Ponongese's vertical pupils, surrounded by thin bands of bright yellow, often startled visitors to the islands, but the werewolves should have been used to them by now. And Ivitch should have known better than to call her people snakes. She let her inner eyelid lower. The bright colors of the marketplace dimmed as her vision clouded.

Ivitch shuddered and looked away.

A satisfied smile curved the corners of her mouth.

"You heard me. The Devil says to come. Now," Casmir ordered.

QuiTai flicked her long, black braid over her narrow shoulder and headed for the nearest tamtuk stand. Even though Ivitch and Casmir growled, she bought one of the fried dough balls. As her teeth cracked the golden crust, spicy steam curled up to her nose. She strolled through the spice merchants' stalls below the stairs of the Thampurian government building while she savored the pork and rice stuffing.

The Devil – she rarely allowed herself to think of his real name in public – would be furious that she'd kept him waiting. While she knew she should have immediately returned to his den with Casmir and Ivitch, something gave her pause. This close to a full moon, she and the Devil didn't usually talk. Why did he want to see her? The question paced fretfully on the edge of her thoughts like a hungry street cur.

As she licked the last salty crumb of tamtuk from her fingers, she headed for the jellylantern merchant's stall. The light in the Devil's den had grown so dim in the past few weeks that she could barely see inside, which was perhaps more of a blessing than a curse, but nonetheless someone had to buy them. She lifted a jellylantern to inspect the tiny bioluminescent medusozoa floating in the glass tube. She turned it to the light and gave the tube a gentle flick. A few dead creatures settled to the bottom. The delicate, transparent bodies of the live ones glowed faint green.

"The price went up again?" she asked the merchant.

Color rose in his cheeks and he lowered his chin so that he seemed to answer his rounded belly instead of her. "It's typhoon season. Shipping rates always go up."

"Ridiculous, considering we raise the medusozoa right here on Ponong."

The merchant said nothing. He'd probably had this argument with too many customers. It wasn't his fault the occupying Thampurian government had made it illegal to sell the harvest to anyone but the Thampurian-owned medusozoa monopoly. It wasn't his fault that half the harvest died on the long ocean voyage back to Thampur, where the jellylanterns were manufactured, or that the people of Ponong had to pay shipping both ways. It was the price they paid for being a colony. And paid. And paid. In land, in coin, in justice.

QuiTai scanned the crowd. Shoppers seemed to have sudden urgent business elsewhere as Casmir and Ivitch, lured by the scent of blood, wandered to a butcher's stall several yards from the jellylantern seller. Soon there were no other shoppers to be seen. The men were too far away for her to hear their conversation, but the butcher clearly didn't want werewolves rubbing their noses against the pigs' heads hanging from his awning.

Still scanning, she turned in the other direction. Her expression hardened the moment she glimpsed the Thampurian spy Kyam Zul standing among the wide, spreading limbs of the banyan tree across the town square. He seemed to be trying to hide, which was ridiculous: his broad shoulders and height set him a head higher than most Ponongese.

Of course Kyam had to ruin her afternoon. He was always the mosquito in the dark room.

As usual, he was between shaves, and his glossy straight black hair fell into his eyes. From the distance, his thigh-length shewani jacket and tight trousers seemed impeccable, although she knew up close she'd see frayed hems and missing buttons. None of that diminished his good looks, which only irritated her more.

While she couldn't hold the jellylantern merchant responsible for the price of jellylanterns, she was more than willing to point the finger at Kyam Zul and all his kind. As a scion of one of the privileged thirteen families of Thampur, he shared their blame. His grandfather was one of the thieves who had stolen her country from her people.

Kyam stopped a boy playing tag around the banyan tree and spoke urgently to the squirming child. His gaze met

QuiTai's before he looked away.

The jellylantern merchant cleared his throat. She turned back to him.

"How much for the blue light ones?" she asked.

He named a staggering price.

QuiTai carefully stacked tubes of expired green jellylanterns on his counter with a rueful shake of her head. Yelling at him wouldn't solve anything, even if it would make her feel better. "More green, then. What are you giving for the old tubes?"

"Same as always."

She clenched her jaw. "At least give me fresh ones. There are too many sinkers in these."

Perhaps if she were not the Devil's concubine, he might have told her in rough language where she could take her business. Instead, he opened a crate in the back of his stall and put twelve strong green jellylanterns on the counter. She counted out the coins and gently placed the tubes into her basket.

A sweaty little hand pressed something scratchy into her palm and then tugged on her sarong. She looked down into the yellow-ringed eyes of the boy she'd seen with Kyam.

"Pui, auntie?" His front teeth were almost too big for his mouth, and he smelled of salted earth, as if he'd been playing hard in the sun all day.

Her breath caught. Despite the heat, icy fear shot through her. She glanced quickly at Casmir and Ivitch. Their backs were to her as they held a dripping pig's liver high above the butcher's reach.

Surely someone had warned the boy to stay far away from werewolves. Unfortunately, he was at that age when boys were fascinated by the things that scared them. She quickly handed him a coin and pushed him away. "Go, before the Devil's werewolves see you, little brother."

His eyes widened as his smile faded.

She shielded him from Ivitch and Casmir's sight as she shoved him again, harder. "Obey auntie." She meant to sound terse, but a warble of fear made it more of a plea.

A woman with a basket of fish yanked the boy's arm and

dragged him further away from Casmir and Ivitch. When she let go, an old man weaving straw hats urgently beckoned the boy to duck into his stall. From across the square, Kyam Zul nodded curtly at QuiTai and then disappeared behind the banyan tree.

Their sport with the butcher over, Casmir and Ivitch headed toward her.

Even though the boy was gone, her pulse still raced. She hoped the slight tremor in her hands wasn't noticeable as she put the last of the tubes into her basket.

"That better be the last of your errands," Ivitch said.

QuiTai tucked a cloth around the jellylanterns so they wouldn't clank together. A broken tube couldn't be returned for credit.

Followed by the werewolves, she walked past the bank and cafés where the business district gave way to a residential neighborhood. The noise and scents of the marketplace grew fainter as the hush of wealth enveloped her. The limbs of tall trees formed a shady canopy over the dirt road as the tropical sun beat on the low tile roofs of the houses behind their compound walls. She shook her head at the stupidity. Leave it to Thampurians to get things so entirely wrong. They seemed to think they still lived in their blustery capital.

"What did that brat want?" Casmir asked.

Despite her alarm, QuiTai shrugged. "Pui."

Ivitch chuckled. "You should have let us have him."

It felt as if he'd plunged his fist into her chest, but she drew air deep into her lungs as if it were perfumed.

A few servants walked on the wide lane between the compounds, but they were far away. The Thampurian neighborhood slumbered through the afternoon heat.

She took her time looking at their surroundings and sighed with great satisfaction. "I love this part of the city. So private; and yet, still close to the marketplace." She opened her mouth and let her fangs spring forward. Never one to waste what she might need later, she held back the flow of venom, but the werewolves wouldn't know her fangs were dry.

The color faded from Casmir's face. He walked away quickly. She pressed her fangs back against the roof of her mouth then followed at a slower pace. Ivitch fell behind her.

When both men were at a distance, she unfolded the note from Kyam. Only a Thampurian would use such fine stationery for a clandestine note.

Mister Zul asked that she hire him to paint her portrait and suggested they meet at the Red Happiness. His words were amusingly polite, given that he was asking to meet her at a brothel. If he thought she would be insulted by the implication that she was a whore, he was wrong.

While at first glance it seemed a simple enough request, QuiTai and Kyam Zul both operated in a world beneath the surface. She found his note rather cryptic. Normally people begged her to plead with the Devil on their behalf, but he'd called for the Devil's arrest too many times to dare beg for that kind of favor. No, Kyam Zul wanted to discuss something with her. How intriguing. If he'd resorted to asking his biggest enemy in Levapur for a favor, he must be desperate.

Desperate enough to send a child within a few feet of the werewolves. The bastard.

The werewolves had been too far away to see the boy slip the note into her hand, but it would be best to be rid of it before they arrived at the Devil's den. She tore the thick stationery into tiny pieces and dropped them one by one into murky puddles left behind from the monsoon rains. If Ivitch saw them fluttering to her feet like night spirit moths, he didn't say anything.

What was Kyam up to?

She shook her head. She couldn't dwell on Kyam's note; she had to prepare herself to face the Devil.

The town of Levapur clung to the edge of a cliff high above a turquoise harbor on the Sea of Erykoli. The narrow band of flat land close to the cliff edge had been seized by the

Thampurians colonists. Beyond their compounds, the hillside began a steep ascent to the Ponongese neighborhoods. Past the buildings, the cloud-cloaked mountains of the interior range rose to sharp peaks.

The border between the jungle and Levapur was indistinguishable in places. Troops of monkeys and lizards and colonies of bats lived as comfortably in town as outside it. Brightly plumaged jungle fowl scattered as QuiTai walked through the small flock foraging in deep weeds between two apartment buildings. She hoisted the hem of her sarong above the deep, meandering rut of orange slurry that ran sluggishly downslope. When monsoon rains fell, the tiny trickle became a river.

Casmir huffed as he led the way through the increasingly steep alleys.

Her shoulder blades itched every time Ivitch grunted behind her. She hated being followed. They did it for their safety, not hers. She couldn't decide if that amused or annoyed her. As they climbed upslope through the alleyways, the space between the buildings became too narrow to walk side by side, but even where the gaps widened neither of the men drew closer to her.

Finally, the hills grew so steep that they had to leave the alleys and take the road that climbed the hillside in sharp switchbacks.

By the time QuiTai and her silent escorts neared the stone bridge over the Jupoli Gorge, the closely packed buildings of Levapur had given way to lush plants. Pink blossoms the size of her hand fell from overhead to cover the path with wilting petals. Although shaded, the torpid air under the jungle canopy was much hotter than in town, so thick with humidity that it felt like a weight against her chest.

Far below the stone bridge, the Pha River churned between narrow limestone cliffs. Anyone foolish or unlucky enough to fall into the river would be swept several miles downstream by the torrent before hurtling off a cliff and dropping three hundred yards into the treacherous waters of the Ponong Fangs, where the Sea of Erykoli met the Te'Am Ocean.

Over the sound of the water thundering through the gorge, she could hear the chug of the steam engine at the base station of the funicular that ran in stages up the steep mountainside to the plantation terraces carved into its slopes. Before she reached the station plateau, she veered from the upslope road onto a narrow path that ran along the southern rim of the gorge. She went around a stand of banana trees and stepped onto a wide timbergrass bridge that jogged left, right, and then left again to thwart demons and spirits who could only travel in straight lines.

She heard Ivitch step onto the bridge behind her as she passed through a vine-covered moon gate. Then he shouldered past her, knocking her hard enough that she had to grab the bridge railing.

The werewolves threatened and blustered, but knew better than to take their posturing beyond that. She had the Devil's protection, and she was his most ruthless weapon against any werewolf who dared challenge his authority.

The scent of damp dogs and mold hit QuiTai's nose as she entered the Devil's house. She was glad that he didn't insist that she live with the pack. The feeling, she knew, was mutual.

The clatter of tiles came from a corner where four men sat around a game table. Another dozen large hairy men slumped on stained sleeping couches, as if drunk on humidity. They panted in the stifling atmosphere but didn't dare open the windows to allow the breeze to flow through. Yet something had changed in the den. The men didn't bicker. They lolled on the furniture as if a collective sigh of relief had eased their tension; and yet, eerie discomfort prickled over her as it did when the jungle went suddenly silent. What they waited for was a mystery to her.

The pack slowly came to their feet as QuiTai stumbled over a pair of muddy boots abandoned in the middle of the floor. She could feel their low growls creep over her skin. The men circled and sniffed, a habit that grated on her nerves. After two years, she'd have thought they would have grown used to her, but some races could never overcome the primal fear her scent and fangs evoked. Not to mention the more specific reason they had to fear and hate her.

"Slayer," a narrow-eyed wolf spat dry, as if he wouldn't even waste fluids on her.

She placed the fresh jellylanterns around the room in their wall holders; when the room was illuminated, she almost wished she hadn't. Beer bottles, muddy clothes, and bones littered the floor. That didn't surprise her. She'd seen their stone fortresses back in their mountainous homeland Rujick, and understood why their women lived in their own keeps.

"I smell QuiTai. Don't keep me waiting any longer, woman," a deep male voice barked from behind a sliding door at the far end of the room. The door panels had once been rice paper, to allow light between the two rooms, but were now been boarded over.

She raised an eyebrow to the men who still circled her. The pack parted.

She left the sliding door open when she entered the Devil's chamber.

The room had once opened onto a deck that cantilevered over the Jupoli Gorge, offering breathtaking views of the Pha River below and the waterfalls thundering off the opposite canyon wall. QuiTai had stood there to marvel as clouds of iridescent blue butterflies clung to treetops and flocks of bright birds flew past. Occasionally, a troop of monkeys would climb the long, thick stilts that secured the house to the hillside to play on the deck until the scent of the werewolves scared them away.

But a few months after the full moon massacre, the Thampurian soldiers had captured Petrof during a hunt and dragged him down to their fortress. Four agonizing days later he limped back to his den. He never said what happened, but in the past year, the doors to the deck had been shut off with thick wood screens, then covered with blinds, and finally boarded over. The ocean breeze no longer penetrated the stuffy room, but beams of sunlight squeezed between the warped window boards. Motes of dust drifted through them and disappeared into the deep shadows.

Casmir and Ivitch followed QuiTai as far as the open door. It was odd that the others didn't press close to steal a glimpse of their leader like they usually did.

A shadowy figure on an ornately carved, high-backed chair at the far end of the room stirred.

The power of his presence flooded through her as it always did. She felt so alive with him. He was impossible to please, but she alone shared his most private side.

"I sent Casmir and Ivitch to fetch you over an hour ago," Petrof said. He leaned forward into a faltering ray of light. Blond highlights glinted in his red beard. Thick, dark auburn chest hair curled over his shirt collar. Much brawnier than the average Ponongese, his build was almost lithe for a werewolf. He was not the largest of the pack, but he was the most cunning, and by far the cruelest.

"Your business required my attention, Petrof."

His eyes narrowed. Good. She wasn't the only person in the house who knew the Devil's real name, but only she dared to use it.

"The way she defies you, she must think she's in charge around here," Casmir said.

"Remind her of her place," Ivitch said.

She knelt beside Petrof's throne on a thick maroon carpet. His red-rimmed eyes had gone feral, never a good sign. The moon was already in him even though it was not yet full. Flies buzzed over the remains of a meal left on the floor. The scent of mountain trails and blood clung to his skin. Fear stole her breath. Had he worked up the courage to leave his room? She paused to gather control over her voice before speaking.

His hand shot out. Ragged nails scraped QuiTai's throat. He came to his feet and lifted her by her throat as he growled. From the corner of her eye, she saw Casmir and Ivitch laughing at the threshold of the room.

Petrof bared his teeth at them. The crushing pressure on her neck increased. He'd grasped her throat many times, but this was different. Panic spiked through her. His big hand could easily crush her neck, and he always kept his elbow stiff so that she couldn't lunge at him with her fangs and inject her poison into him.

"Petrof... there's a disturbing rumor that independent smugglers brought a shipment onto the island," she croaked.

He slowly sank back into his seat, but didn't release her. He focused on her face again. She said, "Smugglers who dare to openly challenge your power."

"What did they bring?" Petrof asked.

She swallowed against the pressure of his hand. "Rumor says a few big crates, but no one seems sure. I've told all my sources to bring me news."

His grip tightened. "Who are they? Did they bring it in through the harbor, or did they use one of the coves?"

QuiTai coughed as her lips tingled. He eased his hold enough that she could gasp fresh air into her bursting lungs. "That, also, I do not know," she was finally able to say.

"She's wasting your time," Ivitch said to Petrof.

QuiTai wished she had shut the door. "Someone dared to challenge the Devil. Rumors now are as elusive as maishun spirits, but as with any good tale, they will be repeated, and someone will remember something they saw. We will find these smugglers and make examples of them."

Ivitch snorted. "She acts like they're smoke wraiths."

"Answers don't simply come to me. I have to hunt them down." She gave the wolves a challenging stare. "You understand," she said.

"Kill her now." Ivitch reached for the doorjamb and leaned over the threshold into the room.

The low rumble of Petrof's growl made QuiTai's hairs stand on end. She made an effort not to show it. "Ivitch, if you have the names of the smugglers, tell us. Better yet, bring them before our master. But remember: the last time you chased monkeys up a tree, they flung their shit at you."

Petrof chuckled, and his grasp on QuiTai's throat finally dropped. She laughed too: it was always safest to match his moods. Since he'd shut himself away from the world, he'd become even more unpredictable.

Ivitch stepped back. He might be stupid, but he had at least the sense to rein himself in. After the last killing, no one dared enter the Devil's private chamber without his permission.

QuiTai picked up one of the bones on the rug near her with her thumb and forefinger. A scrap of bloody sinew dangled off the end. She tossed it onto a brass tray and reached for another. Clouds of flies spiraled up and then returned to crawl over the grisly pile.

"Information will cost money, Petrof."

"The Devil takes money; he doesn't give," Petrof said.

"Think of it as an investment," she said.

"I said no. Don't try to use your wiles to make me change my mind."

It always amazed QuiTai that he had no idea how his own syndicate worked. Every time she was forced to use her own coin to keep his business running, she resented it a little more. If only he'd stop hoarding his fortune.

She forced herself not to glance at the wall behind Petrof's messy bed. What appeared to be an intricate wood mosaic beyond the mosquito netting was actually a puzzle. With the right moves, the center of the design would open, revealing his safe. Over time, she'd worked out the complex sequence of sliding pieces, but the biolock inside could only be opened by the touch of his fingertips. If she ever figured out how to break that lock, she'd pay herself back the thousands of coins that the Devil owed her.

Her temper flared. Usually she had no problem controlling it, but for the past week she'd been restless and couldn't seem to quash her rebellious thoughts. Worse than not understanding his own business, Petrof didn't understand her. He demanded her advice but never respected it. It had always been so; but now she sensed that their long alliance was strained to the point of breaking.

She could survive without him if he cast her aside. But it would be difficult to find a lover to replace him. There was something addictive about bedding someone so dangerous, even though it was foolishness to let her desires overrule her brain.

And the idea of the Devil was as important to her future plans as was the actual man. Sometimes even more important.

Until then, she hadn't been sure whether she would answer Kyam Zul's note. Now she realized how much she needed a brief escape from the werewolves. She might not like Kyam, but at least he could argue with her without getting violent. And he was always interesting.

She forced her voice in a casual, light tone and said, "On an unrelated note, I've decided to hire that itinerant Thampurian artist to paint my portrait."

"The good-looking one?" Ivitch asked.

She didn't dare show how furious she was with him. Had he seen Kyam in the marketplace? Maybe Ivitch simply remembered seeing him around Levapur, or had witnessed one of their verbal battles.

The Devil's eyes narrowed. "QuiTai?"

"Ivitch seems to fancy him." She forced a blatantly fake yet innocent smile.

"I like Thampurians less than you do," Ivitch said.

"Not possible."

"What does he look like?" Petrof asked.

QuiTai tossed the furry skull left over from Petrof's dinner onto the tray and wiped her hand on the carpet. "He's a typical Thampurian snob. Surely you've seen him."

"You know I haven't left this room for over a year."

So he didn't want her to know that he'd conquered his fear of the world outside long enough to leave his den. He was the only person she knew who had ever left the fortress alive, but something horrible had happened behind those stone walls, something bad enough to make a werewolf too scared to hunt with his pack – until now. Maybe enough time had passed that his terror had faded. Or perhaps that fear had never been real; she had only his word for it.

Perhaps he thought she still accepted the common wisdom that werewolves could only shift under a full moon. In the years they'd been together, she'd figured out the wolves could shift anytime they wished. That was fair; she had secrets from him too. She hoped hers weren't as easy to figure out.

Petrof's glazed eyes moved from Ivitch to QuiTai. "I don't like you being alone with anyone."

"In his bedroom," Ivitch said.

Ivitch, she decided, should have a fatal accident – and soon.

QuiTai peered into the gloom over Petrof's shoulder. For now, she'd drop the issue of the portrait. Eventually, she'd convince him, or she'd find another way to meet Kyam Zul. For some perverse reason, she felt that she had to talk to the Thampurian. As if it were fated.

"QuiTai!" Petrof snapped.

She knew now how sea captains felt as they negotiated the treacherous currents of the Ponong Fangs, the only deep water passage in the Ponong Archipelago that linked the Sea of Erykoli to the Te'Am Ocean. As with the Fangs, there was only one safe path through this conversation. One false step, one wrong word, could spell disaster. Whatever Kyam wanted from her, he had better be prepared to pay handsomely for it, because she would surely pay a price herself for meeting him.

"Why don't you accompany me then, Ivitch? If Mister Zul acts improperly, you can rip out his throat."

Ivitch tugged on his attempt at a beard. "You think I'm stupid? If I do that, the Thampurians will know a werewolf killed him. I'd strangle him so they wouldn't know who to hang."

"How very cunning of you. Did you come up with that on your own, or did you have help?"

"The Devil told us – "

"Shut up, Ivitch!" Petrof said.

There were times when it was safer to act as if she hadn't heard anything. "If you're against the idea, Petrof, I won't have him paint my portrait. It was a whim, one that I can easily forget." She shrugged, as if it were of no concern.

"Is he handsome?"

She held back a sigh. Once Petrof fixed on an idea, he rarely let it go. It was better to be truthful, in case he had seen Kyam. "The sea dragons are an attractive race, when they aren't sneering. He's tall and broad-shouldered. His face is not so plain as to be ordinary, but not too pretty either. He keeps healthy and fit. Is that what you wanted to hear?"

Petrof lunged from his chair, took her down, pinned her to the carpet. His nose bumped hers. "Keep taunting me and one day you'll regret it, you cold-blooded bitch."

The game between them had begun as it always did.

A grin slowly spread across her face as desire for him welled through her body. His big hands crushed her thin wrists. He didn't rub or grind against her, but the anticipation had both of them breathing hard. Petrof was dangerous and unpredictable, traits she knew she should despise, but she'd developed a taste for the edge he brought to the bed.

"It's my nature to be cruel," she said.

Petrof stroked her hair. His lips pressed close to her ear. "Yes, my little avenging demon, you did warn me when we first met." His fingers clutched her hair. "How I wish I could see your mind working. I imagine it's a sliding puzzle with thousands of little moving pieces."

"Crack her head open and find out," Ivitch said.

Petrof's growl rumbled through the room. If Ivitch had been smart, he would have closed the door and walked away. "Leave them alone now," Casmir told Ivitch as he reached for the door. "The master will decide when the time is right."

Ivitch shoved him back. Casmir leapt onto him and dragged him to the ground. She heard furniture knock over. Petrof flinched when the wall between the rooms shook from the impact of a body against it. Soon the pack was merrily brawling.

"Click, clack. I can hear the gears in your mind whirling from here, QuiTai. Why are you quiet?" Petrof asked.

"It's hard to appreciate your touch with the boys roughhousing in the next room."

Petrof grinned as she struggled to free her wrist from his grasp. Finally, he let go. "Your tale of smugglers had better be true."

"Send your pack to question their dealers. Someone will fetch the same rumor I heard."

Suspicion lingered in his eyes, but he rolled off her. "Close the door, woman. The moon isn't the only stirring in my blood."

Petrof sank onto the small stool in the bathing chamber with a drawn-out sigh. QuiTai dipped a sponge into soapy water and scrubbed mud smears from his neck. Dark auburn hair covered his muscular chest, thighs, and back.

"I assume from the state of your floor that you've eaten," she said.

"The pack hunted for me."

The dirty suds trailing down his wide shoulders told a different story. She didn't mind that he lied to her. She wasn't even offended that the pack kept secrets from her. They were his men, not hers. They made their loyalties clear in any number of ways, including making sure that no one else on the island dared sell black lotus to the Devil's concubine.

Petrof captured QuiTai's hand and brought it to his lips as he twisted around to face her. "You're quiet. When you're quiet, it means you're thinking, and when you think, wise men reach for weapons."

"I'm thinking about the smugglers." One lie in exchange for another.

"I want results."

He tugged her close as he stood. She felt him stir against her. His wet hand grasped her bottom. She closed her eyes as his beard scraped her cheek.

"I have further business tonight," she said.

"With whom?"

"No one in particular. It's just that something feels odd in town, but I can't put my finger on what it is. I'm... if I observe, maybe it will come to me. I don't know. It's so elusive that I can't even be sure that it's real."

That was the part that bothered her most. A faint suspicion that Kyam Zul was somehow involved flitted on the edge of her thoughts. It could simply be coincidence that he turned to her now; but she did not believe in coincidence.

QuiTai slightly shook her head. Kyam was the last person she wanted to think about when she was with her lover.

"You're imagining things," Petrof said.

If it wasn't something he could touch, he decided it didn't exist. She knew better. "It might be important," she said.

"Does it have anything to do with the smugglers?"

"I'm sure you're smart enough to figure that out."

He released her from his hold. "When you flatter me, I instinctively check my balls, and then my safe."

QuiTai gave him a playful push. "Now who is flattering whom?"

Petrof rubbed his head with a towel until his hair stood up in spikes. He wiped water drops from his thighs and then wrapped the cloth low around his waist so that his muscles showed to their best advantage. He stalked toward her. "Every morsel of lies from you is wrapped in only enough truth to make it easy to swallow. I'm not sure why I keep you around."

QuiTai ran her finger down the trail of hair from his navel to his groin. At the top of the towel, her hand stopped. She tilted her head and smiled at him. "You knew what I was when you chose me."

Petrof shoved her to the wall. The heat of his body rolled over her in a soap-scented cloud. "I chose you because I believed you knew where the Oracle was. Now I think she's another of your lies."

Ah, that had been a mistake, telling him when they first met that the Oracle had led her to him. Over the time they'd been together, he alternately wooed and threatened her for more information. Now she answered him as she always did: "When do I speak of her? She's a vapor dream. Don't waste your time chasing oblivion."

What Petrof did not know was that the Oracle had spoken through him many times. He simply didn't remember. That was perhaps for the best; if he had been able to recall the voice that spoke from his lips, he would have been driven mad by it.

"You're the key to finding her," Petrof said.

QuiTai knew how to evoke the Oracle, as did all the women of her clan; but the Oracle was their goddess, not a tool for Petrof to bend to his bidding. And he would not like her; her answers seemed to make sense only in retrospect, when it was too late to change the course of time. Petrof did not like anything he could not control.

QuiTai tugged on his towel and let it fall to the floor. "Enough talking." He glowered down at her. Maybe it was his wolf nature, but he hated it when she initiated sex. Every time had to be a conquest. He only wanted the unobtainable.

She slipped under his arm and sauntered to the bedroom. "Maybe I'll head downslope and see to my own dinner, since the only food you have here is beer and bones."

As she bent to grab her sarong, he gripped her arm. "You'll stay."

"I told you that I have further business tonight." It was getting harder to pretend she didn't want him to take her to bed again. His lips tickled her neck, and she trembled as his breath sent a chill down her spine.

"And I told you that you're staying," he said. He dragged her to his bed and pushed her onto the mattress. "Cold, cruel, devious QuiTai. What does it take to melt your reptilian heart?"

Even though his hands weren't on her throat, she felt as if she couldn't breathe. Warnings flashed through her brain. If she struggled against him in earnest, she'd never escape his touch. This called for a subtler approach. Luckily, there was a temptation he could never resist.

"Shall we take the vapor first?" she asked.

Thirty minutes later, she sped across the timbergrass bridge, leaving Petrof lost in vapor dream. His memory of the evening would be hazy; he wouldn't remember if he'd let her go. Halfway to the funicular station, she paused: In her hurry to escape, she'd forgotten to scrape the remains of the black lotus from his pipe. And perhaps she should have taken the opportunity to summon the Oracle and ask for guidance on what might be amiss in Levapur.

No. To summon the Oracle she had to inject Petrof with

a non-lethal dose of her venom. The Goddess of the Hunt fated the Ponongese to feel a connection with the animals they poisoned, so they'd have empathy for their food. QuiTai couldn't bear linking her mind and emotions to Petrof, especially this close to a full moon. His thoughts were ugly enough when he wasn't completely unhinged. Besides, she could find the answer without the Oracle's help.

And maybe Kyam Zul was the first place she should start looking.

CHAPTER 2: THE RED HAPPINESS

Over the next few days, Petrof became more furious that no information was forthcoming about the smugglers. He threatened QuiTai; he beat his pack; he broke things. But none of it made any news happen. And that made it harder to talk him into allowing her to have her portrait painted. But tonight she finally had his permission, and she wanted to act before he changed his mind. She hurried from the wolves' den toward Levapur, intent on making her way to the Red Happiness.

While Levapur didn't have official boundaries, the apartment building squatting near the Jupoli Gorge was considered the outskirts. QuiTai grimaced as she neared it. She never liked to pass by the hovel, but there was only one path into town from upslope. The sun and humidity had long ago peeled the paint from the graying wood where ferns sprouted like hair on the ears of old men. There were gaps in the upstairs veranda where the wood had rotted away. The jungle had consumed the houses that used to stand near it, but the old dwelling refused to go away. Someone should have burned it down long ago.

Silent children with suspicious eyes darted onto the veranda to stare at her as she walked down the center of the dirt trail. She never saw them play during the day, but at night they stirred to life. A woman leaning against the veranda railing left her watchful sisters to duck behind the sheet hanging in the doorway. QuiTai often wondered if all these aloof people were related to each other, or if the town pushed everyone like them to the margins.

"Auntie QuiTai!" A whiskered man with bowed legs pushed aside the sheet and headed toward her. She would never set foot on that veranda, so she did not stop, but slowed her steps to give him time to catch up. She hadn't planned to contact her spies this evening, but she couldn't ignore LiHoun.

He pressed his hands together. "Auntie QuiTai, have you eaten?"

She was no more the man's aunt than he was her uncle, but respect was a balm for many woes. QuiTai returned the bow. "Yes, uncle LiHoun. Thank you for asking. And you?"

"Yes. Very well," he said.

"You must have an appetite for air."

He laughed, showing teeth that sprouted from his jaw like the monolith stones in the harbor. His pupils were vertical like hers, but his iris was like the jungle under the canopy, muted green with patches of brown. He had no inner eyelid and no fangs. His people were from a cluster of volcanic islands several hundred miles south of the Ponong archipelago. Despite their similar coloring and language, the Li weren't related to the Ponongese.

He stopped at a glade of banana trees at the foot of an eroded hillside. After pushing the back hem of his homespun sarong into the front waistband, making billowy shorts, he squatted. "I heard a story."

Despite the fancy Thampurian style dress she wore, with a heavy velvet jacket that reached her knees, velvet leggings, a long scarf that draped across her chest and shoulders, and a hat from the finest milliner on the continent, QuiTai squatted beside him in Ponongese fashion and set down the black box she carried. Both faced the road. They watched the turning shades of twilight draw across the sky and the night spirit moths flutter through the thicket of trees. She lit a tightly rolled kur, inhaled deeply, and passed it to him. Then she rested her hands on her knees.

"A good story is meat for your rice," she said.

"This story is a plump chicken." He took a long drag on the kur, pulling the orange line of embers close to his curved fingernails, and held the smoke in his lungs before slowly releasing it in a plume. QuiTai quietly coughed. He smiled shyly, took another drag, and handed the roll back to her with an apologetic shrug.

QuiTai pulled the hot smoke into her mouth and returned the nub to him. The stimulant made her blood feel hot. "I'd rather have meat than smoke anyway, uncle." She exhaled.

Time slowed as it always did during these meetings. They leisurely discussed LiHoun's family, the price of rice, working conditions in the upslope plantations, and rumors of another typhoon forming over the Te'Am Ocean. Thankfully, impatience wasn't a Ponongese vice. It was always better to let matters unfold at their own pace.

Finally, LiHoun came around to it. "PhaNyan regularly sticks his finger into a dirt Thampurian's bowl, without giving the Devil his share. Several weeks ago, the dirt Thampurian, by the grace of gods in a capricious mood, smuggled several large crates onto the island. When he didn't share his bounty with PhaNyan, PhaNyan cried to a cat, who whispered the story to the wolf slayer. But somewhere in the retelling, PhaNyan's name was lost to the story."

QuiTai could imagine where. She'd deal with that later. For now, she wanted to know more about the Thampurian who aided the smugglers. His name hadn't been attached to the rumor either when it reached her, which meant that someone down the line had held back information. That person would regret his foolish decision.

If she'd passed by LiHoun, it might have been another few

days before she heard his information. Manners, she reflected, were never wasted effort.

"The gods love and protect their fools," she said.

A rasping cough shook LiHoun's thin shoulders. "So it's said. I wonder how a dirt Thampurian talked anyone into trusting him with their shipment, and how he managed to do everything right except get paid?" His cunning eyes narrowed as he tilted his head.

Unless he was paid in some other way than coin. There were few ways for a Thampurian to sink to dirt: the most assured route was becoming a vapor addict. If PhaNyan's source knew smugglers who brought black lotus onto the island outside of the Devil's syndicate, she wanted to talk to him.

"I wonder what was in those crates," she said.

LiHoun nodded. "That would be a story worth telling."

She handed him several coins. "It would be a story worth hearing, uncle. Worth ten times this tale." She held up another coin between her fingertips. "Those crates went somewhere. Find them." She put a second, larger, coin with the first. LiHoun's eyes widened with appreciation. "For me alone. Not the wolves."

He took the coins. "Wolves eat cats." She flinched, but he didn't seem to see it. He went on, "I don't do business with them."

"The wisest hairs are gray." QuiTai gripped the black box by her ankle and rose.

"May your bowl always be full, auntie."

"May yours be full of anything but sorrow, uncle."

"Or air!" He laughed heartily as she headed down the road in search of PhaNyan.

She found PhaNyan drinking among a row of plantation workers at a plank nailed to the railing of a veranda. Like the other men in the back alley bar, the weight of the day hunched his back. His hand curled around his beer as if someone might snatch it away. The fragrant haze of kur rose in heavy tendrils that reflected the sickly green light of an aging jellylantern.

The man beside him saw QuiTai first. He nudged PhaNyan with his elbow.

PhaNyan bolted down the alley, but stopped running after only a few steps. His shoulders slumped as he turned to face her. Tall for a Ponongese, he was delicately featured, except for his flattened nose.

As angry as she was that she had to hunt him down, QuiTai knew better than to talk the Devil's business in front of the bar's patrons. She gestured for him to walk with her deeper into the maze of alleys off the main road.

"Little brother PhaNyan, have you eaten?"

PhaNyan licked his bottom lip as he cast side glances at her. "Yes, auntie. And you?"

"Alas, no. When the Devil does not eat, neither do I."

He made a face. "He's from the continent. Why do you share a bowl with him, auntie QuiTai?"

"You question my loyalties?"

"I'm not the only one."

"Ah." The last thing she needed was that sort of trouble. The werewolves were good at enforcement, but her network was mostly natives who were far better at the subtle art of intelligence gathering. If they questioned her, they wouldn't continue to help the Devil.

She stopped in a dark alley with a dead end. "Setting aside my choice of bedmates for the moment, you're fortunate that the Devil hasn't heard of your betrayal yet. There's still time to replace the meat in his bowl before he notices it's gone."

His head snapped up. She could see understanding dawning in his eyes. It wouldn't matter to the Devil why he'd withheld information. Her protection was the only thing standing between him and a painful death.

His Adam's apple bobbed as he swallowed hard. "I would be grateful."

She cupped his chin in her hand. "Gratitude becomes you.

But, of course, he'll be ravenous when I do tell him, so it's best to make sure he has extra to feast on."

"I have to eat too."

"Don't we all."

"But they haven't sold anything to our fences yet, so I have no cut to offer the Devil as penance."

The crack of QuiTai's fist hitting his jaw echoed through the alleyway. He staggered back against a wall, and shook his head as if to clear it.

"I name your penance. Not you," QuiTai said.

PhaNyan's fingers traced over his jaw. She gave him cool silence so that he would know she wouldn't strike him again. He grimaced before grasping her hand and bowing over it to place a reverent kiss on her knuckles.

Knowing that her displeasure would spur his efforts, she soured her smile. "Bring me the names and movements of every stranger on the island."

Still bent in his bow, he lifted his gaze to hers. "Are you searching for the Ravidian smugglers to make an alliance against the Thampurians?"

So the smugglers were Ravidians. Many shipments that passed under the harbor master's greedy eye weren't legal, but as a Thampurian, he would have drawn the line at aiding Ravidians. Or maybe not: the dirt Thampurian had worked for them, after all. Still, chances were that the Ravidians used one of the smugglers' coves to bring their crates ashore. If so, LiHoun would find out.

PhaNyan said, "I knew it! You're only working with the Devil until you can start the revolution."

She grabbed his hand and bent it back until he dropped to his knees. "Foolish little brother! Don't ever speak of such things where we might be overheard. Spies are everywhere."

He screamed as she broke one of his fingers.

"That's for withholding information. Refuse to tell the werewolves if you must, but never try to hide anything from me."

"Forgive me, grandmother QuiTai!"

She wrapped her hand around his thumb. "Dirt has a name. I want it, and where I will find him. Now."

He sobbed out an answer as his thumb snapped.

As she headed for the Red Happiness, the scent of a thousand different dinners wafted from hibachis on verandas. People leaned over the railings of the upstairs verandas to chat with neighbors below. Lovers gathered in alleyways to smile shyly and share long silences. Only the full moon could drive Ponongese to seek shelter inside their apartments.

The line between the Thampurian and Ponongese neighborhoods was visible at night as a change in the color of light that filtered through their intricate carved wood window screens. The blue jellylanterns the Thampurians could afford were much stronger than the cheaper green, but they were still too weak to conquer the night's shadows. Like a giant jellyfish floating in a misty ocean, Levapur glowed everywhere she looked. Beyond the town, the Sea of Erykoli was a different sort of darkness, one that seethed with the remnant power cast off by the last typhoon.

QuiTai's Thampurian-style clothes were ridiculous in Ponong's tropical climate, but it seemed to irk Kyam Zul when she dressed like his people, so she endured the layers of undergarments and heavy fabrics. With every breath, the corset under her jacket tightened around her ribs like a constrictor: that explained why Thampurian ladies, who wore such outfits every day rather than a sensible sarong, swooned so often in the streets of Levapur. No matter how hard she fought to breathe, QuiTai refused to faint. She wouldn't give anyone the satisfaction, especially Kyam Zul.

Standing in the light mist, she opened her dainty umbrella and watched the Red Happiness brothel from across the road. The scent of damp plants and Ponong's rich soil filled the air as clouds released warm, fat raindrops. Customers and workers sat on the wide veranda of the Red Happiness in white wicker chairs, the veranda's roof protecting them from the rain while allowing the cooling breezes from the ocean to waft over them.

Conversations stopped as QuiTai entered the brothel through the open typhoon shutters. She shook the water off her umbrella and closed it. Kyam sat toward the back of the long, narrow room where small cabaret tables clustered. He had been waiting three days for her to answer his message. By now, he was probably furious. She didn't let her gaze linger on him long enough to find out.

In Thampur's capital Surrayya or one of the other glittering cities on the continent, the Red Happiness would have been considered vulgar. The red velvet wallpaper curled from the humidity and the brass fixtures around the room featured illustrations from the ancient *Book of Carnal Bliss*. Blue light jellychandeliers and wall sconces bathed the bar in stark light. It was an outrageous, almost obscene luxury, but QuiTai considered it part of the cost of doing business with the clientele the brothel attracted.

The brothel was too empty for her taste, even if every room upstairs was in use. Most of the crushed velvet divans lining the public room's walls were unoccupied. Kyam and two other men were the only customers at the tables. The barkeep at the far end of the room ran a cloth over the bar in a pretense of work. It would rain almost every day for the next four months, but at the beginning of monsoon season, Thampurians tended to stay at home when the clouds gathered. The typhoon that had just passed probably had something to do with the lack of business too. Until she knew what Kyam wanted, she wasn't sure if she was glad or not it was a slow night.

Belts slowly churned ceiling fans over head. Lizards skittered down the walls. Two redheaded Ingosolians giggled before kissing, to the delight the chubby Thampurian who sat between them on a divan. And Madame Jezereet perched on the banister of the staircase that led to the upstairs rooms. She wore a brown and tan striped waist cincher over a deep purple dress that fell in ruffled layers to the floor, and paprika curls piled high on her head that fell in ringlets to her creamy décolletage. Her skin was pale as the daytime moon. Such coloring was common for the Ingosolians, but her pallor was as unnatural as her bright garnet lips. Her once famously curvaceous figure had shrunk so that every rib in her sternum stuck out. Two years ago, every customer from the continent recognized her from her days on the stage. Nowadays, no one did.

As QuiTai watched, Jezereet slowly raked her fingernails from her wrist to her elbow, leaving long angry welts.

She roused as she saw QuiTai.

QuiTai quickly shook her head and motioned for Jezereet to be patient. She pointedly turned away, but not before catching Jezereet's furious stagger up the stairs.

A rangy, white-blond customer sat at one of the small tables in the center of the room, ignoring the woman who tried to talk him into buying her a drink. At first glance, QuiTai thought his frock coat had a raised collar, but when she drew closer, she saw the blue veins that branched between the knobby bones that supported the frill. Until she saw a dewclaw on his toe she couldn't be sure that he was a Ravidian, but she didn't know of another race with a neck frill like that.

The expatriate at the next table could have been the Ravidian's twin. He daubed his sunburned forehead with a folded handkerchief. An ugly red scar ran between two fingers, across the back of his hand, and disappeared under the lace cuff at his wrist. When he saw her looking at it, he hid his hand under the table.

These two weren't familiar to her: In a small town like Levapur, that was unusual. It seemed odd that they'd choose to come to Ponong now, since it meant crossing the Te'Am Ocean during typhoon season. Besides, the history of the continent was written in Thampurian and Ravidian blood. Why would Ravidians come so far from home to a small island controlled by their enemies, unless they were the Ravidian smugglers PhaNyan had promised to deliver to her?

After admonishing herself for jumping to conclusions, QuiTai reminded herself of the task at hand. The smugglers could wait until after her business in the Red Happiness was complete.

Kyam glowered as she threaded her way between the tightly packed tables toward him. He'd missed a spot on his cheek whenever he had last shaved, and his straight black hair was sorely in need of a cut. The tropical sun had turned his skin a healthy golden brown and etched a few lines around his dark eyes. His only defect was the impatience that set his face into a permanent scowl. Tonight, she could match his mood and then some.

His easel sat before him and he held a brush, but QuiTai had observed him long enough from across the road to know that he had yet to apply the orange paint to his canvas. That was in keeping with his cover as a dilettante artist and wastrel son. In the year that he'd lived on the island, she'd never seen his façade drop. Her admiration for him was grudging, though. After all, she'd played her part for far longer. Only his bitterness seemed real to her, although she couldn't imagine what he had to be angry about.

His sleeves were pushed back to reveal powerful forearms and his open collar showed more of his broad chest than was proper. When she reached his table, he dropped his paintbrush into a glass filled with murky liquid. "What's with the fancy dress?"

She flicked a raindrop from her soft velvet sleeve. What a delight that her pains to dress for this meeting hadn't been in vain. It was as if some cruel god had plucked her from an afternoon stroll in Thampur's lush Suvat Park and dropped her in a sweatbox. She hoped it reminded Kyam of his home: she took such pleasure in poking the snarling Thampurian in his tender spots.

"I'm surprised you haven't noticed. I always dress like a Thampurian when we conduct business, Mister Zul."

"Business!"

His grudging laugh hinted at mockery, but his gaze slid to the Ravidian nearest him. She knew it was a signal to her to make any watchers believe that the animosity between them had not changed. That was easy enough. It hadn't, except that he wanted very much to speak with her. There were plenty of dark alleyways in Levapur where they could have conducted any business he had in mind, so he must want witnesses. That was enough to pique her curiosity.

"I don't like it any more than you do, sea dragon," she said.

He picked up a bottle of rum, but paused before taking a swallow. "The Devil has enough thugs to commit his crimes, and he has you to do his really dirty work, snake. So what business could your master possibly have with me?"

She'd called him a sea dragon first, so she supposed he thought was only fair to call her a snake, but the terms weren't equally derogatory. Thampurians bragged about being sea dragons; the Ponongese didn't think of themselves as snakes.

QuiTai turned to the typhoon shutters. Outside, rain fell in misty swirls that obscured the world beyond the veranda. He wanted everyone to think she'd sought him out: That didn't mean she had to make it easy for him. If he wanted a favor, he'd have to earn it. Then he'd have to atone for calling her a snake.

Kyam grunted. The chair scraped across the wood floor as he kicked it toward her.

QuiTai said, "I see that one can send a scion of the thirteen families to the finest schools in Thampur, but even they can't make a gentleman out of him." She settled into the seat, put the box she carried at her feet, and hooked her umbrella's handle onto the edge of the table.

"If I wanted to be a gentleman, I would have stayed in Thampur." Kyam took a long swig from his bottle.

"I didn't think you'd had a choice about leaving."

Kyam took long, deep breaths, as if trying to calm himself. He failed. "Whatever business your master has with me, tell him I'm not interested. Go away!" He pointed to the door.

QuiTai crooked a finger at Kyam as she leaned across the table. He glared at her but met her halfway. The Ravidians, she noticed, tried to act as if they alone in the room weren't eavesdropping on the conversation, even though QuiTai could have reached out and touched both of them. She gave him her wickedest smile, as if she planned to say something that would make even the workers of the Red Happiness blush; then she whispered, "Now what am I supposed to do?"

"You're smart. You'll think of something," Kyam said through gritted teeth.

"I may be smart, but I'm not a nice woman and I grow tired of this game. I could leave. That's something." Her teeth barely nipped his ear.

Kyam slammed back in his seat as if stung. He slowly lifted his fingers to his earlobe while watching her.

QuiTai chuckled quietly. "Come now, Mister Zul. Those weren't my fangs, only my teeth. Too many witnesses, and I don't particularly care to hang." She rose.

Kyam gripped her arm. "What do you want, Lady QuiTai?"

Briefly, she thought about leaving anyway, but curiosity won. "Ah! Excellent! You found your manners." She pointedly stared at his hold on her arm until his grip eased. She sat back down, but didn't say anything.

Kyam's impatient growl only made her smile more. But as fun as it was to irk him, she decided to play nice – for now. "My master requests a portrait."

"A portrait?"

Kyam's acting skills impressed her. He sounded genuinely surprised.

"You are an artist?" Her tone implied doubt as she flicked her hand toward his canvas, evoking and dismissing it in the same gesture.

"Tell the Devil that I only paint flowers."

"Is that what those lurid whirls are supposed to be?" She held up her hand to stop Kyam's outraged comments. "I told him you don't do portraits, but I'm afraid I was unable to dissuade him." She wondered how long she was supposed to continue this scene, and to what purpose. While it showed that Kyam had some respect for her intelligence, it was maddening that she didn't know where the conversation was supposed to lead.

Kyam glanced at the Ravidians. He picked up his drink and sent the contents swirling inside the bottle with a slight flick of his wrist. The sight seemed to mesmerize him. She stabbed his foot with the pointy tip of her umbrella. He held back his yelp as he tapped on the table with his forefinger. When she glanced down, he looked away while turning the paper under his finger. She recognized the chop of the Dragon Pearl. If she wasn't careful, she was going to admire his ingenuity.

QuiTai's small velvet purse dropped onto the table between them with a solid thunk. "It's a long time between remittance payments, Mister Zul, especially when you have gambling debts." She rose. It was time for him to come to the point.

His eyes widened a bit too much, but it was for the benefit of the audience, not her. "How the hell did you know about that?"

"I have my sources."

"Exactly," he muttered.

Her eyebrow rose. Had he finally mentioned the reason he wanted to speak with her?

He grabbed her purse and shoved it into his pocket without counting the coins. Then he ran his fingers through his hair until it was tousled, and grinned as he stretched. QuiTai could feel the other patrons poised for a demonstration of his cutting wit.

"I guess if I can paint a flower, I can paint the Devil's whore."

"A whore, Mister Zul? That's the best you can do? Not up to your usual level of banter. Are you feeling unwell? A dose of the cleanse should clear up that little problem."

While she was poised to go, there was a point that had to be made now, before they pursued whatever it was he wanted from her. QuiTai leaned over him again and whispered, "This is a game for grownups. If you ever involve a child in your plots again, you will not live to see the sun set."

He nodded slightly.

She picked up her box and umbrella, even though she still had no idea what Kyam wanted. It had something to do with her sources, but that was hardly enough for her to go on. She wasn't sure what sitting for a portrait entailed, but it seemed to her that ought to take several sessions, which meant that he expected them to consult a few times. Interesting.

"I will call on you tomorrow morning, Mister Zul. Try to be sober by then."

And now she had to pay the price for Petrof's permission to meet Kyam. Normally, she entered the Red Happiness by climbing a vine in the back alleyway to the second floor veranda; but Petrof surely had her watched, and she wanted him to know that she'd obeyed him.

Kyam and the other patrons watched her with varying degrees of astonishment as she walked up the brothel's main staircase to the bedrooms on the second floor.

The second floor hallway of the Red Happiness wasn't as garish as the first; by the time customers walked up the stairs, the décor no longer mattered. Doors were clustered in threes down the long, wide hallway. The two side doors of each cluster led to the bedrooms where the workers plied their trade: the narrow center door opened to a passageway between the rooms where patrons could peek through spy holes. Peeping was cheaper, and some patrons simply preferred watching.

Two men came out of a room, exchanged friendly nods with QuiTai, and headed downstairs.

QuiTai knocked on the last door to the left.

"I'm not taking customers tonight," Jezereet said wearily from within.

QuiTai knocked again. "It's me."

The door flew open. Jezereet gripped QuiTai's wrist and yanked her into the room.

The walls were covered in rose and cream striped silk. The furniture was white wood trimmed in gold, a truly Ingosolian fashion. Rose silk draped over a table and cascaded to the floor; framed pictures and mementos crowded the lace doily. Little machines for playing music and other clever gadgets of entertainment sat abandoned on shelves and tucked under the divan. Although Jezereet rarely took customers anymore, a large bed filled most of the room.

QuiTai held out her arms. "Forgive me for staying away so long."

"Did you bring any?"

QuiTai bit her lip. Then she forced a smile. "I brought you a present! I think you'll like it." She showed Jezereet the black box with crisp corners.

Jezereet scratched her arm. "You always give presents when you won't let me have what I need." Her underskirts rustled as she moved across the room. Short black tassels bounced enticingly against her backside with each step. Jezereet had always favored her female form.

She sank onto a chair before a dressing table with the slow grace of a tightly corseted woman, but from the loose laces on her cincher, QuiTai could tell that Jezereet had lost even more weight.

Jezereet checked her make-up, then picked up a pot of lip rouge and brushed some on her lips.

QuiTai placed the box on the low table and sank onto the pink silk divan where she could see Jezereet's reflection in the mirror. "Would you like to see what I brought you?"

"You dismissed me."

Jezereet had been a notorious diva and star of the stage before she came to Levapur. Now she was simply a diva. There was a time when her slightest frown sent actors, directors, and fans scrambling to please her; now there was only QuiTai. No one was more forgiving of Jezereet's habits, though, and QuiTai knew that no one else had ever worked so hard to keep her happy. Once upon a time, it had been out of love. Now, it was more complex than QuiTai cared to reflect upon.

"If I had black lotus for you, I would have come up immediately," QuiTai said sadly.

That was the Devil's bargain. She had to torment Jezereet with the promise of black lotus and then not deliver it. His jealousy had a cruel edge. Now she saw how foolish it was to think a gift could soften the blow. All that Jezereet cared about was her addiction.

"I don't want another damn gift! I need the vapor. Look at me!" She held out her pink-streaked arms.

Grief washed over QuiTai. The Devil was probably chuckling with glee right now, picturing QuiTai's despair and Jezereet's hysterics. He didn't know Jezereet like she did, though: after the storm, there would be calm.

QuiTai patted the box. "This was imported all the way from Rantuum."

Jezereet's gaze met QuiTai's in the mirror before she returned to fixing her makeup. "I haven't even read the fashion magazines you brought me last time."

"Let me save you the trouble. They're showing a different silhouette in Rantuum. The skirts are quite narrow." She flipped open one of the magazines. "Here it is. *The ladies must take mincing steps, which creates a movement pleasing to a gentleman's eye.* The old pervert apparently likes some sway from the hips and a bouncing bosom."

QuiTai saw Jezereet roll her eyes. "Leave it to my fellow countrymen to come up with something scandalous. Next thing you know, they'll get rid of corsets."

QuiTai wriggled, and pinched her waist where it itched: she could barely feel her own fingertips through the corset. "That's a wonderful idea."

Jezereet turned around to face her. "You used to get so impatient while your maid buttoned your bodice."

"I should have been more grateful to her. It's impossible to put on these stupid clothes by myself, and werewolves make terrible lady's maids. Casmir had to lace me up again, with Petrof growling at him the entire time. If Casmir could have pulled the strings tight enough to suffocate me, I'm sure he would have."

"So why are you dressed like that? That sexy Thampurian downstairs? He's from a rich family, you know," Jezereet said.

"And a remittance man. He's as close to being disowned as you can get."

Jezereet held up a curl and dissected it with her fingernail. "They don't do that. Noble blood and all. They only want to teach him a lesson." Her brow furrowed. "Although you should be careful. We know what the Devil does to people you love."

That wound Jezereet always kept fresh. She had willingly taken the vapor with Petrof, but she'd never accepted her responsibility for it any more than she'd apologized for dallying with QuiTai's lover. But as soon as she was addicted, Petrof's visits stopped.

"I can only apologize for what he did so many times," QuiTai said. After a while, no matter how much she meant it, the words lost their power. She didn't want to say it anymore because it didn't change anything. The past was the past, and no regrets could fix any of it.

Perhaps sensing that she'd sent QuiTai's thoughts down a path strewn with recriminations neither wanted to revisit, Jezereet sat next to QuiTai. "Let's open my gift. Although that is the ugliest box I've ever seen. I shudder to think of the hat inside it."

"It isn't a hat."

The sturdy handle swung down so QuiTai could lift the top. From the box, she pulled a pair of big copper opera glasses with a long brass handle and one red and one green lens.

Jezereet gave QuiTai a doubtful look. "That's hideous. What is it?"

"It's a bit heavy, so be careful. Put it to your eyes and peer through the openings."

Jezereet still seemed unconvinced, but she put the contraption up to her eyes.

"Now watch." QuiTai wound a knob between the two lenses.

"Oh! Pictures. But they're moving! They look so real." Jezereet's free hand reached out before her and grasped at the air. "It's like I can touch them."

"It's a kinescoptic motion picture, the latest thing from Ingolsol. Your people are so clever. It's like being at the theater for a show."

"Only I can't hear what they're saying."

Leave it to Jezereet to pay attention to what it wasn't, not what it was. "There's no sound. After a while, you learn to read their lips. Watch out for the Houltoness. I think she improvised her lines. At least, I don't remember anything about sex with animals in the original script, but I might be mistaken. It's been years since we were on stage."

"It hasn't been that long."

"It feels like a lifetime," QuiTai murmured.

"A card popped up with words on it. Wait! Now we're back to the actors." Jezereet's hand went to her mouth. "That's Gernert." She lowered the device from her eyes. "He's playing Kenertate? But he's such a ham."

QuiTai tipped the device with her fingertips so that Jezereet would keep watching. "Wait till you see who they've cast as Inaza."

She didn't have to wait long for Jezereet's outraged squeak. "That little no-talent bitch!"

"She never had your presence."

Jezereet sat in entranced silence while QuiTai tried to figure out a gift that might please her more next time. Then she lowered the device. "That was wonderful. Except Gernert. He wouldn't know restraint and subtlety if they kicked him in the balls."

"He looks good."

"Looks seem to be their only criteria for picking the actors. But it was nice to see some of our old troupe."

The first time QuiTai had watched, the familiar faces nearly made her cry. How could they be so little changed when she felt as if decades had passed? "I'm glad you liked it," she said. "I bought every story they have, and I hear that they're making more every day. Fashion isn't the only thing changing in Rantuum." She showed Jezereet the stack of cartridges in the bottom of the box.

Jezereet hugged QuiTai. "You spoil me."

"It brings me pleasure to see you smile. Would you like to watch another?"

Shaking her head, Jezereet set the contraption back into the box. Her eyes were weary. "I'm sorry. I seem to be fading quickly today." She rubbed her arms. "You have an umbrella. Is it monsoon already?"

"It has been for weeks. Don't you hear the rain? It's cleansing the air. Would you like to open your window and smell how fresh it is?"

Jezereet gripped her wrist. "No, no, no." She shook her head. "I can't bear it. The breeze makes my skin itch."

"All right. We'll leave it closed."

"I wish monsoon would come. How can you people stand this heat?"

QuiTai bit her lip. She hated the circular discussions, but it was useless to correct Jezereet. "We dress for it. If you'd only learn to wear a sarong... Turn around and I'll loosen your laces."

Jezereet stood and let her overclothes slip to the floor. She removed the wire frames that supported her skirts. "Freed from the burden of civilization." Her delicious curves had turned to bones. The once-famous luster of her skin was gray.

"Your camisole is damp. Shall I wash your neck? It would cool you down." QuiTai pressed her lips to Jezereet's pale shoulder.

Jezereet turned with a grin. She placed a quick peck on QuiTai's lips then lingered on her second kiss. "Let's take the vapor."

"I don't have any."

"Just a little bowl." Jezereet's kisses lingered longer. "I'll shift male if you'd like."

QuiTai's mouth bowed in a frown. No, she did not want Jezereet to waste precious energy on a shift. "I have business to attend to."

Jezereet's eyes grew cold as she dropped onto the divan. "Always." She shoved the kinescope away as if she couldn't bear the sight of it. The cartridges spilled to the floor. "Toys, but never your time. I know you take the vapor with Petrof. Sometimes I can smell it on you."

"I bring you what I can scrape out of his pipe after he's in vapor dream. Jezereet, the dealers are too afraid of him to sell to me. If I could, you know I'd give it to you right now."

"Liar!" Jezereet's fingernails dug into QuiTai's slim forearm.

"You're hurting me, love."

The pain of the nails was only part of the ache. Jezereet used to be such fun, but the black lotus had stripped away her spark and left only ugly need. It was getting harder to pretend she was who she used to be. Guilt made QuiTai try, but even that had its limit.

"It's like bugs crawling under my skin. I can't scrape them out. I've tried." She showed QuiTai the open sore on her thigh.

"I promise I'll bring you some next time."

Jezereet's eyes were full of cunning hope. "Tonight?"

"Next time," QuiTai said patiently.

"I hate you." Jezereet's grip tightened. QuiTai gently, but firmly, pushed her back onto the bed. Jezereet gasped when she saw blood trickle down QuiTai's arm. "I didn't mean it! You know I didn't."

"I know." QuiTai eased onto the mattress and cradled Jezereet's head to her bosom. She smoothed Jezereet's hair as she rocked her. "I know."

CHAPTER 3: A PROPOSITION

QuiTai stood back as Ivitch pounded on the door for the fifth time. "What?" she heard Kyam bellow from inside, and then the door flew open.

Kyam stopped short when he saw Ivitch's fist before his nose.

QuiTai could see he was trying to appear as if he'd just woken, although he'd shaved. His long black bangs fell into his eyes, but his hair gleamed as if recently washed and brushed. While he usually left the top buttons of his shewani jacket open and the sleeves pushed back, today he'd buttoned all the way to his neck and left the sleeves down. He wanted to make a good impression. Of course, his grumpy demeanor ruined that. QuiTai wondered if he'd known Ivitch was with her before he opened the door.

For her first sitting, she'd chosen a simple kebaya blouse and batik sarong in the style of the QuiYalin Provence. Her black braid wound over her shoulder and dropped to her waist. If she had to have her portrait painted, she'd be damned if she'd dress like a Thampurian.

"You were expecting us, weren't you, Mister Zul?" She strolled past him into his fourth floor apartment.

Stacks of canvases leaned against the mold-mottled walls. The mosquito netting over his crisply made bed had been mended in several places. A wardrobe, two rickety chairs, and a small desk were pushed aside to make room for an easel and a table splattered with bright globs of paint. A drop cloth was thrown over the floor, but yellow flecks speckled the bare wood around it.

Kyam turned his attention to Ivitch. The men were about the same height, both with muscular builds, but there was no real resemblance between them: Ivitch looked as if he belonged behind a plow, where Kyam had an easy grace as if comfortable no matter his surroundings.

"What's with the bodyguard?" Kyam stifled a yawn as he stretched.

She lifted a filthy cloth from the back of a chair, wrinkled her nose, and let the cloth drop to the floor. "That's Ivitch. He loathes me."

"Who doesn't?" Kyam slammed the door shut.

He had a habit of standing too close so that he could glower down at her. If he thought that intimidated her, he was wrong – it brought out her fighting instinct. She folded her arms across her chest. "This studio isn't fit for a beast, even a Thampurian."

"If you don't like it, you shouldn't have forced me to live here."

Ivitch's suspicious eyes slid from QuiTai to Kyam. "What's he talking about?"

"Nothing of importance," she told Ivitch. "Really, Mister Zul, It's been a year. You could have moved."

"Does the Devil know?" Ivitch asked. He seemed eager for tales to tattle.

With mischief dancing merrily across his face, Kyam looked down at QuiTai. "Yes. Does he?"

He was the most infuriating man. "You boys have bonded already. How nice."

"The enemy of my enemy..." Kyam said. Ivitch nodded.

She dusted the seat of one of the chairs before settling onto it. "I thought only Ponongese traded stories at gatherings, Mister Zul. You've gone native."

That remark wiped the humor from Kyam's face. She noted how stricken he seemed in the instant before he returned to his usual surliness.

"Do you remember when Mister Zul arrived in Levapur, Ivitch? He was attacked by ruffians – "

"That you sent," Kyam said.

"Am I telling this, or are you?"

Kyam made a gesture for her to continue. She lifted her chin and turned away from him.

"He was attacked by ruffians beyond the marketplace. It seems that he was mesmerized by the sight of a young lady on the veranda of the Red Happiness."

"Who was told to distract me."

"For a jaded debauch from the continent, you were easily distracted."

"The young lady in question hiked up her petticoats. She wasn't wearing any – Well, she made her profession clear," Kyam told Ivitch. "Like Madame Jezereet, she was an Ingosolian."

Whatever Kyam was after, he wasn't going to get it by trying to make Ivitch his chum. The idea of the two men chatting about women was laughable. Kyam's clothes might have been studiously shabby, but they were quality. Social-climbing Thampurians tried to mimic his pedigreed accent. There was no doubt that he was a gentleman despite his reduced circumstances and gruff manners; whereas Ivitch was a thug.

Ivitch proved it by shoving the mosquito netting aside and reclining on Kyam's bed without taking off his boots. Kyam and QuiTai exchanged horrified glances.

"Ingosolians. The ultimate shifters," Kyam said in a distracted tone. He seemed unable to turn away from the shocking sight of a werewolf sprawled across his bed. Then he cleared his throat. "So there I was, admiring the show, when two scruffy men attacked me from behind. They knocked me to the ground and were kicking the sh..." – Kyam glanced at QuiTai – "the daylights out of me, when off in the distance, this woman appears ... "

"He means me. Don't get huffy, Mister Zul. You interrupted me too. But go on. Tell your story."

"From her eyes, clearly a native of Ponong, but dressed as if she'd stepped out of my mother's salon back in Thampur. As she came closer, the men grabbed my trunk and ran off. So there I am, bleeding on the street, and she walks to me."

"I did not walk to you. You were in the middle of the street and I saw no reason to detour around you."

"And I said, 'Help, I've been attacked! Call for the police,' and she said, 'Police, Mister Zul? You are a fresh,' then steps right over me as if I'm not even there."

"Can you imagine? He expected me to help," QuiTai said to Ivitch.

"Now I know better, don't I? I'd heard that this island was lawless. I expected some crime. But a man attacked in the middle of the street in front of thirty witnesses, and no one does anything?"

Kyam's outrage sparked QuiTai's anger. He acted as if he didn't know why Levapur was the way it was. "You can thank your government for that, sea dragon."

"Or your master – the Devil."

They were on the brink of one of their vicious arguments. If Kyam didn't have the sense to tone it down, she'd have to be the one who brought them back to the point of this meeting. With some difficulty, she set aside her simmering outrage.

"You forget it was the Devil who made sure that you were reunited with your belongings. Although... " QuiTai wrinkled her nose at an orange and yellow painting leaning against the wall near her. "The rest of the world might not thank me for giving you back your paints and brushes. Couldn't you be a poet instead?"

But Kyam refused to be deterred. "So I finally dragged myself to the bank for the first advance on my remittance, and went in search of a place to stay; only everyone in town refused to house me." He shot QuiTai a jaundiced look, and then went on, "Until I came to this, this... " Kyam lifted his hands to the water-stained ceiling of his apartment.

"Dump," QuiTai said.

Kyam shook his finger at her. "And how do I know she was behind it? Because when my landlady unlocked the door for me, which she refused to do until I gave her a month's rent, there was QuiTai sitting here on my trunk!"

"It was too heavy to move on my own, so why not bring him to his trunk rather than the other way around?" she asked Ivitch.

Ivitch didn't so much as crack a smile. The werewolves never could acclimate to Ponong, either the weather or the culture.

Kyam snatched a pad of paper from his desk and shoved pencils into the breast pocket of his shewani jacket. His temper seemed ready to explode. "This isn't getting us anywhere."

That, QuiTai could agree with.

Kyam stalked to the door.

Ivitch reluctantly rose from the bed. He scratched behind his ear. "Where are we going?"

"I need better light," Kyam said. He headed out of his apartment.

Ivitch gave QuiTai an annoyed but puzzled glance. Equally confused, she shrugged.

The funicular line from the town to the harbor below had been built to move cargo, but passengers were grudgingly allowed to ride rather than brave the steep path that crisscrossed the track a dozen times. There were no seats. The interior was scarred from crates that had broken free from the cargo belts that strained to hold them in place.

"Stinks in here. They shouldn't allow the fishermen to bring their catch up in these," Ivitch said.

Kyam took a pencil from his pocket and whittled the end with a pocket knife.

QuiTai peered out the hazy window that she wished someone would clean. Overhead, thick green leaves longer than her arm created a shaded tunnel. Halfway down, the dense plants suddenly dropped away, revealing the turquoise waters of the harbor, and beyond, the sapphire Sea of Erykoli. Monolith stones far from shore, bleached white from the sun and covered in thick layers of bird guano, jutted from the harbor's water like the sails of ghost ships dredged up from watery graves. Most were bare, but tenacious wind-bowed trees clung to the tops of the biggest stones. On the eastern side of the island, similar rocks formed the dreaded Ponong Fangs.

From this far above the harbor, the round stone fortress squatting on the end of a jetty looked like a crenellated ring with an emerald center. The wharf was a narrow band of commerce on the western edge, near where three- and four-masted junks anchored. Between the wharf and the lower funicular station was a slim crescent of red sand beach that ended abruptly at a cliff.

The funicular creaked slowly down the track. Another thicket of trees blocked her view for several minutes. When they emerged into sun again, it seemed ten degrees hotter inside the stuffy car. The narrow side window screeched in protest as she lowered it to let in the sea breeze.

The funicular bumped to a stop.

Ivitch listed and tried to catch his balance in three quick steps before stumbling into the wall of the car. "There was plenty of sunlight in town, Zul," he snapped as he rubbed his shoulder.

"Not like here. It bounces off the water – "

"Light doesn't bounce," Ivitch said with the absolutely certainty of a man who is often wrong but doesn't know it.

Kyam turned to QuiTai. "Well? I suppose you have some complaint too."

She shook her head. If he'd swathed her in velvet and taken her to an inland valley cut off from the ocean breezes, she wouldn't have complained. She was all curiosity now. It was right there, almost within touch, what he wanted from her. As much as she enjoyed speculating, it was time to find out.

Dock workers lounged along the wharf: Between ships arriving or setting sail, there were many long hours with nothing for them to do. One group squatted at the far end and pitched coins against a wall; Ivitch's eyes lit up, until Kyam led them down the narrow beach. The shouts of the players carried over the noise of the wind and waves. Ivitch kept looking back.

"Lady QuiTai, stand there, looking out at the sea." Kyam pointed to a spot in the sand then perched on a small monolith stone several feet away. He flipped open his sketch pad.

"What am I supposed to do?" Ivitch asked.

"Spy on me," QuiTai said.

"Could you turn? No. Here, let me show you." Kyam stepped over, gripped QuiTai's shoulders, and adjusted her position slightly. "Then turn your head to face me. Good." He returned to the boulder, selected a pencil from his pocket, and began to sketch.

QuiTai had no idea how Kyam wanted her to pose, so she simply stood and looked past him. Across the harbor, red flags emblazoned with the Thampurian Imperial chop snapped above the fortress. Near the wharf, junks at anchor rolled with the incoming waves: The closest to the fortress flew banners with the symbols of Thampur and three of the thirteen families. She assumed that meant the ship was a joint venture. In contrast, the junk anchored further from the wharf, with the single eye painted on its hull, flew only the Thampurian flag and banners with the chop of the Zul clan. Kyam's family owned their own fleet.

She wondered which son Kyam was; had he always known those ships would never be his, or were the banners were a constant reminder of what he'd lost? But he wasn't a real remittance man, she reminded herself: Any day he chose, he could stop playing spy, show his articles of transport to the harbor master, and board a ship bound for Thampur. Except that he wouldn't. No matter how miserable QuiTai tried to make his life, he stayed.

She should know by now that it was useless to try. The Oracle had told her long ago that Kyam Zul would become the colonial governor of Ponong. And the Oracle was never wrong.

Ivitch paced behind Kyam, stopping occasionally to peer over Kyam's shoulder.

"Could you stop doing that? You're distracting me. Can't you watch her from over there somewhere?" He motioned toward the wharf.

Ivitch licked his lips.

"No, he couldn't," QuiTai said.

Ivitch sneered at her and headed down the beach.

"That was too easy," Kyam said as they watched Ivitch join the gamblers at the end of the wharf.

She jutted her chin toward the wharf. "Yours?"

"It's happy coincidence that the dockworkers are here but didn't have cargo to unload. I didn't expect him, after all. I go to all this trouble to set up a private talk, and you bring a chaperone."

"*You* went to trouble?" She had to control her outrage. Unless it would give her leverage, she'd never tell Kyam what she'd done to meet him at the Red Happiness. "The Devil is jealous and paranoid. If I'd tried to convince him not to send one of his men, he would have insisted, so I suggested it first."

Kyam sniffed and bent over his drawing pad. "Don't move if you can help it."

She focused over his shoulder. "Did you really gamble away your remittance just so that you'd have an excuse to accept the commission for the portrait? That was thorough of you."

Kyam scowled. "It wasn't as easy as you think. I kept winning."

She put her hand over her mouth as she laughed. "You should have sent word. I could have arranged to have you robbed right outside the Dragon Pearl, in front of witnesses."

"Once was enough, thank you."

She took a deep breath as she looked out at the sea beyond the harbor seawall. The salted air felt cleansing as she drew it into her lungs.

"Why did you want to see me? Ivitch could come back any moment, so I suggest we get down to business."

Kyam kept drawing. "There are Ravidians in Levapur."

A chill ran through her core. Kyam also sought the Ravidians? Her lips pursed as she composed herself. "And the sky is blue."

He set down his pencil. Dark eyes leveled on her. "What's that supposed to mean?"

"Don't waste my time telling me the obvious. You sat between them in the Red Happiness."

"Lower your chin a bit. You saw two of them. There's a third." He glanced over at the wharf. "Unless you know about him too?"

She did now.

"What exactly do you want from me, Mister Zul?"

"I can't possibly follow all three Ravidians. You have contacts and spies all over town, all over the island. I need to know what they're up to," Kyam said.

"It looked to me as if they were up to a bit of fun with the workers at the Red Happiness."

It was just her luck. As much as they tried to avoid each other, their paths always crossed at the most inconvenient times. If she didn't know better, she'd think the Oracle's hidden hand was to blame for it; but the Oracle only foretold the future, she didn't make it happen. Or did she? There was too much QuiTai didn't know about her goddess. If only she hadn't turned her back on her people and gone to the continent to be an actress; now there were no Qui elders left on Ponong to ask, and every responsibility she'd run from – and then some – was now hers alone to shoulder.

"I would pay a month's rent to know what's making you frown like that, Lady QuiTai. Is it something about the Ravidians?"

He would insist on forcing her to concentrate on his needs rather than leaving her to dwell on her thoughts. Although, truthfully, she didn't mind the jolt back to present concerns as much as she might have under different circumstances. Still, she didn't want him to interfere with the Ravidians until she found out if they had indeed smuggled black lotus onto the island in those mysterious crates. A new source of the drug would free Jezereet from Petrof's clutches. And probably kill her sooner – there were never any good answers to QuiTai's troubles, only ones that led to less suffering.

"It's horrible narcissism, you know." She knew that her voice was too quiet, too tired, too honest. Kyam stared at her, as if it took all his focus to hear her over the waves. If she said something like that to Petrof, he would demand to know what the hell she was on about now, but Kyam only listened, as if he felt able to keep up with her sudden changes of thought, as if he could see the trail leapfrogging across seemingly random bits of information and arrive at the same place she'd gone to. "We go to such great lengths to hide our true goals from their eyes, and they probably aren't even paying any attention to us. You could walk up to me in the marketplace in front of a hundred witnesses and ask me if I know anything about the Ravidians in Levapur, and I could tell you what I know, and no one would care."

"Narcissism? That's rich coming from you. I've seen too many of your grand entrances."

"I move through the marketplace often without being recognized. And even when I do make a grand entrance, as you call it, after the people are satisfied that I have no business with them, they forget me, because there are much more important matters in life than the Devil's concubine. Believe anything you want about me; it's no concern of mine. But don't doubt for a second that I have a firm grasp on my role and position. So next time you want to talk to me, save us both a lot of bother and quit acting like a spy. No one cares."

"Except the Ravidians."

She shrugged, but her mood didn't shake off that easily.

"And the Devil," Kyam added.

"Ah, yes. We must not forget about him." She sighed and stared over his shoulder at the open water. "The Devil and a handful of Ravidian spies. Such an esteemed audience."

"Do you anticipate a return to the stage?" Kyam asked.

So he knew her history. Was he trying to bribe her into helping his government by dangling the prospect of a starring role? That wasn't even close to her price for working with Thampurians.

"Do you anticipate a return to Thampur?" she asked.

Anger settled around his mouth and seeped into his eyes. He set down his pencil and reached for another one. "As long as we're avoiding each other's questions, did you examine my trunk after your men stole it?"

Maybe he'd learned in the fancy salons of Thampur how to steer a conversation back to a safe harbor when it went adrift in treacherous waters. Now they could act as if she'd never let an indecent amount of her soul show. She was grateful, even if the kindness was out of habit. She rallied and clicked her tongue as if scolding a drunk. "Presumption of guilt, Mister Zul."

"You should have been a lawyer. Let me restate my question. Did you examine my trunk before you returned it to me?"

"Of course." She let one corner of her mouth curve just enough to irk him.

"Completely?"

"If you're asking whether I found the secret compartment that held the farwriter, then yes, my search was thorough."

He took off a boot and poured red sand from it. After tapping the heel to make sure it was empty, he put it on again. "How did you break the biolock?"

The almost-supernatural powers people were willing to believe she possessed always amused her. "I didn't. I must commend you on how complete your cover was. Every detail from your clothes to your mementos was perfection, and the workmanship on your trunk first rate. If I hadn't been so persistent, I wouldn't have found the hidden compartment. Once I knew it was there, I surmised the contents from the size. And, of course, a farwriter was the one item that was glaringly absent from the rest of your belongings."

"So you didn't open the biolock."

"Don't talk nonsense. No one can do that, not even me." She'd tried, of course. It wasn't often that she had time to experiment with a biolock without worrying that Petrof might catch her at it.

"Did you tell the Devil about the farwriter?"

QuiTai hesitated. Her gaze slipped from his. "I saw no profit in it."

"So only you think I'm a spy; and for some unfathomable reason, you've helped maintain my cover all this time."

A loose strand of hair floated in the ocean breeze and trailed across her face. She tucked it behind her ear. "When you put it that way, it seems foolish of me."

"That's hardly the word I'd use to describe you, Lady QuiTai. Exasperating, yes. Foolish, no."

She could have said the same thing about him. It was such a pity he sided with the colonial government.

He switched pencils again. "So, what do you know about the Ravidians?"

Them again. She reminded herself that pearls began as specks of grit, but that didn't make the grit any less irritating to endure. "They're foppish dressers, miserly drinkers, and too rough with the workers at the Red Happiness."

"I'm sure you know far more than that."

Two fishermen struggled past them through the sand with a big basket full of their day's catch. Kyam bent over his drawing pad as more men headed from their boats to the lower funicular station. Some men sauntered over to watch the dockworkers and Ivitch gamble. Others spread heavy, wet nets to dry across tall poles stuck in the sand.

After the last men moved far down the beach, Kyam returned his attention to her. "We may not have much time before your werewolf comes back, so let's lay our tiles on the table. If you found something about the Ravidians that might interest me and had nothing to do with the Devil's business, what would it cost to get that information from you? My family is wealthy."

So that's why he had her facing the junks in the harbor, to

remind her of that wealth and the connections that came with it: The Zuls were related to their king by generations of blood and marriage. But that was the wrong tactic to try with her.

"My money doesn't interest you, Lady QuiTai? Most actresses and whores want money and jewels. Don't look so offended. I said most. Try the obvious negotiation first, my grandfather always said. There's no reason to make it more complicated than it needs to be."

"A wise man, your grandfather, even though he is a thief."

"Most people hated him because he always found their price. Of course, he knew his competitors very well, which made it easier. I'll admit that I'm at a disadvantage. I know very little about you. We hadn't even been properly introduced before you began your campaign to make my life a living hell. Since that day, the facts I've learned about you wouldn't even fill out a one-sheet dossier. Oh, I know your reputation, but that's long on myth and short on proof. People here relish a good story, don't they?" He gave her a piercing look. "One thing I am sure of is that you're much more than the Devil's concubine. You're his right arm."

"Such flattery. I may swoon."

"Don't. I need you to hold that pose."

He tapped his pencil on his bottom lip as he checked to see if Ivitch was still at the dock. Then he said, "Have you noticed a subtle change in the mood on the island?" While his tone was casual, he watched her closely.

Relief washed over her. Finally, someone else was saying out loud what she'd been feeling for weeks. It wasn't just her imagination. "Sometimes I think I'm dreaming, but other times, I swear I can feel it. What do your superiors say?"

Kyam laughed as if the joke were on him. "The government has no interest in anything I have to say. That's why I need proof. If they listened to me, I wouldn't need your help. Believe me, you were my last choice."

"Fair enough. You're my last choice for an ally too, but since you gave a little information, I'll return the favor. I always pay my debts."

"A scoundrel with honor. We're not so different after all."

With an admonishing smile, she shook her head slightly. He had nerve.

"The Ravidians aren't the only newcomers. Levapur is overrun with mysterious strangers these days." Mysterious was a bit of a leap, but more travelers than usual had come to the island, considering the time of year.

"Am I focusing on the wrong group?"

"Subtle, Mister Zul, very subtle. I think I've given you enough information today." She couldn't blame him for trying, though.

"Not that I'm keeping score, since this is a debt of honor, but I gave you more information than you gave me," Kyam said.

"In the future, if I hear something that is of no value to me but might be useful to you, I might be tempted to pass it along."

Kyam didn't like that answer. "Coyness doesn't suit you."

"How is this, then? My people are watching the Ravidians and all suspicious newcomers. I agree that the Ravidians are up to something." She put up her hand when he leaned forward. "However, they aren't my enemies."

"That you're aware of. I've heard rumors that you have separatist sympathies, but Thampurians look like the Goddess of Mercy compared to what Ravidians do to the native populations of their colonies."

There might have been some truth to that, but sworn enemies usually exaggerated about each other. She could imagine what the Ravidians said about the Thampurians. It probably wasn't all that different from what she said about them. "There are only three Ravidians on Ponong. I'll take my chances."

Kyam said, "Don't underestimate how determined I am to get what I want. I'd rather have your cooperation, but I have other means."

She sensed the same change in the power flowing around him as she did when the werewolves shifted. She crossed her arms over her chest to hide her gooseflesh.

He said, "Don't force my hand, Lady QuiTai."

"You will never be able to force mine, Mister Zul."

His mouth tightened. Then he hunched over his pad, barely looking up at her as he furiously erased something with rubber gum. He had no right to be angry. She was the one who should have been insulted. Did he really think she'd help the Thampurians?

As his pencil swept along the paper, he said, "The drugs, the smuggled rice, the murders, the burglaries, the extortion – our soldiers could interrogate you about those crimes for hours. They've wanted to get their hands on the Devil ever since he killed his competitors and became the face of criminal activity on this island. Only he's not the face, is he? He's the coward who hides in the shadows while you run the syndicate. I could have you arrested right now. I could have you tortured."

It was true. If not for her generous payments to key Thampurians in the colonial government, she probably would have been taken in long ago. She knew that was an illusion of safety. A bought man wasn't to be trusted. No one would protect her if the soldiers dragged her to the fortress.

But Kyam forgot that she knew he wanted her help. It was the trump tile in this game.

"Go ahead. Have me arrested. I dare you, Mister Zul."

He flipped the cover of his drawing pad closed and stood. "That's enough for today."

She ambled over and extended her hand. "Let me see."

He thrust the pad at her.

In his sketch, there were harsh lines around her mouth, and her eyes were cunning. It was the portrait of an unrelenting, cruel woman. The drawing was quite good, which surprised her. She handed it back without comment.

CHAPTER 4: DEATH OF A VAPOR ADDICT

As QuiTai went to collect Ivitch from his game on the wharf, she saw Kyam head toward the funicular. The attendant shut the door, and the train began to rise up the slope to the town.

"He could have asked them to hold it for us," Ivitch said. He covered his ears as the engine that powered the funicular's drive chain gave off a shrill whistle.

QuiTai pointed to the steep road leading up the hillside. "You could always walk."

"I'll wait for the other car to come down."

"Suit yourself." She walked away from the ticket booth.

"Where are you going?"

"As long as I'm here, I thought I'd pay a social call. Run along. I no longer need you to protect me from Mister Zul."

"I take my orders from the Devil, not his whore."

"I am wounded, Ivitch, simply gutted by your scathing condemnation."

Confusion spread over his features slowly, in keeping with the speed of his thoughts. It was as if his brain were surrounded by thick paste. It was almost painful to wait for her barbs to hit their mark; she used to lose patience and try to push the process along, but that only seemed to confuse him more. It was a mistake to ignore him, though, the same way it would be lunacy to turn her back on a mob.

She was sorry he wasn't Kyam. There was a man who could hold his own in a conversation, and understand an insult, no matter how veiled.

Finally, Ivitch grinned, as if it had been a compliment. She could have wept for him, but never would.

"If you're about the Devil's business, then I should come along."

If she said no, he would tell Petrof, and then she'd have to explain her reasons. It would be easier to let him come. All she planned to do was find out if the dirt Thampurian who'd helped the smugglers was a black lotus addict. If so, she could return later and question him alone.

They crossed the beach to the far end of the harbor where small sailing skiffs and fishing boats moored. She pointed to a skiff at the end of a line of boats tied together; used, weathered wood was bound together to shape a ramshackle lean-to at the stern behind the sail. That matched the information from PhaNyan that the dirt Thampurian lived on his boat, which made sense since his brother was the harbor master. "That one," she said.

"How do we get out there?"

After checking to see that no one watched, QuiTai stepped from the narrow dock onto the deck of the first boat in the line. She reached for the tieline to the next boat and pulled it close; then, carefully balancing, stepped from one boat to the next.

Ivitch tried to follow and nearly lost his balance as he stood with each foot on a different boat and a wave sent them rocking. "This is stupid."

She turned to press her finger to her lips, and kept going.

"Why are we doing this?" Ivitch asked.

"I heard a rumor this man might know something about the smugglers."

Ivitch cracked his knuckles. "It's a good thing I'm along."

She put her hand on his shoulder. "No, it's good that I'm along." He wrested away from her touch, setting the boat they stood on to rocking violently. QuiTai said, "We only want to question him." To be sure that Ivitch understood, she had to be clear. "Don't kill him. Threaten to if he won't cooperate, but offer the forgiveness of the Devil before you damage him too much. He needs to be able to work off his debt."

Ivitch climbed onto the skiff. QuiTai ducked under the boom of the main sail and followed him to the lean-to.

Ivitch already held the skeletal dirt Thampurian by the throat. From the smell of the shelter, the man was a heavy black lotus user, although that didn't explain the sharp scent of vinegar under the sweeter stink of vapor. A spirit lamp and clay pipe with a tiny bowl sat on an upturned crate. The cot he lay on was held together with leather straps and hope. There wasn't much else in the tiny, dank space – probably not even food, QuiTai assumed.

The Thampurian wore only trousers. Every bone in his chest protruded, and his skin barely stretched over his skull. His lips were deep red, in stark contrast to his unhealthy pallor. QuiTai had to bite her lip to stop it from quivering: Eventually, Jezereet would look like this.

"Gently, Ivitch. He probably won't remember any lesson you try to teach him."

As Ivitch hefted at the ghoul in his hands, QuiTai swiped a vial of sticky black resin from the crate by the cot and hid it in her blouse. Empty vials rolled loose on under their feet with several vinegar bottles. The smugglers evidently had paid the dirt Thampurian in black lotus instead of coin.

The Thampurian gurgled.

"What did he say?" QuiTai asked.

"Who cares what the fuck a vapor dreamer says?"

"He looks pretty far gone. We'll get nothing useful from him now. I'll come back to interrogate him later."

The Thampurian gurgled again.

"Let him go, Ivitch."

Ivitch wiped his hand on his trousers. "I already did."

QuiTai knelt before the man. His tongue protruded from his mouth.

"Why are his lips turning purple?" Ivitch asked.

"Because you crushed his throat, you idiot."

"He shouldn't have been so weak."

Red bubbles foamed at the edges of the Thampurian's mouth as he gasped for air. His hand clawed at something only his glazed eyes could see.

"Excellent work, Ivitch. You've killed our only link to the smugglers, not to mention a Thampurian citizen, and the brother of the harbor master."

"An addict and a thief."

"I'm sure that the colonial government will take that into account when they try you for murder."

Ivitch slapped his hands together as if washing himself of the matter and crossed the skiff.

"For the love of – Ivitch, get down. We can't afford to be seen now." QuiTai turned back to the man on the cot. His struggle for air was painful to hear. "Petrof will hear about this. You weren't supposed to kill him."

Ivitch already had a foot on the next boat. "He's not dead."

If only she could keep him alive. She glanced frantically around the bare shack, but even if an entire surgery full of instruments had been there, she wouldn't have known what to do for him. She was overcome with sadness: One day, Jezereet's beautiful face would be like his, her eyes abnormally large, her lips virulent red, her soul lost forever in the nothingworld of vapor.

She risked raising her voice to say, "Ivitch, you bastard, get back here!"

"My orders were to make sure you didn't sleep with Zul. You're on your own now."

QuiTai bit back the insults she gladly would have shouted at him if it hadn't been for the soldiers.

She waited for Ivitch to reach the dock before she leaned over the dirt Thampurian and lowered her fangs. Fear seeped through the fog of the vapor as his eyes darted about in search of help. She pressed her mouth to his, gently parted his lips with her tongue, and milked enough drops of her venom into his mouth for a gentle death that would end his suffering; she stroked his throat to help the poison down.

He gripped her arm with sudden, bruising strength. His eyes widened as his pupils imploded. Fleeting wisps of his thoughts, blurred by fear and dreamer's eyes, pushed into her mind as her venom invaded his brain. Words bubbled from his mouth with the red foam of his blood and burst gently on his lips. *Help Kyam Zul find what he seeks.*

The Oracle had spoken.

Before the Thampurians had brought their black lotus to the island, evoking the Oracle had been an ordeal. The women of her clan gathered rare roots and seeds and cooked them into a red tar that was then smoked, much as the black lotus was. The difference was that black lotus wasn't fatal; at least, not if used in extreme moderation. The red tar always killed. The visions were more potent, but given the price, her clan rarely evoked their goddess.

The dirt Thampurian's head lolled. She felt his waning life. At least he wasn't afraid anymore.

She crawled across the hull and peeked over the side. Ivitch was already at the beach. He bypassed the harbor master's office and went to the funicular station. Thank goodness he wasn't smart enough to send someone to the skiff and frame her for the dirt Thampurian's murder.

She cast a glance over her shoulder at the crenellated walls of the fortress. Two soldiers leaned against the ramparts overlooking the harbor. From the movement of their hands, she suspected they shared a kur. She had no idea how often the harbor master came to visit his brother, but as soon as the body was found, there would be questions, and she couldn't risk the soldiers remembering her crossing the line of boats. And despite growing up on an island, she wasn't a strong swimmer. Not to mention the dark shape gliding through the harbor water, its head swaying gently side to side opposite the movement of its tail. A fin broke the surface. The biggest sharks rarely swam into the harbor, but a man-killer could be lurking near one of the monolith stones. Even if she made it to land safely, the soldiers might wonder why she was swimming through shark-infested waters.

Another glance up at the ramparts. One of the soldiers sat on the wall now. They weren't moving anytime soon.

QuiTai crept back toward the lean-to. Water pooled in the sections along the keel of the skiff, and as she crawled, her hand slipped off the damp wood into a puddle. Fiery pain shot through her palm.

With tears running down her cheeks, she examined her hand. A thick, dark red welt rose along her skin. She squinted at the pool of water: at the right angle, she could see shards of thick glass.

She rolled onto her back and gulped in air. The pain grew worse.

She held her palm close to her face, expecting to see a sliver of glass in the welt. Instead, she saw a long, gelatinous, nearly invisible medusozoa tentacle clinging to her skin. A bright orange stinger, no thicker than a thread, ran through it. Her fingertips burned as she tried to peel it away. Cursing, she crawled to the cot in the lean-to, grabbed the corner of a threadbare blanket, and used it as a makeshift glove to pull the stinger from her hand. Fresh, raw pain seared across the welt. Her face felt hot, her mind dizzy, heart pounding, and now she couldn't stop her legs from churning. She stared at the roof of the lean-to as she writhed helplessly. Sweat dripped down her temples. Tears poured freely down her cheeks.

A bloodied shard of glass appeared in her mental vision as pain once again sliced through her palm. She grasped her wrist and forced her trembling hand closer to her face. There was no blood on the ugly dark red welt. No glass.

Think of anything but the pain.

The welt looked like the scar she'd seen on the hand of the Ravidian in the Red Happiness, the one he'd hidden when he saw her staring. He'd been sunburned, as if he'd spent a lot of time out in the sun. Maybe on a skiff.

She could hear choppy waves slamming against the seawall. The skiff rocked. She could envision the scene: three Ravidians huddled in the hull when a rogue wave hit and a crate tumbled over. They rushed to set it upright and discovered a glass container broken. Perhaps they simply tossed it over the side without noticing that some of the contents had spilled. It would be hard enough to see glass and stinger in the puddle when the water was calm.

The vision was so clear, so specific.

She stared at the dirt Thampurian. This was what he'd seen. And then, with his last horrible gasp, his death cut their connection.

The vision cleared and the real world flashed over her like flames across dry tinder.

Her heart hammered so hard she could feel it in her ears. She could barely catch her breath. She wondered briefly if she might die, then hoped she would, then scolded herself for being so dramatic. The pain would pass. It had to pass. Until then, the trick was to keep her mind occupied.

Sometimes, Ponongese workers fell into the tide pools and suffered multiple stings from the blue-light medusozoa. They might be in pain for days, and the stingers left scars, but nothing like this. The stinger that marked her had to have come from another species. No one fished from a skiff, so it was unlikely something got hauled on board in a net; but why anyone would deliberately bring such a creature aboard a boat puzzled her.

Her heart still pounded as if she'd run miles. She staggered to her knees and reached toward the bottles of vinegar. They clinked together with the dull thud of empty glass, but she shook them over her hand one at a time in the hope that a few small drops were left. Sobs lifted her shoulders as she flung the last empty bottle away.

Then she pushed the tears back down. Her anger shoved the pain away for a moment and cleared her thoughts. She took the vial of black lotus from the pocket in her blouse. A tiny bit of the resinous tar could put her into oblivion for a couple of hours.

Ponongese, for some reason, seemed immune to the powerful addictive properties of the vapor, but not the effects.

But if someone came to check on the dirt Thampurian, she needed to be awake to protect herself.

She unhooked the chain around her neck with fumbling fingers and threaded it through the top of the black lotus vial. It seemed to take forever to make her shaking hands work, and pain shot down her arm with every movement.

Ten minutes. Ten minutes without resorting to the vapor.

With a long sigh of resignation, she began a slow, methodical search of the lean-to. She didn't expect to find any record that the dirt Thampurian had taken the Ravidians and their mysterious crates to a hidden location, but it was something to do.

Finally, the only thing she hadn't checked was the body.

I made it the first ten minutes. I'll make it another ten before I give in. Save this for Jezereet. She needs it more than I do.

She began her examination of the dirt Thampurian at his feet. Across his toes, she found a welt like hers, only not as red.

"Poor ghoul. How you must have suffered," she told the corpse as she closed his eyes. "But at least someone cared enough about you to bring you vinegar."

The sun took its damn time setting. The lavender shades of twilight, which usually delighted her, lingered too long in the sky. A new watch of soldiers had come and gone from the fortress ramparts before QuiTai dared to leave the skiff.

Even in bright moonlight, moving from boat to boat in the dark was difficult. Without using her injured hand, it was almost impossible. QuiTai reached the dock and sank to her knees. The pain hadn't dulled during the four or five hours she'd spent on the skiff, but at least her heart had stopped racing.

The beach sand weighed down her steps. The harbor master's office was dark, and the wharf was deserted. By the time she reached the funicular station, tendrils of hair stuck to her sweaty face. When she found the station closed, she leaned against the station building. Her gaze rose up the long climb to the town square. Cursing, she clutched her arm to her body and forced herself to begin walking.

Bats filled the sky as she stumbled into the town square. A few brave Thampurians gathered inside a café, but no one dared sit outside to enjoy the fine night. Even the Ponongese had withdrawn from their verandas, closed their window screens, and bolted their doors tonight.

She staggered past the little tables outside the café into an alleyway and pounded on the kitchen door.

"It's full moon," someone called from the other side.

It had been two years since the werewolves had terrorized Levapur during their full-moon shift, but it was seared into the memories of the town folk. No one in their right mind would open their door to her tonight. If they only knew that the moon did not control the werewolves' ability to shift, perhaps they'd never open their doors again.

"Please! I need vinegar."

The door cracked open. Fragrant steam, heavy with the scent of Thampurian spices, rolled over her.

"Auntie QuiTai!"

She half-expected the man to slam the door in her face: She loved her people, but they didn't always return her affection. Instead, the heavyset Ponongese cook shouted over his shoulder, "Bring a bottle of vinegar!" as he glanced anxiously up and down the alleyway.

QuiTai wavered. She had no idea how to keep going. She only knew that she must. "Forgive my manners. Have you eaten, uncle?"

"Yes. And you?" he asked. It was a rote response while he uncorked the bottle of vinegar.

She winced as she extended her hand. Her arm hurt all the way up to her shoulder. The sharp pangs ebbed as the vinegar flowed over her skin. She drew her first deep breath in hours.

The cook held the door open to shed more light on her hand

as the other kitchen workers crowded near to look. "I've seen stings before, but nothing like this," one said. "Medusozoa?"

QuiTai shrugged. "That would be a story worth telling, if I knew."

"My brother is a fisherman," the youngest man said. "Should I warn him to carry vinegar on his boat?" Worry furrowed his forehead.

Why did they bother her with questions she couldn't answer? Still, she bit back her sharp tone because they'd opened their door to her. "I don't know."

"Is it something new? Did those damn sea dragons bring a new evil to our waters?"

The Oracle's vision had showed that the stinger came from the Ravidians and their mysterious crates. Whatever it was they transported in glass jars, she never wanted to touch one again.

An older man produced a damp towel. She smiled her thanks. It felt cool and perfect on her face and neck.

"The jellies always bloom for the moon," a short, sweet-faced dishwasher said as he wiped his hands on his soiled apron.

So did the werewolves. There was no reasoning with them while they were under its influence. As much as she wanted to go to the Devil's den and defend herself against any lies Ivitch had told Petrof by now, she already knew what they were capable of once they were in their wolf forms. She'd have to wait.

"Do you need shelter, auntie?" the oldest man asked. He seemed to regret the invitation as soon as he uttered it, but being Ponongese, he'd never take it back. He corked the vinegar bottle and handed it to her.

"Your kindness does you credit, uncle, but I must be on my way." He didn't offer again, although at least twice was custom. She bowed and headed down the alley. Behind her, she heard the door slam shut against the night.

Despite the relief of the vinegar, her hand still hurt. She touched the vial of black lotus on the chain around her neck. Somehow she'd managed to get through these painful hours without its help, but her resolve was ebbing with her energy.

Jezereet would be crazy with need by now. And all Qui Tai

wanted to do was sleep. For once, she could risk spending the night next to Jezereet.

Only three more blocks to go.

She heard a sound behind her. Not paws: a footstep. Ears sharply focused, she kept walking. At the next alleyway, she hurried to the main road.

Another sound.

Tapping deep into the last of her energy, QuiTai ran, weaving across verandas and over railings. By the time she reached the vine at the back of the Red Happiness, she heard no more tracking sounds behind her.

Staring up at the vine, she was tempted to go around through the front doors. Waves of exhaustion swept over her. Then, gritting her teeth, she tucked the back of her sarong into the waistband so the skirt wouldn't tangle in her legs, gripped the vine, and began to climb.

CHAPTER 5: JEZEREET

QuiTai paused on the door of Jezereet's room, leaning wearily against the frame. Jezereet smiled at her: The long scratch marks on her arms had faded, and she had dreamer's eyes.

"I'm relieved to see you so tranquil," QuiTai said. "Do I smell vapor?"

Jezereet wrung her hands together, then darted to her window and knelt on the divan to push open the window screen. "It's hot in here. You must smell my sweat. Isn't that breeze nice?"

QuiTai heard footsteps in the hallway. She stepped into the room and shut the door behind her. "I thought you hated the feel of the air on your skin."

Jezereet hugged herself and rocked side to side.

QuiTai looked longingly at the bed. The soft mattress would feel so good… But until Jezereet got her pipe, there was no chance of sleep.

The footsteps in the hallway were closer. Heavy; a man.

QuiTai turned to the room door.

"Why are you going already? You can't leave. You can't!" Jezereet stumbled to QuiTai and gripped her arms.

"I'm not leaving, I'm locking the door," QuiTai said calmly. "No one will bother us."

"I wanted to be certain. I think I was followed..." But no, she should not mention that. Jezereet might think of wolves and panic.

Jezereet sighed loudly. "I hate it when you think too much. It makes me tense."

Not too far down the hallway, a door closed with a quiet click.

"Anything for you," QuiTai said.

Jezereet laughed merrily: if QuiTai hadn't heard that musical laugh so many times as she waited offstage for her cue, she might have believed it was real. Jezereet kept looking toward the window as if she expected a customer to stroll by on the veranda. It struck QuiTai as a little odd that she hadn't demanded black lotus yet. Then she felt bad that Jezereet always had to beg. "Get the kit," she said.

Jezereet clapped her handed together and bounced. "You brought me some?"

"I promised."

Jezereet rushed to grab a small cabinet from her wardrobe, and then shoved everything on the low table beside her divan onto the floor to make room for it. She licked her lips as she watched QuiTai cross to the divan.

QuiTai opened the cabinet doors and folded down a wooden tray. Delicate clay pipes with tiny bowls and long slender stems clattered out; a short glass spirit lamp nestled inside the purple velvet, but the black leather restraints that held it in place hadn't been snapped closed. She took the glass flue off the lamp and trimmed the wick, something she always did before she put it away.

"You used this," she said.

Jezereet's feet tapped against the floor as she shrugged up at the ceiling.

"What did you do? Scrape it from the bowls and recook it?"

"Um. Yes." Jezereet nodded hard. "That's what I did."

"I wasn't aware you knew how."

"I watch you all the time." Jezereet rose from the divan. "You didn't bring me any for so long, and the bugs were under my skin, and then the wolf came… "

Overcome with guilt, QuiTai rushed over to hug her. "Hush, now. That was a long time ago."

Jezereet seized QuiTai's hands and pressed them to her cheek. QuiTai yelped and pulled away.

"I didn't do anything." Jezereet wailed.

"It's nothing, my love." QuiTai gripped her hand to her waist.

"Then why did you make that sound?"

She didn't want to explain. All she wanted to do was sleep. But she showed Jezereet her hand. "A medusozoa stung me. Then I hurt it again on the vine climbing up."

"I can see the pain in your eyes." Jezereet caressed QuiTai's face. "I wish I could take care of you the way you care for me."

"It's been a very long day," QuiTai said.

QuiTai led Jezereet to the divan. She stuck a long ivory pick into the vial around her neck and withdrew a lump of black paste. As the tar cooked in the small bowl of one of the delicate pipes, it filled the room with a sweet, resinous scent. Dark brown bubbles broke in slow motion around the edge of the bowl. QuiTai moved it on and off the flame to keep it from burning.

Jezereet leaned over the spirit lamp and inhaled. "Lovely."

"Hold your hair back if you're going to do that."

Jezereet sat back. Her curls fell around her face and hid the sharp planes of her cheeks and jaw. In the soft glow of the lamp, she almost looked like she had when she'd graced the stages of the continent's glittering cities. "Is it done yet?"

QuiTai smiled down at her. "Patience."

"You are going to smoke with me, aren't you? You know how much I hate going into the vapor alone."

The temptation was almost overwhelming. In the vapor,

she wouldn't feel any pain. "I shouldn't. Whoever followed me might be waiting for me to leave."

Jezereet's eyes widened. "You were followed? You saw him already?"

"I told you when I arrived that I thought I'd been followed." But Jezereet only looked more confused. "Never mind," QuiTai said. "Everything will be fine. The pipe is almost ready."

Jezereet rose to her knees and pressed her lips to QuiTai's neck. "Please come into the vapor with me."

QuiTai sighed as she turned the pipe.

"Please." Her hand slid between QuiTai's thighs. That was temptation QuiTai could not resist. "All right. A little."

"You first," Jezereet urged her. But Jezereet usually took the pipe the second it was ready. Something wasn't right. The open window, Jezereet's artificial laughter... Everything inside QuiTai told her to be cautious. But Jezereet's hand was persuasive, and QuiTai was too tired to fight fate.

"Don't you trust me anymore?" Jezereet asked. Tears brimmed in her eyes.

Jezereet was the best crier the stage had ever seen.

QuiTai came to consciousness to find someone rhythmically slapping her face. Kyam's voice cut through her fog. "Lady QuiTai! Wake up!"

It was a vapor nightmare if Kyam Zul had invaded it. If she couldn't sink back into the warm comfort of the nothingness, she could at least make him stop. Her fist struck out, but hit only air.

Cold water poured over her head. Sputtering, she forced herself out of her stupor. "What do you think you're – ?"

Kyam put his hand over her mouth. Grimly, he steered her attention to his side.

Jezereet lay on the floor near the door. Pink marks marred her perfect throat. She stared unblinking at QuiTai.

QuiTai pushed Kyam away and scrambled off the bed. She stumbled to Jezereet and gripped her hand. Still warm. "Jezereet!"

Kyam put his hand over her mouth again. "We must get out of here right away," he whispered.

Just blink. Just once. For me. Please, love.

Kyam whispered again, "You can't do any more for her. You've already done too much." He sounded as if he hated Jezereet.

QuiTai yanked away his hand and bared her fangs at him. She felt the heavy tug of her pale green venom hanging from the tips. He had no idea how fast she could drive them into the meat of his hand, or how willing she was to do it.

"Put those away. They make my skin crawl."

The fangs made her lisp slightly as she asked, "Did you kill her?"

"No." He pulled QuiTai to her feet. "Can you walk, or do I need to carry you?" When her legs failed her, he grabbed her roughly around the waist. She couldn't take her eyes off Jezereet. This had to be a nightmare.

"Do you know a private way out of here? You're in no shape to climb down the vine, and the front staircase is a little too public," Kyam said.

QuiTai shook her head hard. That only made it spin more.

Lines around his mouth and eyes radiated anger. Maybe he judged her for using black lotus. "Does that mean no?"

"It means I'm trying to get my brain working again. Have the soldiers been summoned? How many people know – " A sob welled out of her. It burned in her throat; when she put a hand to her neck, the flesh felt tender and swollen.

Take a breath, Jezereet. Breathe for me.

QuiTai bent and pulled the hem of Jezereet's dress to cover her thigh. QuiTai's lips trembled. There was nothing she could do. Everything she'd ever done was a waste now.

"It's too late to give her any dignity," Kyam said. "You're in danger. Do you understand that? We have to get you safe."

QuiTai shoved Kyam's arm away and lurched toward the

divan. He glared at her when she hung the vial of black lotus around her neck, but his opinion of her was the least of her concerns. Then she slipped behind Jezereet's dressing table and slid her fingertips over the silk moiré pattern on the wall. When she felt a bump under a rose print, she pushed. A thin door opened in the panel.

QuiTai headed down the dark, narrow stairs. When Kyam followed and shut the panel, the passage went black.

"Hold still for a moment," he said.

She was angry with him for daring to judge Jezereet; she was also strangely glad he was there. At least she could trust him to do the smart thing. Right then, she wasn't so sure she could. Time seemed to have stopped, and her thoughts were wrapped in fog inside a void.

Water dripped from her hair down the back of her neck. "Did you have to empty the entire pitcher on me?"

"You tried to hit me. It seemed safer than touching you again."

She heard a cracking sound, and then a blue glow filled the hallway from behind her.

"Hold this." Kyam passed a glowing glass tube to her. There was another crack, and then enough light to make out the steps ahead of them. The under-lighting cast sinister shadows across Kyam's face as she turned to him, holding the tube. "Instant jellylanterns. A Ravidian invention," he explained. "They don't give off much light, but it's better than the dark."

She tipped the tube back and forth to mix the rest of the chalky chemical at the bottom of the tube with the thick electric-blue slush that glowed brighter the more she shook it. "How do they work?"

"They dry the blue light jellylantern medusozoa, then grind them up. Half the tube has the dust, the other half water. When I push down the plunger, it breaks a thin membrane between them, and the water mixes with the dust to reconstitute the bioluminescence. But it doesn't last long. Half an hour at most."

Ravidian, she thought.

They took the stairs downward. At the landing, a long, narrow passage stretched before them.

"Where are we headed?" Kyam whispered.

She didn't bother to answer; he'd figure it out soon enough that it was the café next to the Red Happiness, as the sound of clanking dishes and voices came through the wall.

QuiTai held up the jellylantern until she spied a metal slot in the passageway wall. Through the opening, she could see the alley that ran behind the Red Happiness, and a bit of the lane beyond. It was dark outside; she didn't see anyone on the street.

On the floor under the spy hole was a large black box covered with dust and cobwebs. She crouched to open it: The fingers of her injured hand felt as if someone had taken a hammer to them and crushed every bone. From the box, she lifted a jacket, velvet leggings, and hat. Kyam had the good sense to stay quiet as she struggled to button the knee-length jacket over her kebaya blouse, although their voices probably wouldn't be heard over the noise in the café on the other side of the wall. But he chuckled a little as she wriggled into the thick leggings that went under the jacket.

She coiled her dripping braid into a bun and held it in place with her injured hand as she pushed the hat down on her head and jabbed long hat pins through it. When she was convinced it would stay, she withdrew a small box from the larger trunk. Inside were two vials. She willed her inner eyelids down, opened a vial, and carefully placed the contacts on her inner eyelids.

"There. Good enough to pass in the night," she muttered as she pushed away tears and dust from her face. "I can't see well like this. Is anyone passing by right now?"

Kyam moved to the observation slot. "A full moon, not many people out. A drunk is staggering toward the Red Happiness, but after him, it's quiet."

"There's a knob below the slot for the door."

"Why did you climb up the vine when you could take these

stairs instead?"

"There's no way to get in here from the outside. And even if there were, sometimes I'm followed. There are spies everywhere."

He didn't comment on that. She shoved the door open and they stepped cautiously out onto the street.

"Thank you for your assistance, Mister Zul," she said. "Perhaps I'll repay the favor one day."

She turned away from him, but didn't get two steps before he wrapped his hands around her waist and lifted her off the ground. The problem with big, strong men was that they could render you undignified without even straining a muscle. It was cruelly unfair, QuiTai thought, as she struck at him with both fists.

"Put up a fight if you must, Lady QuiTai, but I'm not letting you out of my sight until we've had a long talk."

She kicked as hard as she could. He started to double over, then smiled and shook his head. "That was close."

"Not close enough, apparently. If this is your attempt to make me help you, the answer is still no."

"I have a better proposition, one you won't be able to resist." He set her down and offered his arm. "But we can't discuss it until you're somewhere safe. Come with me willingly, or I'll toss you over my shoulder. It's up to you."

She gripped his elbow hard enough to make him wince. "I hope you know that I despise you right now," she told him.

"The feeling is mutual, my dear."

They strolled as if they were simply Thampurians out for some air after dinner. If anyone had looked closely, they might have seen her puffy eyes or trembling lips, but they might only have thought she feared rampaging werewolves.

They did not speak or look at each other; but a block later, they turned at the same time to check if they were followed. She would have laughed if she'd been able to.

Kyam finally broke the silence. "So, Lady QuiTai, your safe house or mine?"

CHAPTER 6: AN UNLIKELY ALLIANCE

Kyam's compound sat on the outer edge of the Thampurian neighborhood, past the governor's mansion and close enough to the sea that she could hear the constant surge of waves on the rocks far below. The kitchen house where he led her, while small by Thampurian standards, was three times the size of his apartment in town.

She huddled on a stool, arms wrapped tight around her, while he stoked the pit fire. Slowly she began to rock. She sang under her breath; her throat hurt too much for anything louder.

"That's pretty. What is it?" Kyam asked.

"Ingosolian death prayer. I'm singing Jezereet's soul into the arms of her goddess. She taught it to me when she first became addicted, she made me swear – "

Two things: that QuiTai would sing the death prayers, and that she would avenge Jezereet's death. QuiTai had known that Jezereet meant Petrof, who had set her on the black lotus path; but QuiTai fully intended to keep her word now, even though the murderer was still unknown. She would find him, and he would pay.

There was no way to stop the tears now. She hated that Kyam, of all people, saw her break down. If he tried to pat her, she'd rip off his hand.

Every time she thought she had control, hopeless tears poured down her cheeks. She was suffocating on grief.

Kyam went to the sideboard and searched roughly through canisters until he found what he wanted. Agitation seemed to ripple through his shoulders. "I'm making you tiuhon tea. Unless you need something stronger?"

She shook her head.

He filled an iron pot with water and swung it on a hook out over the fire. As he wiped out two cups, he leaned against the sideboard.

"You loved her? Why?"

She winced as her hands clenched into fists. It hurt almost as much as it had on the skiff.

"Put your hand out. I'll wrap it. Maybe that will help."

"Don't be nice to me. I can't bear it."

Kyam wet a thin towel with vinegar and wound it around her hand. "If this is your definition of nice, it explains a lot."

She closed her eyes and tried to will the pain out of her hand into the towel. "You mentioned business," she said. "Tell me what you have to offer."

"Not until you're fit to talk." Steam curled over the mugs as he poured hot water into them. After the tea steeped, he carried the two cups to her. QuiTai took both and poured the tea back and forth between them. When she was convinced they were equal, she handed one to Kyam.

"You think I'd poison you after going to so much trouble to save your life?" he asked.

"It's a force of habit. Drink yours first."

He seemed to struggle to hold back a few choice words before he took a sip.

QuiTai held her cup with both hands even though the heat made her hand throb again. The tea was bitter, but tiuhon was a restorative, something people drank to heal: it wasn't supposed to taste good.

Then she realized her hands were shaking. She willed them to stop. They did not. "What is this?"

"Shock, Lady QuiTai, you're in shock. I'll go find a blanket for you."

She was trembling so hard that she splashed the tea over the floor when she set the cup down. She closed her eyes, but that only brought back the image of Jezereet dead on the floor. By the time Kyam returned and draped a plush blanket over her shoulders, she was wracked by sobs.

"I can't – " A wave of grief stole the words from her. "I knew this day would come. Not murder... but I knew the vapor would eventually kill her. You'd think I'd be prepared by now." She took a deep breath and held it for a moment before slowly exhaling. "Please excuse my excessive emotion."

"You sound like a Thampurian." Kyam pulled a handkerchief out of his pocket and gently wiped her face. He held it to her nose. "Blow?"

She gave him a dark look. "You know what you can do with that handkerchief."

He put the square of silk on top of a solid wood chopping block as big as a tea table. "That sounds like the QuiTai I know and... well, that I'm used to. A gentleman would give you time to grieve, but as you know, I'm not a gentleman. I need the old you, . and I need her quick. The Ravidians disappeared from town hours after we met at the Red Happiness. But no ships have left the harbor for over a week because of the typhoon, and the Ravidians don't have articles of transport even if one had sailed. So they're here, in hiding, and my instincts tell me that they're up to no good. Time is of the essence."

Her temper flared, replacing the grief that had clung inside her. "Jezereet is dead, not even cold yet, and you brought me here to pump me for information?"

"You told me not to be nice."

"Oh, do be quiet. Since when do you do anything I ask?"

She tugged the blanket Kyam had given her closer around her shoulders. It smelled as if had been put away while still damp.

"What have you ever asked of me?"

"I ask you to leave the island every time we meet."

"You seem to forget that I've been told by my family to stay here, out of sight and out of mind."

"You expect me to believe that?"

He made a sound deep in his throat, as if he fought back a reply that welled from the darkest recess of his heart. "If you're going to accuse me of taking advantage of your grief, maybe I should. Tell me about the Ravidians. They had rooms in West Levapur overlooking the harbor, but they moved out several days ago and didn't leave as much as a speck of dust behind."

"I don't give a damn about the Ravidians anymore," she said. Petrof would force her to find them, but her urgency had evaporated with Jezereet's dying breath.

Kyam gripped the chopping block with big hands. His knuckles turned white. "You're going to help me whether you feel like it or not."

Despite herself, she was a bit curious. With their neck frills and velvet frock coats, the Ravidians stood out in Levapur. Why was Kyam having such a difficult time tracking them? He'd had a year to build a network of informants. Wasn't that the first thing a spy did when he went undercover at a new assignment? "Did anyone see them leave?"

"No one who will talk to me. But you could find out. If you don't already know." He waited. "Do you?"

Exhaustion rolled over QuiTai. "I'll give you this; you know how to pick your times. I can't think straight and all I want to do is curl up in a ball and sleep, or cry. First a spy, now an interrogator. Congratulations."

"You can't think that I planned this! You may be the most cynical, conniving person who ever lived, but not everyone is like you."

"Me in a vapor dream with my dead lover lying on the floor. You miraculously on the scene. What am I supposed to think?"

With his jaw clenched, he said, "I told you I didn't kill her."

Did she believe him?

He was rushing her. She needed time to think. She only had his word for it that she'd been in danger. If she hadn't been so muddled by the vapor, she could have examined Jezereet's room and figured out what happened. But he'd hurried her away. Was he hiding something?

He hovered over her as if he could intimidate her into a decision. That wasn't fair – not that anything was ever fair – but he was a Thampurian gentleman to his core, no matter how much he denied it.

If he'd wanted to use Jezereet as leverage, he would have kidnapped her. He would have kept her somewhere safe and maybe even brought her black lotus while he used her against QuiTai. Even Petrof understood that technique.

Her neck throbbed and her eyes itched. She had no energy left to fight Kyam. What would it matter if she gave him a little information?

"Do you have rum?" she asked.

He rummaged through the sideboard and found a half-empty bottle. He poured some into a glass, took a sip, and handed it to her. Then he poured one for himself.

She looked through the kitchen doorway. The moon was reflected in a puddle in the courtyard. As raindrops fell, expanding ripples collided and the moon's image fragmented. Soon the rain drummed steadily on the kitchen's roof.

Kyam rinsed out their tea cups in a stone bowl and put them away. He turned back to her. "I'm sorry for your loss."

His sincerity caught her by surprise. It was amazing how a few words could change the balance. He was probably the only person who would ever offer her any solace for Jezereet's death.

"Thank you." She meant it as much as he'd meant his condolences.

"I couldn't tell from what I saw… how was it done?" She closed her eyes for a moment. "Do you think she suffered much?"

"It was fairly quick. But if you're asking if she was in a vapor dream too, no, she wasn't. She knew what she was doing – " He stopped.

"My poor Jezereet," QuiTai murmured. Then realization

dawned on her. "You know who killed her."

Kyam took another sip of his rum and nodded.

The need for vengeance jolted her out of the fog of grief that had enveloped her. "Who did it, sea dragon?"

"Help me figure out what the Ravidians are up to, and I'll tell you; but not until I know everything. It's the only deal I'll make with you."

Their brief truce was over. It was better that way. Negotiations would keep them at a formal distance. Sympathy would only complicate matters between them.

She sat up straighter. Business. Right. A proposition was on the table and he thought he held all the tiles. That would work to her advantage.

Other people had been in the Red Happiness; maybe a few discreet questions would bring her the name of Jezereet's killer. But until she made her inquiries, it was best to pretend Kyam had won. "It seems that I stand corrected. You are able to force my hand."

Kyam said, "You need food. Is rice-and-eggs okay? It better be. It's the only thing I have stored here, and the only thing I know how to cook." He dumped cooked rice into a skillet and put it over the fire.

He was trying to set the tone for their working relationship. If he wanted to believe that they could be chums, she'd let him, but the moment she had what she wanted she'd drop the act.

She thought for a moment before saying, "Since we agree that you aren't the murderer, I'll assume that you followed me there. I'm still not sure why you risked the streets during a full moon when you couldn't have known the evening would turn in your favor. I know what you think of me. Bitch. Whore. Shiftless. Snake."

Only the word *snake* made him cringe. "If that's all you were, I wouldn't have gone to the trouble to get you out of the Red Happiness alive."

Her mind went back to the brothel. The servants had standing orders to check on Jezereet every morning and evening, but still it would be hours before anyone found her body. And then the Thampurian soldiers would be called in to investigate.

QuiTai's eyes widened as she realized what would follow. "Do you have more rum?"

"Sure. Why?"

"Because my hand hurts unbelievably badly. And because we're about to have the ugliest conversation ever, and I don't want to be completely sober for it."

"Ugly how?"

"There are going to be another two murders tonight."

He frowned. "The Ravidians have a target? Or is there someone else dear to you that you think is in danger?"

"Not people. We're going to have to kill our consciences. Someone has to hang for Jezereet's murder." Now he looked thoroughly puzzled. "You really are a fresh, Mister Zul. Think. The soldiers are called to the scene. I assume even those incompetent bastards will figure out that she was murdered?"

He reluctantly nodded. "It will be fairly obvious."

"There will be an investigation. They have to arrest someone, to make it seem as if they know what they're doing. If not me, and not the real murderer, then who? I suggest we decide rather than leaving it up to your soldiers. As you may be aware, they aren't too particular about actual guilt. So, which innocent is going to suffer for her death, Mister Zul?"

Grimly, he uncorked the bottle and filled both glasses.

Kyam and QuiTai sat on the wood chopping block, back to back. She'd shed her disguise and was much more comfortable in her normal clothes, except for the dull ache in her throat and the sharper pains in her heart.

The homey scent of rice-and-eggs hung in the air. Both Kyam and QuiTai clutched glasses of rum. An empty bottle sat between them, and they'd started on a second one.

Thunder rumbled as rain splattered on the tile roof of the

kitchen building. They kept the door and windows shut, not because of the rain, but so the light of the kitchen fire wouldn't give them away. It seemed unlikely to QuiTai that anyone would dare enter the small exterior courtyard without being invited in, much less go around the privacy wall and pass through the inner festoon gates to the inner courtyard where they could see into the kitchen, but she appreciated his caution.

"Is your hand any better?" Kyam asked.

"No, but I care less about the pain. I guess that's something."

"Did it ever occur to you that the murderer might give your name to the authorities? He might have meant for you to be found in the room with her," Kyam said.

"He? So it was a man?"

"General, non-specific he, the same way you refer to all monkeys as he."

"I refer to the female monkeys as she, but we're getting off topic again."

It was a mistake to spend time with Kyam. Her normal defenses were shattered, and he was too easy to talk to, too reasonable, except for the anger he directed at Jezereet. QuiTai had to think about her loyalties, and they sure as hell didn't lie with a Thampurian spy.

She felt Kyam turn, and she looked over her shoulder at him.

"This is getting us nowhere," he said.

"I still refuse to pin it on a Ponongese. You are aware that my people are *people*, right? Actual thinking, feeling humans. Not snakes. It's not as if we're shifters too."

He bristled. "Shifters aren't animals." When she grinned slightly, she could see him force his temper aside. "Okay, fine. And I won't implicate Thampurians, so quit saying we should accuse the chief justice of the colonial government."

"You have no idea how dangerous that man is. Besides they wouldn't hang a Thampurian for killing an Ingosolian prostitute. They save those punishments for the Ponongese."

"You always have to slip in that lecture about politics, as if I'm personally responsible for everything every Thampurian has ever done."

He had a point. Still, if he would agree that Thampurian rule was unjust, she might back off. And he worked for the government, which certainly made him guilty of something.

The steady sound of the pouring rain made her sleepy. Even though it was warm in the kitchen, she kept the blanket around her shoulders.

It had been a while since her last crying jag. Bit by bit, she pried grief from her heart. She accepted that she was fated to find Jezereet's killer and make him pay for his crime, because the sense of cold calm it brought her was the only way she knew to keep going.

Why kill Jezereet, who had never harmed anyone? Who was doomed anyway? It might make sense to kill QuiTai, but why Jezereet?

"You're awfully quiet. Nodding off?" Kyam asked.

"Thinking." QuiTai sipped her drink. It helped when he talked. It stopped her from spiraling down too far into her thoughts.

"You realize we've limited ourselves to about one percent of the island's population." Kyam hopped off the chopping block and gripped it to steady himself.

"You also narrowed my list of suspects considerably."

Kyam grimaced as if he had just lost a point in a game. Then he pushed away his glass of rum. "I don't suppose you'd be willing to turn in the Devil, would you?"

"That's not an option."

"Why not? Unless he's just a myth."

"What a thing to say. Of course he's real."

"No one has ever seen him. But everyone knows you." Kyam poked her arm with an unsteady finger.

"Stop that." QuiTai clumsily shoved his hand away. She slid off the block to stand up to him. Her brain felt as if it floated. "I think I better stop drinking now."

He picked up the bottle and shook it. "I like you drunk. You haven't insulted me for over two hours."

"More reason to sober up. You should slow down too, or

you'll be too drunk to tell the soldiers who to arrest, and then where will we be?"

"We'd feel like better people."

"Don't fool yourself. Even having this conversation has soiled our souls forever."

"Then decide. Don't you know anyone who deserves to hang? With all those criminals in the Devil's organization, one of them has to be guilty of a capital crime. Someone you don't like?"

"I have nothing against them, but have you thought of the Ravidians?" QuiTai asked.

"I certainly have, but for now, I need them alive. Come on. You know the dregs of society. Who's a villain?"

Ivitch. Of course. Why hadn't she thought of him sooner?

Kyam shook his finger at her again but didn't poke her. "You have that look on your face. Tell me."

Petrof would never forgive her if he ever found out. She grimaced. Ivitch had surely told Petrof some story about how she'd failed with the dirt Thampurian. Petrof might never give her a chance to tell her version; but with Ivitch out of the way, she'd have a better shot at earning her way back into his good graces.

"All right. Don't. Protect people who don't deserve protection. I've decided anyway." Kyam grabbed a hearth shovel and banked the glowing coals in the cooking pit together.

This would be interesting. "Who?"

"Ivitch."

She gasped. "How did you – "

Kyam leaned forward as if he were afraid he'd miss the next words out of her mouth.

"Are you trying to get me to tell you who the Devil is? Never," she snapped. "But I think we've reached an agreement on the official sacrifice. And just in case you have any qualms tomorrow morning when your head is clear and you start trying to have a conscience again, Ivitch killed a Thampurian citizen after you left us at the harbor. So technically he's due for hanging anyway."

"That proves one thing at least. Ivitch isn't the Devil. You'd never give your lover up that easily, even if he abandoned you to suffer alone down in the harbor. You're stubbornly loyal to people who don't deserve your affection."

"Ivitch didn't touch me. He wouldn't dare. I was hurt after he left. He doesn't know."

Kyam raised his hands to the roof as if inviting the gods to join their conversation. "And now you're covering for him too. Unbelievable." His arms fell to his sides. It seemed he couldn't bear to look at her until he swiftly turned back to her, hand outstretched. "Look at the way you're able to predict what will happen when Jezereet's body is found – and yes, I think you're dead right. You're twenty steps ahead of everyone, even in your condition. But for such a smart woman, you're a marvel of selective vision."

"Who should I be loyal to? You?"

"Of all the people you know, I'm the only one who protected you tonight."

"I didn't ask you to." She smoothed her sarong. "If Ivitch is captured alive, he may implicate me in that death, and nothing, not even the Zul family money, can protect me from the rope if he does. So if you want me to help you with the Ravidians, you're going to have to protect me from your government."

Grudgingly, Kyam laughed. "You really are unbelievable." He cleared his throat when he saw her scowl. "Does Ivitch have good cause to implicate you? Are you guilty?"

"If my word means anything to you, no, I'm not. I most explicitly warned Ivitch not to kill the man. The dirt Thampurian was an informant who could have told me about the crates the Ravidians smuggled onto the island. Ivitch ignored my orders."

Kyam set down the iron shovel. "I knew it! You do have information on the Ravidians. What was in the crates?"

"You and the Devil would love to know the answer to that."

"How about you? Aren't you curious?"

"I – " She stopped herself abruptly. She was speaking far too much. Talking to Kyam was effortless, as if the words flowed of their own accord. Either he'd spent the entire last year studying her to find a way through her defenses, or he was unaware of how he affected her.

"Not even the tiniest bit curious? Come on. That's not the QuiTai I know." Grinning, he gently bumped her with his shoulder.

He probably didn't mean anything by it other than a friendly gesture, but that was dangerous enough. She steeled her mind and moved away from him. "I only want to know who killed Jezereet." Everything else – the crates, the Ravidians, everything – were simply coins that would buy that information. She didn't owe it to Kyam to be sweet. Her suspicious nature had saved her life many times, and if it hurt his precious manly feelings, that was just too bad. Jezereet had tried to be the accommodating hostess when a cunning monster showed up at her door, and look where that got her.

CHAPTER 7: TRACKING THE RAVIDIANS

*T*he rum and the sound of the rain that fell through the night worked their magic to lull QuiTai to sleep, but every time she moved, pain shot through her hand and woke her. After a difficult night of tossing and turning, her unbraided hair was a mess. Her clothes from the day before stank of sweat and vinegar. As she reluctantly considered putting them on, Kyam knocked quietly at the door of the cook's quarters. When she opened the door, a soft pink batik print sarong and blouse lay folded neatly on the floor. It wasn't a color she would have chosen, but the blouse fit, and it was better than wearing her soiled clothes another day. He'd even left her a bowl of water, a sliver of fragrant soap, and a wash cloth.

From the pile of blankets on the floor outside the door, she guessed he had slept there while she took the only cot.

When she joined him in the kitchen, he wore fresh clothes too. He offered her a bowl of fritters. "I went shopping right after sunrise. These are cold already, if you trust me enough to eat them."

"You seem to want me alive, for now, so I'll risk it."

QuiTai climbed gingerly onto the chopping block rather than take one of the low stools near the cooking pit. Her feet dangled above the floor. She bit into a sweet fritter, while Kyam frowned at his reflection in a narrow, stained mirror fragment hanging from the roof's support beam.

"Why don't you do that in the house? You can't even see your entire face in that mirror," she said. She got down from the block and reached for his ear. She pinched his earlobe much harder than she needed to. He flinched. "Stay still," she said, "unless a dollop of shaving cream on your ear is the latest in Thampurian fashion. And you missed that spot on your cheek you always do."

His hand slid over his face in search of the errant whiskers.

"I'll do it." She reached for the razor on the sideboard.

Kyam snatched it first. "Only a fool would hand you a straight razor." He turned his head and tried to see the spot he'd missed.

"Don't be an idiot. I won't kill you until you tell me who killed Jezereet." She lightly pushed on his arm. "And share the mirror. Do you have a hair brush? I need to plait my hair." She'd never go out in public with it loose, as if she were a child.

When he gave her space to look at herself, she saw that her throat was bruised. She stepped closer and spread the neckline of her blouse. That explained why it hurt so much. "Mister Zul?" She turned to him.

"I told you that we'd talk about what happened last night after you helped me with the Ravidians."

"You said you'd give me the name of the murderer. That's different."

"You are a sargasso sea." He clipped each word with terse precision.

"I take it that's a Thampurian insult."

"Literally, it means you're seaweed blocking my shipping lane. Metaphorically, it means you're a massive pain in my a— backside."

That gave her more satisfaction than it should have. "Afraid that I'll figure out the culprit on my own?"

"You have a remarkable ability to add one and one and come up with five. The description of the murderer is the only leverage I have. I can't risk slipping up, not around you."

It was strange to be with someone who complimented her, even when he was furious with her. Petrof always said that her abilities were annoying. "How about an exchange? I'll answer your questions if you answer mine."

Kyam shook his head. "If there's one thing I've learned from you, it's that I don't ask the right questions. So I'd rather you volunteered information."

"You're the one with the pressing timetable. Jezereet is beyond my help."

The muscles along his jaw line flexed. Too bad. If he'd let himself speak, it would no doubt have been an impressive string of curses. "Sit down. Let me see your hand."

QuiTai held out her hand. Her head ached a bit from the rum, and the dull throb in her throat still nagged at her, but her heart hurt much more.

Today is my first day without Jezereet. For now and forever.

Underneath her grief she felt a terrible relief, the sense that a great burden had been lifted from her. She wouldn't have to watch Jezereet decline into the vapor like that dirt Thampurian. Jezereet would never strike her out of frustration again. Petrof would never again be able to use black lotus to coerce her. She was free.

She hated herself for even thinking it.

Kyam unwrapped the bandage and held her fingers gently as he turned her hand to the daylight streaming through the window screen. "Why does it worry me when you get quiet?"

"The Devil often says the same thing."

He dripped vinegar over the welt. "And how do you answer him?"

"Sometimes with more silence."

He pulled a stool toward him and sat. His long legs were ungainly in such a low seat with his knees up to his chin, but he didn't seem to care.

"How did you manage to get stung by a sea wasp when they

live off the west coast of the continent? Nearly two thousand miles away?"

She studied her scar. "How do you know what it was? Can you be sure?"

"Yes."

Realizing that was all he planned to say, she said, "It's a long story."

"I'm listening."

He'd changed, she realized. The easy camaraderie from the night before was gone. He seemed more determined. Even though she, for once, towered over him, he still managed to be menacing. That dangerous aura sent a familiar rush through her body, one she normally only felt around Petrof. And Kyam's intense concentration made her nervous. Could he sense her thoughts?

"Do the soldiers know that Jezereet is dead yet?" QuiTai asked.

Kyam looked angry. "Her, again. The Red Happiness was quiet this morning."

"They'll know soon. A servant checks on her every morning."

In a swift movement, he came to his feet. As usual, he stood too close; only instead of making her angry, this time she wanted to wrap her fingers in his hair and bring his mouth down to hers for a kiss. What was she thinking? She couldn't even look at him, because all she saw was the finely tailored shewani jacket that fit his muscular chest like a second skin; all she felt was the promise of danger that set her blood on fire like nothing else.

He still trapped her hand. Her fingers throbbed. He said, "One wonders how you know the daily routine of the Red Happiness. And about the secret passage inside it. But we can discuss that later. Now I'd like to talk about what happened to your hand." Kyam's grip on her fingers tightened. "Lady QuiTai, how did you come by this scar?"

Even though it hurt enough to bring a tear to the corner of her eye, she pushed her hand toward him, twisted it, and escaped from his grasp. She cradled her hand in her lap. "No need to be so primitive."

"You didn't even consider telling me how much that hurt. Are you so used to pain?"

"Are you so used to hurting people?" she asked.

"If I have to."

Something in his tone made her believe him. And the information about her hand was covered in their agreement about exchanging information...

She said, "Yesterday, after you left me at the harbor, I stayed behind to conduct a bit of the Devil's business. Which is rapidly becoming indistinguishable from your business."

He crossed his arms over his chest and nodded.

"We believe that the Ravidians smuggled something onto the island. Not a simple task. Your soldiers and the harbor master are vigilant tax collectors."

That wasn't strictly true. It was easy to bring contraband through the harbor, as long as one were willing to pay the 'enhanced' tax, and didn't care that it went directly into the harbor master's pocket. But Kyam didn't need to know about that; it was, as she often phrased it, the Devil's business.

"The dirt Thampurian rumored to have helped the Ravidians was the harbor master's brother." She tilted her head, expecting him to say something. His expression didn't change. "If the dirt Thampurian had been paid in money, he would have bought black lotus from the Devil's men. But they hadn't seen him. I think the Ravidians paid him directly in black lotus. But for what? They aren't moving goods through the markets as far as we can tell."

"Continue."

"Someone helped them move their shipment, and I'm fairly certain by now that those crates never made it upslope to Levapur. The dirt Thampurian was a heavy vapor user. The living dead. There's no way he would have had the strength to sail his skiff out of the harbor, especially with the rough seas from the typhoon. The harbor master, however... "

"What does that have to do with your hand?"

"I warned you that it's a long story. Don't make the mistake of thinking I'm trying to entertain you. Every part of this story is fulfillment of my end of our arrangement." But QuiTai took a private moment to decide how much of the whole story she was honor-bound to tell. "After you left the harbor yesterday, Ivitch and I boarded the dirt Thampurian's skiff. Ivitch got rough and strangled him before I could question him. Ivitch took off, leaving me behind."

"Get to the part where you got stung."

"I had to hide on the boat until sunset. It was filthy. Little bits of garbage, murky puddles of sea water... my hand slipped into one, and intense pain shot up my arm, and then I saw the stinger, and I knew..."

"Knew what?"

Everything except how to make a profit from the Ravidian's plot. But she wasn't about to tell Kyam that. With a slight shake of her shoulders, she sat up straight. "This may sound melodramatic, but for a while, I honestly thought I might die."

"Many people do die from those stings. If you'd touched a few more, your heart wouldn't have recovered from the shock."

"There were moments yesterday where death looked like the better option."

"That still doesn't explain why you got a sea wasp sting on a boat in Ponong's harbor."

"I think it does, Mister Zul. Now we know what the Ravidians smuggled onto the island."

Kyam's brows furrowed and he stared speechless for a moment. Then: "Sea wasps? Why? They could catch them off their coast."

"It's fairly obvious."

"To you, maybe."

Her lips curved. He really didn't see it. If he needed her to spell it out, it would cost him. "Why do you care what the Ravidians smuggled onto Ponong, Mister Zul?"

"That's my business, and none of yours. Just accept that I'm very interested and won't rest until I find out."

Kyam Zul might have thought his business was all that

mattered, but she had other duties that didn't stop for his convenience. When he was long out of the picture, the Devil's business would remain. She couldn't lose sight of that. She said, "Well, I had several hours on the boat yesterday to mull it over, and I was up most of last night. I'll be glad to take you through the steps."

"Go ahead. I'm listening."

"Not yet, Mister Zul. The soldiers will have been summoned to the Red Happiness by now. Time for you to convince them that Ivitch is their man."

The typhoon shutters on the upstairs veranda of the residential building inside Kyam's compound were closed. Ferns sprouted from the stucco walls. The jungle erupted through the tiles in the courtyard.

They passed the festoon gate that joined the inner courtyard to the small outer courtyard. The red, green, blue, and gold paint on the four pillars was faded, but the carved sea dragons wrapped around them were still visible, as were the small snakes with caricatures of Ponongese faces crushed under their talons.

"That's subtle," QuiTai said.

"We can talk politics some other time. Or you can talk, and I'll ignore you like I always do."

"One day, Mister Zul, you're going to find yourself caring more about politics, and you'll wish you'd paid more attention."

"One of your visions of the future?"

"You could call it that." It was the Oracle's vision, but she'd learned not to mention the Oracle to anyone.

She followed him around a privacy wall covered in aqua blue tiles bearing the Zul family chop. He raised a finger. "You're either about to tell me that a proper safe house isn't held in your family name, or that I'm an idiot for staying in that apartment when I could be living here. Save your breath. This was nearby, and you were in no shape to travel."

"Actually, I was going to say that you're not much of a morning person. I pity the poor man or woman who wakes up beside you." She smiled sweetly and batted her eyelashes. After their odd truce the night before, a return to their regular banter was a welcome normality.

"At least my lovers wake up," he said.

She blinked. She felt the smile slide off her face. For a moment, she couldn't breathe.

After a moment, he said gruffly, "That was unspeakably rude of me. I'm sorry."

When she was able to draw in a breath, it staggered down her throat. People said cruel things to her all the time, and normally, she ignored them; but his words had uncanny aim.

"Lady QuiTai – " He reached for her arm. She sidestepped his touch. He was under no obligation to be civil to her. She chided herself for expecting any Thampurian to treat a Ponongese with dignity; then, chin lifted high, she headed for the Red Happiness.

Kyam let her walk alone until the white verandas of the Red Happiness were close. Then he gripped her elbow and steered her behind a tree. "I think it would be best if you stayed out of sight for now. I don't want the soldiers to see those marks on your neck. They would raise too many questions."

"You were willing to hand me over to them last night."

"That's before you agreed to help me."

She looked down at his grip on her and then raised her gaze to meet his. "Mister Zul, I understand that despite my personal feelings on the matter, we have entered a business arrangement. I intend to deliver the information I promised, as I assume do you. However, please remember that this partnership is not equal. I can find Jezereet's murderer without your help."

"And I can figure out what the Ravidians are up to without

yours."

"With my blessing." She stepped away.

Kyam yanked her back behind the tree. "We have a deal. But if you want to be in charge, be in charge. Tell me what you want me to do, honorable lady." His bow had too much flourish to be sincere.

"Before or after you go to hell?"

"Too late. I'm already there." He blocked her as she tried to go around him. "If I may make a suggestion though, it really isn't a good idea for the Devil's concubine to mix with the soldiers. They might take you down to the fortress for questioning just because they can. You know how those Thampurians are."

"You have been listening, after all."

"More closely than you imagine."

Maybe she should have been alarmed, but she was flattered.

"And when it comes to this particular group of soldiers, I have to agree with you. They swagger through the marketplace and treat the natives as if they own the whole damn island."

She knew exactly which soldiers he meant. They were the worst face of the colonial occupation.

"So, do we have an agreement? I'll take care of this alone," Kyam said.

"While I do what?"

"Weave one of your devious plans. Think. Create new insults to hurl at me. Or maybe – just maybe – rest a little. Yesterday was a long day for you, and I have a feeling today won't be much better."

She wasn't used to such treatment; his consideration would be missed when their business was complete. Resting sounded good. Keeping mentally sharp around Kyam had exhausted the little burst of energy of the morning.

She plucked a snake flower from an overhead branch and sniffed it. The little green fangs of its twin curving carpals tickled her face. "That's your cue, Mister Zul. The stage is yours."

"What do you know? She does listen to reason." Kyam pulled down his sleeves and buttoned his jacket all the way up.

"Showtime."

QuiTai leaned against the tree. Leaving Kyam to his own devices was tempting, but where would she go? Her safe houses were even more barren than his. Why was it that everyone else had someone they could turn to in moments like this? There wasn't a single person she trusted to give her help and restful shelter. She couldn't think of a lover who had ever offered her comfort. Maybe it was the kind of people she tended to take to bed. Petrof wasn't a tender person, and even before Jezereet was addicted to the vapor, she always had to be the center of attention.

Perhaps QuiTai needed to find a friend.

She chuckled at herself. A friend. The very idea was absurd.

Her palm still ached. When she brushed her fingertips lightly over the wine-red welt, it was like stroking burned flesh.

"Where have you been, QuiTai?" Petrof said.

QuiTai jumped as she turned to his voice. He shoved aside leaves in his path as he strode toward her.

Her hand pressed to her chest. She'd never been so stunned. He'd come out of his room. He'd walked through the city to find her. She searched his face for signs of panic, but he only looked annoyed.

"Jezereet... died," she said.

"Where have you been? I searched for you all last night."

"You already heard?"

His clothes were damp, as if he'd been caught out in the rain while she'd spent the night inside. No wonder he was grumpy. And yet, instead of returning to the house for a bath and dry clothes, he'd still hunted for her. More than any soft words, that proved he cared.

She pressed her face against his chest. The familiar scent of him almost made up for the way he stiffened when she wrapped her arms around him.

He paused almost a moment too long, as if he mulled over the news, but he finally stroked her hair. "Poor QuiTai. How your heart must be breaking." From his tone, that seemed to please him.

Suspicious, she leaned back and searched his face. He was jealous enough of Jezereet to addict her to black lotus. It was a slow, cruel death sentence and he'd enjoyed making QuiTai watch it. She'd never fooled herself about that. Maybe she shouldn't have been so quick to believe that he'd come to her now out of love.

Soft concern flowed over his face like a mask. "You can't blame me for hating sharing you with her."

Blame and recriminations were the last things she wanted to think about right now.

"You're my woman."

His hand slid down her back and pushed her groin against his. The hard glint of possessive sexuality was in his eyes now. It radiated from him as if it covered his skin and flowed onto her. His seductive charms could sway her, but they wouldn't make her forget her loss.

"Why would anyone kill her, Petrof? She never hurt anyone."

"It was a mistake."

She nodded. Of course it was a mistake. She held tighter to him and pressed her lips to his chest.

His hand moved from her buttocks to her neck. He said, "Were you alone last night?"

If she told him the truth, he might kill Kyam, and she'd lose her chance to find out who murdered Jezereet. But he'd come to comfort her. Didn't he deserve the truth from her, for once?

His thumb pressed against pulse at the jugular. "Were you alone?" His voice was quiet with menace.

She almost shook her head… but then his fingers curled over the bruises on her neck and woke the points of pain.

"Were you with a man?" he said.

The pain steadied her. Once Jezereet's murderer was dead,

she'd rededicate herself to Petrof and never try to play both sides again. She swore it.

"I slept alone," she told him. That much was true.

He flicked the collar of her blouse. "I don't remember you ever wearing pink before. Did you fuck that Thampurian? Did he buy this for you?"

A shiver went down her back. Who had seen her with Kyam? She said, "You know how I feel about Thampurians."

"Yes. I do. So I'll believe you, about that." Petrof's thumb stroked her pulse. "Tell me about the smugglers."

"Ivitch probably told you that the dirt Thampurian died, but I have a new lead. As soon as I have news, I'll bring it to you." Unwilling to let to moment pass, she hugged him hard again. "Thank you for leaving your den to come find me."

I never knew I could count on you until now.

"It was no – Soldiers!" Petrof shoved QuiTai away. "They're coming after me!"

QuiTai peered around the tree to see Kyam and four Thampurian soldiers step off the veranda of the Red Happiness and head toward them then stop in the middle of the muddy street. She couldn't hear their words, but it looked like a terse exchange. Usually Thampurians carried on with flowery protocol that took forever, but after a curt bow, Kyam stepped away and headed toward the town square instead of returning to her.

She exhaled in relief. "No, Petrof, they're going back... "

But he was gone. She didn't blame him for being wary of the soldiers. Whatever torture he'd endured at their hands haunted him still. He'd never liked jungle's bugs and humidity, but afterwards he couldn't even bear to walk through it. He refused to talk about what they'd done to him, but while in the grip of nightmares, he sometimes screamed about ants. Thousands and thousands of ants swarming over him...

She leaned against the tree. Who would have ever suspected Petrof of being so concerned that he'd overcome his fears to comfort her? Not her. It was such an unexpected, out of character gesture... and she had needed it so much. She would not examine it and twist it until she turned it into something with darker intent, the way she always did. Sometimes she ruined everything by thinking too much.

When Kyam finally came back, he had a small package in his hand. "I'm almost sorry you missed my performance. I played the obnoxious scion of the thirteen families to the hilt. Swaggered in there as if I owned the place." He tried to catch her gaze. "No comment? Come on. I know you want to say something."

"This is your story, not mine." She hated the way Kyam interrupted the spell Petrof had woven around her. Her nerves felt as raw as her hand.

"You couldn't have called that scene any better than if you'd written the script. Major Voorus and his men were already beating a confession out of one of the barkeeps in a back room. They weren't happy about the interruption until they found out they could go after one of the Devil's thugs. Then they were all ears."

"That doesn't surprise me," QuiTai said. She found it hard to summon any interest in his story.

"I told Voorus that everyone knew the werewolves' blood lust ran high the night of the full moon, and that yesterday while we rode on the funicular down to the harbor, Ivitch had muttered dire threats about teaching Jezereet a lesson for some slight. And I warned them that Ivitch was crazy and they should knock him out the second they capture him. It's the only way I could think of to stop him from bringing up your name."

That was smart. It was a relief to work with someone who didn't screw up all the time.

"I, um, bought something for you." Kyam thrust the package at her.

The polite thing would be to extend both hands and take the gift with a bow. She kept her hands at her sides. It wouldn't do for Kyam to think they were friends.

"Okay then." He ripped the packaging away to reveal a mocha silk scarf. He lightly wound it around her throat. "It doesn't match what you're wearing, but it will look nice with the colors you usually wear." He fussed with the ends. "It hides the fingerprints."

She could feel tears for Jezereet welling up inside her. She said, "If time had any manners, it would stop when someone dies and let the mourners catch their breaths. But it doesn't."

His movements slowed but he didn't look up. "I never suspected you had such melancholy moods. You're usually so confident. You saunter around town with that wicked smile playing on your lips... your scathing wit is always ready to draw soul blood."

"Moods pass." Grief ended. The world went on. She took a deep breath.

"If I didn't need your sharper side so much right now, I wouldn't mind this softer QuiTai."

She jerked back from his touch. "I'm not soft, Mister Zul. Never soft."

A glimmer of humor lit up his eyes. "That's my girl."

She tried to wither him with her glare. He grinned. "Let's pay a visit to the harbor master," he said, and offered her his arm.

CHAPTER 8: A NARROW ESCAPE

The harbor master's office was locked. While Kyam rattled the door, QuiTai headed for the wharf. The normally tranquil waves of the protected harbor were white capped, breaking hard on the beach sand, leaving behind a meandering line of foam, broken shells, and kelp when they ebbed. The stiff wind rocked the junk at the dock and whipped her thin sarong around her ankles. Dock workers cast loaded crates onto a net of heavy rope.

She watched a crane lift the net full of crates, the rope creaking as the crane swung towards the junk, where waiting sailors sprang into action, grabbing guide ropes and straining to keep them in place as the ship rolled in the rough waves. The crane lowered the crates through an open cargo hatch into the junk's hold.

Kyam joined her. "When will the harbor master's office open?" he asked the dock workers.

"He hasn't been in since yesterday morning," a dockworker replied grudgingly. It was clear that was all he meant to say.

"We should look into his office," QuiTai whispered.

Kyam nodded.

They strolled to the weathered single-story building. Like all Thampurian structures, the eaves of its roof curved upward at the ends, but that was its only nod to style. It was an ugly, squat building in much need of paint.

As they tried to peer through the salt-caked windows, another worked asked, "What are you two up to?"

"Colonel Kyam Zul of His Majesty's Intelligence Services. I will be entering the harbor master's office to ascertain whether or not he is inside and in need of assistance. This is a matter of Thampurian national security."

QuiTai put a hand over her mouth to hide her smirk. Thampurian national security indeed. As if a corrupt minor local official meant anything to them.

Kyam knocked on the door. "Harbor master, are you inside?" He cocked his head as if listening. "In the name of His Majesty, I command you to open this door if you are able." QuiTai thought he was in danger of overplaying his part. Still, the dockworker seemed impressed, until Kyam took a small black fold out of his pocket, selected a pick, and jiggled it in the lock.

"Aren't you going to kick it in?" the man asked.

QuiTai faked coughing to cover her laughter. Kyam shot her a dirty look. "How would I lock the door after I leave if I kick it?"

The lock clicked open. "That wasn't very exciting," the dockworker complained. He peered through the doorway. "Is there a body in there?"

"Please, sir, stay back." Kyam stepped into the office and slammed the door behind him.

The dockworker nodded toward the door. "If he's in there, wake him up and tell him our boss needs him to sign papers on this shipment we're loading." He walked away.

QuiTai knocked gently on the door. It creaked open. She looked inside. "He's gone. Find anything interesting?"

Kyam stood behind the desk, shuffling through papers in a file. "No. Unless one of these papers has *clue* written across it in bright red letters, I won't find anything without spending hours reading through them."

QuiTai leaned against the doorjamb. "He wouldn't have left a paper trail if he were helping Ravidians."

"Unless the ship's captain knew it was smuggled goods, he would have insisted on an official receipt," Kyam said as he lifted files off the desk. "This would go faster if you helped."

"Our business agreement strictly forbade paperwork," she said.

He almost smiled as he gaze rose to hers.

"It's an implied clause. I invoke them only as the need arises," QuiTai added.

From his reluctant chuckle, Kyam was as amused by her as she was by him. "I have a feeling you could swindle a con artist. My grandfather would adore you."

"If he ever returns to Ponong, I should like to meet the old rascal. I might even like him."

Kyam tossed the file onto the desk. He leaned on his knuckles. "This is work for a team with some expertise in harbor management. Finding the harbor master is a better use of our time." He gestured her toward the door.

"See? You don't need my help. You're doing fine on your own."

They stepped outside. "But it wouldn't be as fun," he said. He shut the door and re-locked it.

"This is business," QuiTai said.

"That doesn't mean it's boring. This morning was the first time I woke up on this island with something to look forward to."

"Only a Thampurian would be giddy at the prospect of digging through a mountain of forms."

"You know that wasn't what I meant." Kyam stepped up to the ticket office for the funicular. "Two, please."

While they waited for the funicular to make the slow

descent from the town square, QuiTai squatted in the shade and plotted her next moves. She would go back to Petrof and tell him her theory about the Ravidian smugglers – which he probably wouldn't believe – and hope he didn't get too angry with her. She touched her throat. The scarf was like water through her fingers. It must have cost Kyam a small fortune. All because he'd upset her and wanted to apologize. For a man of such brusque manners, he had his moments of charm.

And he was right: In spite of her grief, this investigation was fun. And she had no right to enjoy herself right now. She should simply tell Kyam why she thought the Ravidians had brought crates of sea wasps to Ponong. If he really thought about it, he would figure it out: Once he did, he'd also have a good idea where to find them. To save them both time and trouble, she should tell him the theory she'd worked out while on the dirt Thampurian's skiff; then he could tell her the name of Jezereet's murderer, and they could go their separate ways.

The funicular's cable twanged as if plucked. Although she couldn't see the cars yet, that sound was always the first warning that the funicular was near. Kyam offered his hand to pull her to her feet.

The brakes screeched as it slowly slid into the station.

The station master unlocked the doors of each car. Even though Kyam was a Thampurian, they had to wait while crates from the wharf were loaded and strapped in first, and then squeeze in past the cargo. Once they were on board, the station master shut the door and locked it. Moments later, the shrill whistle sounded and the funicular started the steep ascent uphill. The crates strained against the frayed belts that held them in place.

QuiTai leaned against the lower window to watch their rise from the harbor. She always liked this view. The water was the same color as jewels in the windows of expensive shops back on the continent. It seemed so very long ago that she and Jezereet had walked arm in arm through paved streets, dressed in the latest fashions, always happy. Sometimes admirers followed them and bought Jezereet anything she desired. There had been so much wine, so much laughter. If nothing in life was free, then QuiTai was sure she was paying for those carefree days now, with interest.

She shook her head. She was growing melancholy again, and it wouldn't do. She had to stop clinging to this brief respite from the world that Kyam offered and take up her duties again. She owed that to Petrof. It was time to move on.

"Mister Zul, let me save us both a lot of trouble. I'll tell you my theory about the Ravidians. Then you can go your way, and I'll go mine."

"Oh, no. Our contract clearly states that you'll continue to help me until I have all the proof I need."

She arched an eyebrow as high as it would go.

"It's an implied clause," he said.

He thought he was so funny. QuiTai gritted her teeth. "There's ample evidence that you've discovered something important. At the very least, the sea wasp stinger in the dirt Thampurian's boat should raise questions. Get out that farwriter you have hidden in your trunk, and inform your superiors."

"I need proof, not theories."

Frustrated, she folded her arms over her chest. "What is Ponong's primary export, Mister Zul?"

Clearly confused, he said, "Medusozoa for jellylanterns."

"And what – ?"

The funicular car lurched to a halt. The belts securing the crates at the end of the car squealed. A rhythmic clang of metal on metal began somewhere on the track uphill, and the car began to bounce in time.

Kyam and QuiTai exchanged a silent, worried look.

The car dropped several yards downhill. Kyam rushed to the door. Then the frayed end of a cargo belt ripped from its hook. The crates in that stack groaned. The top one slid forward.

A vision of a shard of bloody glass leapt to QuiTai's mind. This was like her vision of the Ravidian's crates sliding across the skiff as they sailed to their hiding place.

"Mister Zul?"

"I'm on it. Why did he lock this?" He reached into his pocket for his picks.

"They do it to keep people from jumping on and riding for free."

"And everyone knows that, don't they?"

QuiTai worked the cranky window down far enough to stick her head out. They were far above the harbor now. The station below looked tiny. The jungle along the uphill tracks was too dense to see past the first car. Whoever stopped the train probably couldn't be seen from the town square either. The station masters would figure it out soon; but not soon enough.

The sound of strained metal grew louder.

"Someone is going to a lot of trouble to stop our investigation, Mister Zul."

"And the sky is blue." He kept his attention on the pick.

She inspected the belts holding back the crates. If they gave, the crates would slide down the car and crush them. "They haven't cut through these, so they weren't at the harbor station."

Kyam said, "The real plan, I assume, is to cut the funicular's cable."

The metallic clanging grew louder and faster. The car slid dropped several yards before jolting to a stomach-churning halt. QuiTai grabbed a belt to stop from sliding to the end of the car; another belt flew snapped loose and flew at her. As she ducked, she saw the belt strike Kyam's arm. He dropped his pick.

"Damn it!" Kyam searched the floor. "Can you climb out the side window?"

"It would be tight. You'd never fit."

Kyam strode to her, lifted her up to the open window, and shoved her through it feet-first. Her head hit the frame, and then she landed hard and slid down the slope beside the track, grabbing frantically for a handhold among the plants. Leaves shredded through her fingers. She saw a thick vine and stretched desperately with both hands to grasp it. As she jolted to a stop, she felt the muscles in her shoulders tear. Her injured hand seared with pain.

She heard a loud snap.

The funicular barreled downhill, picking up speed as it went. The loose cable whipped through the air, slicing small trees in half as QuiTai flattened herself and kept her head down. Moments later, she heard a horrible screech of metal and loud booms as the funicular hit the bottom of the hill.

Then everything was quiet: even the birds and monkeys were stunned into silence. The quiet made QuiTai feel as if a predator stalked her through the wild undergrowth. The hairs along her arms rose.

She crawled to a tree and rested against it while she checked herself for broken bones. Then as she took a deep breath and tipped back her head to look at the sky, she saw Kyam smiling down at her.

"Survived, did you?" she said.

He squatted beside her, a wild grin on his face. "Opened the lock with seconds to spare. Jumped off right as the cars started to fall. It was very dramatic."

"Good. I hate a boring escape from near death."

"Should I be worried?" Kyam asked. "You have that wicked grin."

"I was only thinking, my dear Mister Zul, that I'm in danger of liking you."

His lips twitched. "How perfectly horrid for you."

She felt a pang of regret for her old life, where she could banter with interesting men for hours and the only thing at stake was a night of pleasure. In that world, she and Kyam might have been lovers. He was probably the kind of man who lingered in bed. She gave a rueful half-smile. She had to stop thinking of that. She had a lover. Even if Petrof had never really been enough.

QuiTai tried to rise, wincing. Kyam slipped his arm around her waist to help her. When she was standing, she brushed the broken leaves and dirt from her arms and hands and said, "Well. Where were we? Ah yes. Paying a call to the harbor master."

Kyam still grinned stupidly at her. "You're a tenacious little demon."

"I don't suppose this is simply a horrendous vapor dream?"

She checked her blouse. As far as she could tell, it had survived her downhill slide in fairly respectable condition. The pattern on her sarong was busy enough that the smears of red clay near her knees blended in.

He shook his head. "Not unless we entered the vapor together."

"Right now, I wish we had. And I wish I would wake up before I really hurt myself."

"Are you hurt? We can rest longer if you need to."

QuiTai swatted his hands away before he could coddle her like an elderly aunt. "We can't risk climbing up the tracks if the saboteurs are still there, so we should hike through the jungle." She stared up the hillside. "If I'm right, we're downslope from old Levapur. Once we're there, you can conduct your Thampurian spy business while I talk to my contacts. One of them will know where the harbor master lives."

Kyam finally stopped smiling. "Is the Devil a werewolf?"

Confusion was rare for her; she didn't like it. "Where did that question come from?"

"You're not the only person who can add things up."

"Such as?"

"I'm not giving you anything until you help me find the Ravidians."

"Fine, as long as you stop fishing for information about him."

"Ivitch is a werewolf, and I've seen you around town in the company of a big brute who looks as if he's the model for werewolf heroic statues." Kyam struck an ironic pose. He had to mean Casmir, although a few other werewolves fit that description too.

"Still fishing? If you've been following me, Mister Zul, you've probably also seen me talk to Ponongese, Ingosolians, and a few mixed-blood folk too. On occasion, I even stoop to Thampurians."

"If I asked you not to meet your regular contacts alone until we have this Ravidian situation cleared up, would you?"

"I'm not sure how the spy business works back on the

continent, but around here, we don't send engraved invitations asking people to kindly stop by for an afternoon water pipe and interrogation. If you want to talk to the harbor master, I have to ask my people where we can find him. That is why you dragged me into this little adventure, isn't it? My contacts?"

His face flushed with anger. "At least let me come along to protect you."

Tired of staring at his chest, she shoved him back. "Quit doing that. I'm not some docile daughter of the thirteen families in need of a gentleman to catch me when I faint."

He made the mistake of reaching for her shoulders as if to shake sense into her. In one fluid movement, she yanked his arm and used his forward momentum to shove him to the ground. She dropped onto his chest as he rolled over.

Kyam grunted. "Get off me."

She leaned down to stare into his eyes. "I don't need your protection."

A long moment passed when she couldn't read his face. His mood shifted. She'd never seen him without his swagger.

"Maybe you're right. Maybe you don't need me, but I need you. It's only natural that I'd want to protect – "

"Such a valuable asset?"

He shook his head.

Something about the soft, almost sad look in his eyes told her he was going to do it, so she wasn't surprised when he kissed her. Resisting him never entered her mind. It had been far too long since someone had kissed her like that. Petrof knew how to excite her, but he never bothered with pleasantries. Kyam kissed like he could spend hours on her lips alone. The stroke of his hand down her back felt nice too, and it was increasingly clear that he was ready to do more than kiss.

"I've wanted to do that for months." He sounded a bit breathless, but that might have been because she sat on his stomach. His voice was low and quiet in that earnest way men had of talking in bed, the kind of voice that made her want to peel off his clothes.

Instead, she climbed off him. "We should get moving."

He propped up on his elbows. As quickly as it had drained from him, his impish glint was back. "That's it? No outrage? No triumph? No warning that the Devil is a jealous man who will kill me for touching you? Not even a prim, 'That was terribly forward of you, Mister Zul, even though you saved my life?'"

As he got to his feet and smacked leaves off his trousers, she wondered if she really sounded that cold. And then she saw the mischief in his eyes. The cheeky bastard was teasing her.

She threw a light punch to his chin. "Better?"

He grinned as he rubbed his jaw. "You pulled that. Or at least I hope you did. Otherwise, you're not nearly as tough as your reputation."

It really was a pity he was a Thampurian. He was the best time she'd had in years.

CHAPTER 9: THE HARBOR MASTER

From the look on Kyam's face when they emerged in the center of old Levapur, QuiTai guessed he'd never set foot in the maze of tin-roofed shacks that clung to the hillsides. That didn't surprise her.

As they headed down the deeply rutted main road, a young boy ran to them with his hand out. "Pui, auntie QuiTai?"

QuiTai folded her arms across her chest. "Why aren't you in school, little brother?"

The boy shrugged as he raised his hand higher.

"Pui is for good students only," she said sternly.

Still grinning, he skipped away.

Although she wished they would teach in Ponongese instead of Thampurian, QuiTai had to admit that the Thampurian's zeal to educate her people was a good thing. Every parent on the island knew that if they couldn't afford tuition, the Devil would help, even though the Devil himself wasn't aware of that. It was one of the many details of his business that QuiTai felt he didn't need to know.

"You're a strict little mother," Kyam said.

She shuddered as his words once again hit hidden marks with surprising accuracy. Maybe she came across as strict, but she was only trying to protect the children. Danger could race out of the darkness without warning and rip your world into pieces in moments.

Some lessons you only needed to learn once.

It wasn't something she wanted to discuss with him or anyone. From their brief time together, she'd learned the surest way to make Kyam's penetrating gaze glaze over was to share her political views. So she said, "Since when is ignorance the best way to arm children for the future?"

"Arm? You make it sound like war."

Shaking her head, she gestured to the shacks of old Levapur with contempt. "Look around you, Mister Zul. Sewage running down the middle of the slope. Shacks that will collapse in a typhoon. Look how exhausted even the young men seem, how dull their eyes are, as if the world has beaten them to dust. Of course I'm at war with this."

"Let me guess. You blame the Thampurians."

Old Levapur always made her feel hopeless. Her rage had long ago subsided to a numb ache. She did what she could, but it was like trying to build a wall of sand to protect the beach from the sea. "I blame everyone who accepts it."

"That's oddly fair, coming from you."

"There are plenty of other things I blame on your people."

"Good. I was almost worried."

People were beginning to set aside their chores and approach them. Kyam said, "We seem to have attracted a lot of attention. How dangerous is this place?" He moved closer to QuiTai.

She nodded to a group of men who smoked a kur outside a leaning shack. "You're perfectly safe here, something you can thank the Devil for. He rules old Levapur with an iron fist."

"How is that any better than the iron fist of the colonial government?"

"Politics, Mister Zul? How delightful that you've finally

taken an interest. I'd be glad to discuss that with you at any other time, but as you mentioned, we have company." QuiTai put her hands together and bowed to the people ambling closer to her and Kyam. "Greetings, uncles and aunties. Have you eaten?"

Casting shy smiles at Kyam, many of the people returned the bow. An elderly woman hobbled through the group.

"Grandmother." QuiTai bowed more deeply.

"We heard a loud boom. Some are saying that the harbor funicular is destroyed."

"I will tell you." QuiTai squatted. The crowd squatted too. QuiTai reached for Kyam's arm and tugged him down beside her. His knees popped as he crouched.

There were two types of Ponongese stories. There was lore, and then there was an oration. For the Ponongese, an oration was their source of news, and the first telling was important because it would be repeated verbatim. While QuiTai thought about the best way to begin, a buzz of happy anticipation went through the crowd.

"The sea dragon Kyam Zul and I traveled to the harbor, little knowing that enemy spies had picked today to attack and destroy your livelihoods."

It was, she thought, a decent beginning. Many Ponongese would love to rebel against Thampurian rule, and a few well-chosen words from her could incite them to it. But today she wanted them to be angry with the saboteurs, not feel that the attack on the funicular line was a good idea. While she didn't like that the plantation terraces had been stolen from her people and given to Thampurian colonists; stopping all transport of the vital medusozoa crop would spell economic disaster for her people. As she often reminded herself, better the devil they knew...

Kyam had the good sense not to interrupt her as she spun the story for her wide-eyed audience.

"...and as we leapt from the car, the funicular hurtled downslope to explode in a wreck." QuiTai put her hands on her knees and slightly bowed her head to indicate her oration was done.

The crowd leaned together and whispered. After a long consultation, the grandmother spoke. "Do you know who sabotaged the funicular, little sister?"

QuiTai spread her hands. "No, but they are the enemy of everyone who makes a living on the sea or the plantations." That included almost everyone in old Levapur.

A man at the back of the crowd asked, "How long before the funicular works again?"

"I came here to tell you what happened as soon as we escaped. I haven't even seen the wreckage up close. It was more important to tell you this story before your enemies spread gossip and point the finger of blame."

Many of the men rose. "We will go help. The sooner the wreck is cleared, the sooner we can repair the line," a man said.

"Work is honorable, uncle. May it put rice in your bowl."

Like QuiTai, Kyam pressed his hands together and bobbed his head until the crowd dispersed and they were alone in the middle of the dirt road. Then he groaned as he stood, and put his hand against his back. "My foot is asleep."

"When I first returned to Ponong, it took me a month to get used to squatting again. As you can imagine, it was frowned upon on the continent," she said as she tried to decide which of her informants in old Levapur she was willing to let Kyam meet.

"I'll admit I'm a bit surprised by your story, Lady QuiTai. You didn't make me the villain."

"You didn't cut the cable."

"But I'm Thampurian."

"I'm aware of your unfortunate lineage." She peered into the dark opening of a shack facing onto the main road. It was a bar whose owner had a good view of the road Thampurians used to move between west Levapur and the town square: If anyone in old Levapur knew about the harbor master, she would.

"So why not take the opportunity to make me look like a fool?"

She couldn't tell him that it was because of the Oracle, or about the scheme forming on the edges of her mind: if he were truly destined to become the colonial governor, it would be better for her people if they and Kyam had some respect for each other. So she only said, "The reason I didn't make you look like a fool, Mister Zul, is that you didn't act like one."

Squinting with suspicion, he drew back. "Have you been drinking again, Lady QuiTai?"

"No, but it sounds like a lovely idea. And look, here's a tavern. How convenient." She swept into the metal shack ahead of Kyam.

"I thought you said we'd have drinks." Kyam gave the murky liquid in the mug a doubtful look.

Like the back-alley bar where QuiTai had met PhaNyan, this place had few furnishings beyond an old door balanced on stacks of bricks on which to serve the drinks. The floor was dirt, and there were no chairs or tables. Ocean breezes blew through the wide gaps between the four metal walls and the thatched roof, keeping it cool inside. The short, curvaceous barkeep wore a faded blue kebaya blouse and a bored expression, although her yellow ringed pupils seemed to glow with curiosity.

QuiTai sipped the slightly salty mix of yogurt and tea. "This is a drink, it just isn't alcoholic."

Before the funicular crash, she'd been about to tell Kyam everything she suspected about the Ravidians. Now, she had a better idea: reveal enough to intrigue him while keeping a few steps ahead. She had a couple of trustworthy and resourceful assistants in mind to help her profit from the situation, if she could keep Kyam busy and distracted in the meantime. She'd talk to LiHoun, of course. He was old, but he always delivered. Most of her younger informants only wished they were as accomplished. PhaNyan was a calculated risk. He was resourceful, strong, and reasonably intelligent. Since she'd broken his fingers, he'd sent several ardent messages begging for her forgiveness. As a sign of his desire to please her, he'd discovered a few tantalizing bits of information and promised to bring more. He'd willingly take on a dangerous mission and do his best to bring her what she asked.

Kyam took a sip of the yogurt drink and made a sour face. "It must be an acquired taste."

"A beer for the sea dragon, please." QuiTai put a coin on the door. It disappeared before the beer appeared.

Kyam gulped down a long drink of the dark beer.

"Happy now?" QuiTai asked.

He nodded.

"Good. Then go stand over there" – she gestured to the corner – "while auntie and I have a little chat." She saw an objection rising to his lips. "I'll be perfectly safe with you standing ten feet away. And if you don't go, I won't get the information."

She forced him to turn around and gently shoved him toward a corner. To his credit, he went without a fuss.

She slipped behind the bar and squatted.

The barkeep jerked her head toward Kyam. "Is it safe?"

"He's the one buying the information. The Devil might not be happy that you talked to him, though."

The barkeep hissed as she leaned away.

QuiTai grabbed her wrist. "I could have lied to you, but I didn't. The sea dragon wants to know where the harbor master lives. If the Devil or his men ask, that's what you tell them. And give them the answer too if you want."

She laid out a trail of coins between her and the woman. The barkeep's eyes widened as the coins increased in denomination.

QuiTai lowered her voice. "This is not for the sea dragon or the Devil to know. You will also deliver a message to PhaNyan and LiHoun. Tell them to meet me, and only me, in about an hour in the town square. I have a task for them." She picked up a coin half way between her and the woman. "I will return this after I have spoken to them."

The woman nodded.

QuiTai took the two biggest coins. "And these I will return to you after your son brings me a report from the teachers saying that he's been in school every day for three months."

The woman scowled as the coins disappeared into QuiTai's purse. "He is in school."

"He tried to beg pui from me ten minutes ago."

The bar owner's look of shock wasn't convincing. "The address, and the message," QuiTai said.

The woman snatched the coins out of the dirt. "I'll have to talk to some people."

"The sea dragon and I will wait here. Go."

West Levapur was a spur of the city built on low hills overlooking the harbor. The buildings reminded QuiTai of the town houses in Thampur's capital. None had verandas. No one sat outside and chatted with their neighbors. The street was empty even at midday. The jungle had been clipped back with vigilant thoroughness, leaving the dignified, stuffy buildings in stark relief against the red hills.

"It's one of these," QuiTai told Kyam.

"That was an awful lot of whispering between you and that barkeep for only an address."

QuiTai walked quickly down the road. The numbering sequence made no logical sense. Finally, she pointed to one of the buildings that clung to the cliff overlooking the harbor. "This one. Seventeen dash three. What idiot decided that seventeen falls between forty-three and two hundred?"

"In Thampur, we number houses by when they were built, not by where they are. Eighteen and sixteen could be two streets upslope."

"You are aware that only makes sense to Thampurians, aren't you?"

"These apartments weren't built for Ponongese. And by the way, seventeen dash four is the apartment the Ravidians lived in. Right next door."

"What were they doing in such a thoroughly Thampurian neighborhood? They would have blended into the background better in a mixed neighborhood such as yours."

Kyam spread his arms and turned in a half circle. "Look how still it is. How quiet. They ignore each other here. 'A family's apartment is their compound,' or some other such nonsense that helps them cling to their Thampurian identity. I've seen it before. People who fight so hard to stop cultural contamination that everything becomes a sacred rite." He gestured toward the apartment buildings. "What's sad is that no one in Thampur really lives like this. This is a grotesque exaggeration."

"So their mortal enemies could live among them, and the Thampurians would pretend they didn't see? No wonder why I have so few informants on this side of town."

"But it makes breaking into his apartment a lot easier." Kyam brandished his lock picks.

"Why don't we try the simple, obvious answer first, as that old thief Grandfather Zul would advise?"

When she knocked, the door creaked open under the gentle force of her fist. The coppery smell of blood and the sickening stench of rotting meat made her gag.

Kyam pushed in front of her.

A narrow staircase led from the foyer up to the second story of the apartment. Kyam gestured for QuiTai to follow him down the hallway of the first floor as he moved forward.

A swarm of flies buzzed angrily around a jellylantern sconce.

The smell grew stronger as they came to the end of the hallway, which widened into a room furnished with divans and soft chairs. Daylight streaming through the carved window screens made shell patterns on the rug covering the dark wood floor.

QuiTai pulled her scarf over her nose as they moved to the kitchen.

Flies zigzagged through the air. A Thampurian man with broad, muscled shoulders lay face down in thick, syrupy blood.

A wide smear of blood was near the blood puddle. It looked to QuiTai as if something had been dragged through it. Nothing around the body looked as if it had been moved.

Kyam rolled the corpse over. The throat wasn't the only part of the body torn open. "Werewolf?" he said.

QuiTai didn't mind Kyam's shorthand speech. She planned to open her mouth as little as possible too, or the taste of death would coat her tongue. She pointed to the cuts in man's thighs and arms. "Cut, not bitten." Werewolves ate the stomach and entrails first, all of which were intact on the corpse.

Kyam nodded to a knife on the sideboard then found a towel to lift it with. "Blood on the blade, but the handle is clean. I doubt they'll find fingerprints." He set it down almost exactly where he found it.

QuiTai's gaze jumped, taking in glimpses of the carnage without the details. Her thoughts were in similar disarray. She saw that near the corpse, blood spray peppered the lower cabinets to either side of a clean space. Flies walked across congealed stew in a pot. A lone clean bowl sat on the counter by the cooking fire...

She took a steadying breath and forced herself to methodically look at the floor inch by inch. Her mind grabbed onto the sense of order.

She knew she wasn't looking at a werewolf kill. It was possible a Ponongese killer had mutilated the victim's throat to hide fang marks, but the spray of blood on the cabinets didn't fit that theory. That narrowed the list of suspects to Thampurians and Ravidians.

Her eyes were drawn to the body on the floor. She squatted and forced herself to take her time looking over the rest of the evidence. The answer was there.

A path of blood drops led from the body to the window. Three distinct circular spots of blood about three feet apart formed a line parallel to the blood drops.

The sequence of events began to fall into place for her.

"There, there, and there," she pointed to the three drops.

It wasn't a vision, but everything she saw fit the picture that formed in her mind.

"From his throat?" Kyam asked.

She shook her head. Her fingers fanned out along the line

of the spray on the cabinets then swung over to the dots to show that they weren't the same trajectory. Then she pointed to the steady track of blood drops from the separate smear on the floor to the window.

Kyam lifted his hands as if he saw but didn't know what to make of it.

The stink made QuiTai's head spin. The flavor of old blood clung to the back of her tongue. "Seen enough?"

They hurried away from the harbor master's apartment, gasping the clean, ocean-scented air. They slowed after a minute, and then QuiTai decided that the building with the number eight painted above the doors was a lucky spot, so she sat on the front stoop. Kyam groaned as he sat next to her. His shoulders rubbed against hers. She moved over a bit.

"That was the harbor master, yes? I don't think I've ever talked to him," she said. The werewolves handled that side of the Devil's business. Her nose wrinkled. The harbor master's replacement would doubtless be as corrupt as his predecessor, but if he wasn't it could cause problems. Petrof needed to know about the situation.

"That was him," Kyam said.

"Just making sure. He was fit enough to captain a skiff."

They sat in silence for a while. She sniffed her clothes and the scarf. They smelled of bruised leaves and churned earth; the scent of death hadn't had time to work its way into the fibers. The sarong and blouse she didn't care about, but she would have been sad to part with the scarf. She ran the silk through her fingers. Not only was it the highest quality, but it would, indeed, match most of the colors she usually wore. How flattering that Kyam paid attention to such things. Maybe he truly had an artist's eye.

She looked up and surprised him studying her with a hint of a smile.

If she was going to talk to PhaNyan and LiHoun, she had to convince Kyam that they needed to go to town square for some reason. She pretended to him that all their misdirection and sleight of hand was narcissistic, that no one cared what they did, but she knew that Petrof had her watched. And she knew that she was in a race against Kyam and the colonial government to reach the Ravidians first.

And the Devil. She mustn't forget the Devil. Who had said that? Kyam had.

She was in a race against Petrof too.

Where had that idea come from? Surely she meant to think that it she was in this race *for* Petrof. She was supposed to be rededicating herself to him, and proving her loyalty. Yet there it was, that unbidden thought with its ring of truth. So for now, she had to keep everyone looking the wrong direction while she... well, she wasn't sure what she'd do yet, but she believed the answer would present itself soon. There were hazy details to her vision of the future, like exactly how the Ravidians planned to use the sea wasps. She knew how she'd use them, and that was all that mattered.

The Ravidian's plan was quite elegant, she mused, and executed with precision she admired. But they shouldn't have killed the harbor master. The greedy bastard had probably blackmailed them, but they should have paid him anyway. How else would they get supplies? From the harbor master's brother? That's where her admiration dimmed; everyone knew that you couldn't trust an addict, ever. No doubt the Ravidian killer found that out the hard way, after murdering the harbor master and returning to the harbor only to find the brother lost in vapor. QuiTai could picture the Ravidian's panic. And then he would need to avoid being seen by the soldiers on the fortress' ramparts. Perhaps he had waited on the skiff for nightfall, as QuiTai had.

And then what? One man could manage to sail a skiff alone, but why steal such a large boat when so many small, one-man fishing boats were within arm's reach? She'd have to ask the fishermen if any boats were missing. No Ponongese would report such a theft to the Thampurians, who would simply pick another Ponongese to blame and kill him; but they would tell her. Then they'd expect her to bring it back. Information always had a price. Her nose wrinkled. Maybe this time she'd skip the verification and simply trust her vision. This was no time to go hunting for an errant fishing boat.

"Oh, no," Kyam said. "You're thinking again."

"Let's go get your farwriter. Someone is trying to kill us. I know that you want more proof, but honestly, what if we *are* killed? Then the Ravidians get away with everything. Your superiors don't even know that anything is wrong. Send a preliminary report."

Kyam sat forward and watched the empty road as if he expected someone to come along at any moment. "What should I say? You started to tell me something before the funicular cable got cut. What do you know?"

"Someone tried to make it look as if the harbor master was killed by werewolves. You certainly wanted to believe it."

"No, at that point we were talking about medusozoa, not werewolves."

It would ruin everything if he started asking the right questions, because she sensed he'd know if she lied to him. Sticking to the truth would be safer. But she needed more time.

"Do you want a lecture about colonial economics, Mister Zul, or do you want to know why this murder proves that you're on the right track?" She didn't give him time to answer. "It doesn't take long in this town for someone to sit down and regale you with the story of the time the werewolves rampaged through Levapur. You know how we love our stories. I'm sure someone related it to the Ravidians within days of their arrival. But of course, they didn't pay attention to some of the important details."

"Such as?"

"Normally, the werewolves head for the inland valleys when they shift. After all, they don't want anyone to bring them to trial in case they attack a Thampurian instead of a boar."

"Don't you worry about them attacking Ponongese in the

inland villages or on the plantation terraces?"

"They won't."

"You sound awfully confident about that."

"May I continue? Good. A couple months after they came to Ponong, some of the werewolves came across the Jupoli Gorge Bridge and into town. But only the fringes of Levapur, you understand. It's not as if they were running wild in the marketplace. They were after food. When they're in their animal states, they don't think like people. The destruction wasn't deliberate."

"You're making excuses for them."

"No. I'm explaining why that time, when we knew it was the werewolves, is different from this time, when we're being led rather sloppily to believe it's the werewolves again."

"You parse words like a Thampurian merchant measures silk. As I said before, the legal profession lost a great mind when you took to the stage."

"And the stage lost a comedian when you took up painting. Be careful, or I might take up the law in the third act."

Kyam cupped a hand over his ear. "Did you hear that? Judges from here to the continent shrieking in terror."

She chose to take that as a compliment.

"Explain why you're so convinced that the werewolves aren't involved. Facts that prove it, not simply your opinion this time, if you please," he said.

If only they could stay away from topics that cut deep. QuiTai took a deep breath and hoped her mastery over her voice hid the quiver of emotion that rose in her chest. "As I was saying before, the night of the full moon massacre, several werewolves came into town. At the first apartment building on the fringes of town, they attacked a group of neighbors sitting out on their veranda. It was horrible, horrible carnage. Children, adults, elders. The wolves gorged. Nine people almost entirely devoured. Fact."

She was proud of how steady her voice sounded. Talking about that massacre always reopened a wound that would never heal properly. The trick was to keep it distant, as if it were something she'd heard about long ago and half forgotten.

She went on, "So you understand why it couldn't have been a werewolf that killed the harbor master? The wolves kill at their first opportunity. The harbor master's house is much too far from their den for that. And they don't carve steaks." She held up her hands and wriggled her fingers. "No hands, just paws. They tear off chunks off the body as they eat. Again, fact. Not opinion. And I'm sure that you noticed that the body and the apartment were a fairly tidy murder scene. Believe me, werewolves aren't neat, even in their human form."

"You need to keep better company." Kyam mulled over her words for a while. "What about a werewolf when he's human?"

"Then they're common murderers. No excuses. They know right from wrong in the human definition of morality."

He scoffed. "I haven't seen much evidence of that."

"If they were mad killers while in their human forms, they wouldn't go to the trouble to strangle their victims rather than rip out their throats. Madmen don't think about hiding their crimes."

"Strangle. I find it interesting that you know that but don't – sorry. You were saying?"

Concentrating on the current murder helped her push the past back where it belonged. The challenge electrified her brain. While she knew it was morbid to dwell on the harbor master's body, and even worse to enjoy the challenge, the murder scene presented an interesting tableau of facts. She was eager to share them with someone who could appreciate her observations rather than obsess on the death.

She hugged her knees. "There's more. Want to hear it?"

He leaned on his elbow and stretched his long legs down the steps. "Yes. Amaze me."

"Three dots of blood. The low spray."

"You pointed them out."

She rested her cheek on her knees. The sarong he'd given her to wear was the softest cotton she'd ever felt. "Come on, Kyam. Put it together."

"You called me Kyam."

"Forgive my familiarity. I got carried away."

"You're enjoying this."

"Only on an intellectual level. I've seen more than my share of mutilated bodies. One gets used to it. The smell, never, but the blood and brutality...either you go mad, or you pretend it's merely a cerebral exercise."

Or you sell your soul to the Devil for vengeance.

Kyam seemed a bit taken aback, but then lightly touched her hand. "I understand. And you can get as familiar with me as you like."

"If I get into the habit, I might slip in front of another Thampurian, and I don't need that kind of trouble, *Mister Zul.*"

He nodded, even though it was clear he didn't like agreeing with her.

There was no need to pound him over the head with that lesson, so she said, "The blood. It told a story. Tell it to me."

His forehead furrowed as he concentrated. "The spray was low, so he was on his knees."

"Very good."

"Someone stood in front of him, which explains the break in the spray pattern, so his throat probably wasn't slit from behind. And Ravidians have those neck frills... if you want to slit their throats, you almost have to come at them from the front to be sure you'll get the right angle. So a front attack could be the way they're trained to kill."

"Excellent, Mister Zul."

"You sound like my music tutor, except that you haven't smacked my knuckles yet. She suffered for years before she gave up on me. You could save yourself a lot of time too if you'd simply tell me everything you know."

That was something she couldn't afford to do, not until she'd had a chance to speak to PhaNyan and LiHoun. "I don't drop compliments like a lace hanky in front of a gentleman, so take me at my word. You're doing fine, but I'll give you a hint since you're in a hurry. The trail of blood drops fell from the meat they cut off the harbor master's body. They're not important. However, the three distinct blood marks are. Tell me why."

Kyam cleared his throat but said nothing.

"Evenly spaced, about a yard apart. Parallel to the line of dripped blood," she prompted.

"I was in the same room you were, and I saw the circles you talk about, but I have no idea what they mean. How do you do this trick where you see things I can't?"

No one had ever asked, so she wasn't sure how to explain it. "Everything is a pattern, or not part of a pattern, or it's completely random. Those are the only options. So you find something that doesn't fit in the pattern, or what's missing from it, and figure out why. And don't allow yourself to imagine a pattern when what you see is truly random. You have to see, really see, what you're looking at, rather than what you're meant to see. The clues are a story, Mister Zul. Find the beginning and follow it to the end."

"That was enlightening." He made a 'hurry up' gesture. "Let's just assume that it would take hours of our valuable time for me to figure it out, if ever."

"What I saw was the bloody dewclaw of a Ravidian. After he sliced open the harbor master's throat, he walked to the window. Probably to toss the meat he cut from the body over the cliff to the water below. The bloody marks – not drops – aren't a footprint, but they're better than one in a way, because Ravidians are the only race I know of with dewclaws."

"Are you sure that's what made those marks?"

"We could go back and examine the harbor master's neck more closely to be sure that the fatal wound was caused by a dewclaw-shaped weapon and not something meant to make marks like wolf teeth, but we're not making a case to present for a judge," she reminded him. "Besides, I don't want to stick my hand into his neck. It's probably filled with maggots."

"I wonder if the print of a Ravidian's dewclaw is unique, like a fingerprint," Kyam asked. "Not that it matters. As you pointed out, we're not making a case against a specific Ravidian. All we need to know is that a Ravidian did it."

She smiled benignly at him. It was so nice for once to talk

to someone who could almost keep up with her. "So there's your proof that the Ravidians are, indeed, guilty of something. That should be good enough for your superiors." She stood. "Let's go back to town. You can make your report while I take care of a bit of business."

He came to his feet. "I'm afraid I can't do that."

"Stubborn man. You could have the Ravidians arrested for the harbor master's death right now and save yourself a good deal of trouble. Bring them in for questioning."

She stood too.

"You forget that I don't know where they are exactly, but I think that you do. Something to do with medusozoa, I believe." He had the effrontery to wink at her before taking her hand and placing it on his arm.

The marketplace was in chaos as people squatted in groups and talked in excited voices about the funicular. People streamed downslope, as others returned to share their reports of the damage.

QuiTai caught a glimpse of LiHoun from the corner of her eye as she and Kyam passed the government building, but he disappeared quickly into the milling throng. She didn't see PhaNyan, but if he knew what was good for him, he also hovered close.

Kyam moved with determined speed through the crowd, nearly colliding with a woman who balanced a basket of fibrous jikal roots on her head. If he didn't want to attract attention, he was doing it all wrong: he should have stopped to listen to the gossip.

Since they'd left the harbor master's apartment she'd been too busy managing his train of thought to keep far enough ahead of him. The priority now was convincing him to leave her alone long enough to talk to LiHoun and PhaNyan. Unfortunately, he loomed like a jealous lover. Maybe another demonstration of her defensive moves was in order. They might end in a compromising position again, though, and she'd enjoyed the first time too much to trust herself a second. Besides, one of the wolves might see, and the thought of facing Petrof's anger sent a cold jolt of fear through her.

She touched the vial of black lotus on the chain around her neck as if it were a talisman. With a lot of luck, she could dope him long enough to carry out her plan. Kyam would never forgive her... but she'd warned him that she wasn't a nice woman.

Then the hair at the nape of her neck rose, and a shiver went down her back even though it was the hottest time of day. She rubbed her arms. "Stop that."

"Stop what?" Kyam asked as he pulled her past an abandoned fritter stand. Her stomach grumbled; they hadn't eaten since breakfast.

"You're growling at people. I can't hear it, but I can feel it."

He gripped her elbow hard and dragged her down a side street while he cast suspicious glances at everyone they passed. She barely kept up with his long stride.

"You know one thing that bothers me?" she finally said. "You haven't seen the Ravidians in town for several days. As far as I know, my people haven't seen them either. If they aren't here, who brought down the funicular?"

"I have my theories."

His grim expression worried her. And for once, she didn't have a theory herself. It would take a gang of brawny men to hack that cable apart. The only men fitting that description in Levapur were the werewolves, but she would know if they were working with the Ravidians. It had to be someone else. She simply couldn't imagine who.

"Are we heading back to your safe house?" she asked.

He shook his head. "Rule of safe houses: only use them once."

She knew no such rule. She used her safe houses many times.

"I need to make inquiries about who might be working

with the Ravidians. Give me a few moments to talk to a couple of informants," she said.

His grip on her tightened. "Not alone."

"Quit trying to stick your finger into my rice bowl. This is outside the scope of our business agreement, which clearly stated that I would help you find the Ravidians and their crates, not that I would solve a murder. That's purely a Thampurian matter."

Kyam craned to see if anyone had followed them out of the marketplace.

She saw LiHoun, but the old man blended so well with the rest of the people on the street that he didn't draw Kyam's attention.

"I thought that the Devil was interested in those crates too."

"With the evidence we'll find, he'll understand that there is no profit in this scheme for him. As for me, I get to bring Jezereet's murderer to justice. My justice. The murderer is going to be very sorry that he killed her."

"I'm pretty sure he already is, Lady QuiTai."

They reached Kyam's apartment building and walked up the short flight of steps to the doorway. LiHoun barely darted out of sight before Kyam's watchful gaze swept across the street. He was so close. How could she buy time? All she needed was a minute away from Kyam.

Kyam slammed open the door and shoved her into grimy foyer, then herded her toward the staircase. LiHoun would probably wait for her to come down, but with the clock ticking, she wanted as much of a head start on Kyam as possible. She pulled away from his grip. "Mister Zul, if you don't mind, I need to make a short stop before we go upstairs."

"For what?"

She stared at him as if she expected him to read her mind.

Then she raised her eyebrows. Finally, she rolled her eyes. "A gentleman can heed the demands of nature anywhere…"

He took his time thinking, as if he'd been given a difficult puzzle to solve. "Come on, then." He led her past the stair and down a hallway to the back door of the building.

"I don't need an escort."

"Someone could have seen us come into this building." He opened the back door.

They stepped out onto a veranda whose uneven steps led down to a small yard. A faded ball nestled in a curtain of vines that cascaded from the hillside above. An old woman raked the dirt inside a wire coop while jungle fowl pecked at the ground around her ankles.

"Little brother! I have eggs for you," the auntie called out. Her eyes disappeared into the folds of her cheeks as she smiled. After a brief glance at QuiTai, she clucked at Kyam and wagged her finger at him. "I'll give you extra since you have a guest."

QuiTai stepped into the outhouse and held the door open a crack to watch Kyam make his way to the coop. He said, "Eggs? You spoil me, auntie. Have you eaten?"

As the auntie ducked into the coop, a rooster with an iridescent green-black tail flew at her with his talons out. "Stop it, ChuChun!" she scolded. Kyam stepped inside the coop and grabbed the angry bird.

QuiTai heard a scratching at the side of the outhouse by the vine.

"*Psst.* Auntie QuiTai."

She closed the outhouse door and leaned to a large gap between warped boards in the side wall. "Uncle LiHoun! I'm impressed."

"Cats have their secret ways."

"I don't have much time, so listen closely, favored uncle." She spoke quickly. "The Ravidian smugglers took over a medusozoa plantation. A remote one. Cay Rhi has the highest probability. They're raising special medusozoa that don't glow at night in the tide pool beds. I want you to capture several medusozoa in a glass container with a strong lid and take them to my estate. Take lots of vinegar with you to neutralize any stings. Look." She held her scarred palm through the crack and heard his intake of breath. "One sting did this. Two will kill you. And the stingers don't have to be attached to the medusozoa."

"I understand," LiHoun whispered.

"Ravidians will be guarding the pools. Their dewclaws can gut a man in seconds, so watch their feet. I think there are three, but there may be more." She fed coins out through the gap in the boards and heard them clink into his hands. "Not for the wolves to know. Speed matters."

LiHoun recited the entire message verbatim. "Anything else?" he asked.

"PhaNyan was also supposed to be here. I expected him to help."

"No one has seen him for several days. And an angry wolf is searching for you, auntie. He was furious when word reached the marketplace that you escaped from the wreck."

Ivitch, no doubt. She hoped the soldiers would arrest him before he found her.

"Are you done yet, Lady QuiTai?" Kyam called out.

"Go. Be safe, uncle," she said.

"Lady QuiTai?" Kyam pounded on the door.

She flung it open. "Your manners are atrocious."

"Save the lecture for when we're inside and safe." Kyam yanked her across the yard as if she were a disgraced child.

A sour auntie backed out of an apartment on the first floor with a huge basket of laundry. She sniffed when she saw QuiTai, but her eyes lit up at the jade eggs in Kyam's hand. "Eggs, little brother?" She plucked one from Kyam's hand. "Three is an unlucky number." Satisfied that she'd saved him from peril, she tucked the egg into the corner of her basket.

"My landlady," Kyam explained to QuiTai. "Although you two have met, I think."

"It's been a while," QuiTai murmured. "Have you eaten, auntie?"

The woman cupped her hand to the side of her mouth but didn't bother to whisper. "I know nice Ponongese girls. I could introduce you. For a fee," she told Kyam. Her nostrils flared as she looked over QuiTai from head to foot.

"This is business, auntie. I'm painting her portrait." Kyam pushed QuiTai toward the stairs.

The landlady grunted and called out, "She lives with werewolves! Too good for her own kind, not good enough for yours."

As they climbed the stairs, Kyam said, "Don't take it to heart. She hates everyone."

"And as you said last time I was here, everyone loathes me."

Kyam winced. "That was for Ivitch's benefit."

"Oh, certainly." She enjoyed his discomfort.

They rounded the landing and stopped with their feet on the first step of the last flight of stairs. The door to Kyam's apartment was ajar.

Kyam put the eggs into her hands. "Wait here." Then he crept up the remaining stairs. He flattened against the wall, peeked through the door, then threw it open fully and rushed in.

QuiTai sauntered in behind him. Either the place had been searched, or he'd dumped all his paints on the floor. She lifted her sarong as she stepped carefully over a canvas.

"I told you to wait," Kyam said.

She put his prized eggs near the cooking fire, then righted a chair and sat. "I see you're in the habit of running into dangerous situations on your own, Colonel Zul of His Majesty's Intelligence Services."

"Me? I'm the one who rushes in? My dear Lady QuiTai, I think you're ignoring your own penchant for trouble."

His overly polite words didn't match his tone. He glowered at her as if she'd done something to anger him. She wondered why his mood had turned so quickly. Then she saw his sketch book was on the ground near her foot. She picked it up and flipped through the pages. While preliminary sketches of her were there, the full drawing was gone.

"Someone took a memento," she said. "I meant to tell you yesterday that you're quite talented with a pencil. I was surprised."

Kyam searched under the piles of clothes and canvases. "My art tutor had more luck than the music tutor."

He didn't do it on purpose, but there were times when he made it so clear how very different they were. Even the best school in Levapur didn't teach drawing or music. She wondered suddenly if he missed his home as much as she'd missed Ponong when she'd been away.

Stay focused. Every minute she could buy for LiHoun was precious now. The trick was to keep Kyam talking. "Do you have a handler on the island, or do you report directly to Thampur? If I were you, I wouldn't let the colonial government know about this just yet. Maybe never." There was nothing specific that she could point to, but the more she thought about the colonial government, the more uneasy she grew. It was as if she'd seen or heard something that raised a warning at the back of her mind.

"We may be partners in this investigation, but there are some matters that must remain confidential. Aha!" He triumphantly waved a handful of instant jellylanterns. "These might come in handy." He dropped them on the mattress and reached further under his bed.

"I keep the Devil's business from you, so it's only fair if you withhold Thampurian business from me. However, I'm curious about something," she said.

Wariness hooded his eyes.

She waved her hand. "Nothing top secret, I assure you. It's just that I have a, shall we say, personal curiosity about biolocks. I know that your farwriter is protected by one. May I observe you opening it?"

He leaned against the mattress. "What's it worth to you?"

"Worth?"

"You're the one who treats life like a series of business deals, so consider this a side negotiation. What would you be willing to give up for a chance to inspect my biolock?" There was a hint of teasing in his voice.

"What do you want?"

"The truth. There's a biolock somewhere you want to crack. Why?"

He was the most infuriating man. A worthy adversary, and an even more worrisome ally. Still, she wanted to see how the lock worked.

"I've paid several necessary business expenses out of my own pocket. The Devil is reticent to reimburse me, even though he knows I invest it for his benefit. Unfortunately, his fortune is protected by a biolock." She folded her hands in her lap. "I have no intention of robbing him. I only want what's mine."

Kyam laughed. "So you're financing the Devil's crime syndicate and you get nothing in return? I thought you were smarter than that. But where the Devil is concerned, you've proven yourself to be exasperatingly blind."

"There's no need to be unkind, Mister Zul. It's merely a difference of management styles."

"Oh ho! Management!"

One of their arguments could rage for hours if she managed it right. "The Devil's business is just that, Mister Zul – a business. As a sea dragon, you should appreciate that. Other nations built navies; Thampurians built a merchant fleet, and conquered the Sea of Erykoli with it."

"That's the nicest thing you've ever said about Thampurians."

"Respect where it's due."

It used to be so easy to goad him into fights. If she hadn't been so thoroughly tired, she would have done a better job of provoking him. Certain there'd be another excuse for harsh words, she decided to let this line of discussion go. If she tried to revive it now, he'd get suspicious.

"So, are you satisfied with my reasons? May I see the lock?"

He kicked scattered clothes aside on his way to the trunk that lay open and on its side near the wardrobe. Then he knelt and reached for the lower of the two recessed metal bands that encircled it. "Come over if you want to see."

QuiTai's braid slid over her shoulder as she leaned down for a closer look. If she saw how it worked, maybe she could find a way around it.

"I put my fingers into these copper-lined grooves. You can't see them, but there are indents I have to line up with."

She'd felt similar grooves on Petrof's biolock.

"It's rather advanced technology. My fingers react with the copper to form a signature electrical circuit. It's very weak, but it's enough to – " The metal bar inside slid back to reveal a narrow gap between the false bottom of the trunk and the side. "It triggers a simple latch that slides back."

"And the biolock can't be opened by anyone else?"

"It doesn't read my fingerprints, but the grooves were molded to my fingers. The lock has to receive a certain current that I'm told only my body can produce. That may not be true, but I doubt that a biolock keyed to a male werewolf would yield to a Ponongese woman. Your hands are far too small."

"Would you please stop trying to trick me into telling you who the Devil is?"

"I think I already know everything I need to about him."

She tried to remember any hints she might have dropped, but she'd been careful. She knew she had. Maybe Kyam was bluffing.

"Do you have to be alive to complete the circuit?" When he flinched, she said, "A hypothetical question."

"You wouldn't kill me for a farwriter. At least, I don't think you would. Would you?"

QuiTai put her finger to her chin and pretended to think about it. Finally, she shook her head. "Too many witnesses have seen us together."

"Sometimes I'm not sure if you're joking."

He lifted a small black iron machine with round brass keys from the compartment and placed it on the small desk that had been pushed against the wall. The desk looked as if it had originally belonged to a lady in a grand house. For all she knew, it had once sat in Kyam's family's compound.

"Since it's the Devil's safe you want into, I'll tell you that – hypothetically – if it was soon enough after his death, the lock might still open. Try it and find out."

"That option was never really on the table. Merely curious."

Although if the lock would open for a corpse, it would certainly work for someone in vapor dream. She was a little irritated with herself for not thinking of that before.

He took a smaller box from the trunk and removed a small device with a crank that reminded QuiTai of a pepper mill. At the center was a copper coil. Wires stuck out of the bottom.

"Is that a generator?" she asked.

"Mobile units need a source of power." Kyam attached wires from the generator to the small farwriter then cranked the handle. "So. The lock. Did you see any way around it?"

"Most certainly."

"Aren't you going to tell me?" Kyam asked.

"I shouldn't, but I'm sure that it's occurred to you too. That lock is like putting seven bolts on a door made of rice paper. If, for example, I desperately wanted to get into your trunk, I'd break open the bottom with an axe rather than waste time fiddling with a lock. The only problem with my method is that you'd know I'd done it. I prefer a subtler approach, something that wouldn't arouse even a whiff of suspicion that the safe had been breached."

"The Devil would kill you if he caught you stealing from him?"

She looked at her hands. "He wouldn't react well." That was an understatement, but she was sure Kyam knew that.

"Has he caught you trying to open his safe?"

"How careless do you think I am?"

"Everyone runs out of luck at some point, QuiTai. Even you." Then he turned his attention to the farwriter. Using two fingers, he began to peck out a message.

QuiTai lifted her hand to her mouth to cover a yawn.

"If you're tired, you can stretch out on my bed. I promise to stay over here," he added quickly when she shot a look at him.

"If I eat, I'll be fine."

"You had a rough day yesterday, and today hasn't been any easier."

"Thank you for your concern, but I prefer to keep moving. Then I don't have time to dwell on matters best forgotten for now." But even saying that brought the dull ache back to her heart.

She forced herself to pay attention to Kyam's farwriter. Maybe it was possible to see the frequency he used from across the room; then she could monitor Thampurian government messages. She squinted. But then he fiddled with knobs on the side of the device.

"It wasn't set to the right frequency?" she asked.

He glowered at the machine as he hunted for the next letter. "You know how it works."

His slow typing seemed to drag on forever. Watching his fingers, curved high over the keys and moving across them before he found the next one to press, drove her crazy. It was everything she could do to stop herself from offering to type it for him.

Her stomach growled loudly. Kyam had the manners to cover his smile.

She rose and went to the cooking fire. He had no plates, which was unusual for a Thampurian, but he might have adopted the Ponongese habit of using bowls. Bowls made poor pots and pans though, and he didn't seem to have any of those either.

"Do you eat your eggs raw?" she asked.

"I either share my neighbors' cooking fire out on the veranda, or grab a bite at the Red Happiness. You have an excellent cook and the prices are reasonable."

She hadn't understood how dangerous it would be to spend time with him. While his mind didn't work as quickly as hers, he still put the pieces together. She wondered what other information she'd inadvertently given him that could come back to haunt her. "So you figured that out."

"You knew too much about the brothel to be a casual visitor. And that secret staircase went behind the café next door, so I presume it's also under your control. Are they the Devil's businesses, or yours?"

"I'll answer any question about the Ravidians, as per our original agreement, but that's the extent of what I'll tell you."

Kyam finally sent his message. Then he turned the frequency dials, a precaution she would have approved of even more had she been able to read the settings before he changed them.

"You're not going to wait for their reply?" she asked.

"It'll notify me of incoming messages." He pulled a chair over to face hers and sat. "We were talking about the Red Happiness. I could check government ownership documents, or you could just tell me."

Or she could drag out the conversation by only hinting at answers.

He cast a glance at his door, then turned back to her. It was only a little gesture. It might not have meant anything. But she gave no indication she'd seen it, only saying, "It would be a pity if the documents were stored improperly or filed incorrectly. It could take forever to find the information."

"I'll find the time. The more I learn about you, the more I want to know. For example, why you accept as normal what would horrify the average person."

"More flattery, Mister Zul? You've made it clear how you feel about me and the Devil, which makes me wonder why you're taking such great pains to be nice now."

"Because you know where the Ravidians are, and what they're up to. And you're going to tell me."

They had a business agreement, which meant that no matter how he treated her, he'd get what he'd bargained for. But she wasn't about to tell him that. She crossed her arms. "Not until I get some food." That would buy LiHoun another half hour, maybe.

Kyam went to the typhoon shutters that led out to his veranda. "Wait here. I'll ask one of the neighbor boys to run out to the café around the corner."

"While you're at it, ask them if they saw who ransacked your apartment."

He paused at the door. "No need. I know who did it, and so do you."

CHAPTER 10: BETRAYAL

Kyam pushed his mosquito net to the far side of his bed and set the bowls of food on the bedspread. He reclined at one end, propped on an elbow, and chewed a slice of pan bread dipped into fragrant pork stew. Qui-Tai sat at the other end. Steam curled out of a tamtuk when she cracked it open. The purplish dough, made from jikal root, and the sweet, heavily-spiced pork tucked inside smelled like dinner at her grandmother's home. She dipped it into a tart sauce and bit.

"So good." She sighed with satisfaction.

"FalLoun makes the best tamtuks, although I like PhaChiu's dipping sauce more."

"I never would have suspected you of bring such a connoisseur of Ponongese cuisine, Mister Zul. You've gone native."

Days before, that same comment had angered him. Now, he popped a delicate morsel of rice-paper-wrapped fish into his mouth and grinned. "Back when I was an active agent, I traveled the continent. Some countries, you wonder how their people can stand to eat the food."

"I love the Ingosolians, their culture, their passion for art, their spirit, but would it kill them to use a little spice? I've never tasted anything so bland," QuiTai lamented.

"Except their wine. It's strong enough to make rum blush."

Her appetite suddenly gone, QuiTai put down the piece of pan bread she'd torn off the small loaf.

"You're thinking of Jezereet again."

"I made it through almost the whole day without crying." She wiped a tear from her eye. "If I keep busy... I've had enough food. Let's go." She wiped her hands.

"Not so fast."

"You were in a hurry this morning."

"But you weren't an hour ago."

He noticed far too much. She didn't even try to deny it, although he seemed to be waiting for her to explain.

"I was hungry. Now I'm not."

The farwriter dinged. Kyam ambled over to the machine with a tamtuk clenched between his teeth.

"So many messages. What are you Thampurians chattering about?"

"You know Thampurians. We love our protocol." He spun the tuner dials. "All this chitchat back and forth is a bunch of flowery formality." He frowned at the readout for a while before angrily jamming his fingers down on a series of keys. Then, as with the other messages that had come in, he immediately burned the paper over his cooking fire.

The Thampurians might have been all about formalities, but Kyam's responses to the incoming messages were fifty or sixty keystrokes at most, and his mouth set into a grim frown as he typed them. Something didn't feel right. She'd been stalling, but now it was clear that he was too. It made her uneasy.

"Why don't I give you some privacy? I'm sure your superiors would feel better if I weren't sitting in the same room as your farwriter."

Kyam pulled his chair over to the bed, effectively blocking

her. "You said the Ravidian crates never made it into Levapur. You suggested the harbor master helped load them onto his brother's skiff. That means we'll have to sail wherever it is you think the Ravidians took them. I know my way around a sail, but you probably don't, which means I need to rest before we get under way."

She didn't like feeling trapped by him. He was jumpy, and it unnerved her: as if the barometer were falling and a storm hovered out at sea, ready to unleash its fury.

"If the Ravidians have accomplices in Levapur, they might know by now that we found the harbor master's body. They could be moving their operations."

"So you've known all along where they are."

"I never said that I didn't have a good guess."

"Has anyone told you that you don't play fair?" He leaned across her knees to dip another piece of bread into the stew.

"I wasn't aware we were playing, Mister Zul."

"Let me try a direct question. Do you know what the Ravidians are up to?"

"That's where my ideas get a bit hazy. It's a lot of speculation."

"I'll take your speculation over most people's facts. We dropped an interesting conversation earlier today. You were about to lecture me on medusozoa. So, the Ravidians smuggled sea wasps onto this island... how's your hand, by the way?"

"It twinges from time to time, unless I forget and use it. Then it hurts quite a bit."

"That will fade over time. Now, the medusozoa."

QuiTai had no problem telling him a bit more. It would hold his interest and keep him looking the direction she wanted him to focus on.

"This story is meat for your rice. The green light medusozoa are native to this island and will only grow here. You can't even raise them on other islands in the Ponong archipelago. Plenty have tried. Because of this quirk of nature, my people perfected the methods for farming green light medusozoa. Then the blue light ones were imported here to increase our profitability as a colony. Right? But the blue lights won't live in the plantation terraces because they need ocean water and fish to survive, whereas the green lights feed off the bioluminescent algae in their own bodies. So we invented the tide pool hatcheries for the blue lights. Are you with me so far?"

Kyam nodded. Then, although it was clear he was listening, he stood to put the farwriter back into the trunk, and began to pick up his scattered paintings.

"And what is a sea wasp?" she asked.

"A type of jelly. A medusozoa."

"Are they a forbidden import?"

Kyam shrugged as he cleared the bowls from the bed. "Who would ship them anywhere? You only make laws against things you can imagine someone doing, and I doubt anyone foresaw Ravidians importing sea wasps. It's insane. And why in the world – "

"So the only reason to go to the expense of smuggling would be to make sure that the government back in Thampur doesn't find out they've been brought to Ponong."

But I plan to find out if the colonial government knew.

She said, "Then the crates were taken from the harbor on a skiff to where, Mister Zul?"

He glanced toward his window as if he could see them. "A tide pool plantation. On the leeward side of the island!"

"Very good. Where they can be farmed just like blue light medusozoa."

Of course the Ravidians hadn't taken over one of the leeward plantations. But it was close enough to the truth to suffice for now. She'd tell Kyam what she really thought after they'd wasted some more time checking the plantations on Ponong. That was as much head start as she could give for LiHoun without being obvious.

She said, "You said that the Ravidians are far ahead of the Thampurians in medusozoa technology. I'm going outside my area of expertise here and into yours. Why would anyone want quick, easy access to a steady supply of sea wasps?"

Kyam shoved his bangs out of his eyes as he sank back onto

the bed. She could see the amazement in his face as he came to the same conclusion she had on the skiff. Then his brows drew together as if he doubted his intuition. A fleeting moment later his eyes widened.

Dawning horror hushed his voice when he finally believed it enough to say out loud. "The Ravidians weaponized the sea wasps."

She held up her scarred hand. "One sting is enough to stop you in your tracks. Two or three can kill. And now they're going to mass produce them in farm pools."

"Weaponized sea wasps. I thought they were up to something, but this is huge." Stunned by the scope of the vision, he rubbed his chin.

Petrof would have told her that she imagined things. He would have ignored her warnings. Yet this Thampurian colonist, scion of the thirteen families, treated her with respect. When he got angry, he didn't grab her throat. He listened to her. It was sad that over the past two days, her biggest enemy on the island had drawn closer to her than any other ally. If only she could leave Petrof and form some sort of alliance with Kyam.

But Petrof would never let her leave him. His pride wouldn't let him lose one of his possessions. As if she were a possession. Petrof didn't own her. She owned herself.

Kyam jumped to his feet and paced the room. She'd never seen him so animated. "Yes! They won't be able to dismiss this back in Thampur. I'll get my – " Not another word could have passed through his tightly pressed lips. A bright grin spread over his face though as he plopped down beside her.

"Your what?"

He chuckled. "I may admire you, but I still don't trust you enough to give you leverage. Just be content that this is of vital importance to me."

Me. Not the Thampurians. He wasn't as exacting about his word choice as she was, but she sensed that was a telling slip. And her loyalties were slipping too.

He might not trust her, but he was giddy enough to grab her hand and press his lips to the back of it. The warmth of his touch traveled up her arm as he held her hand a moment too long.

She wanted him. Forget the Ravidians, the Devil, everyone else. Intense desire pushed aside every reason she had to stay away from him. Sex with him would be such a delicious mistake.

Looking Kyam in the eye, she leaned close to him. He didn't pull away, but he didn't encourage her either. Maybe he was still trying to protect her? Maybe he worried about what the Devil might do. That was her problem, not his.

"I was thinking, Kyam..." She caressed his face and kissed him.

He placed a gentle hand over hers and said against her mouth, "Now is not the time, Lady QuiTai."

He was rejecting her? But then she heard the footsteps on the stairs, and the hushed voices. Someone pounded on the door. "Colonel Zul!"

She looked at him, shocked. Kyam spread his hands in apology.

All the hatred she'd ever felt for him rushed back into her heart. She'd been a fool. The humiliation set her temper aflame. Kyam had betrayed her. Why was she so surprised?

QuiTai bolted for the veranda. A soldier blocked her way. She backed into the room as he came at her. Kyam opened his door to three more waiting soldiers.

QuiTai recognized Major Voorus, head of the elite colonial military force. One of the bullies. His silver epaulets dripped fringe. She'd seen him before, at a distance, but until now she'd never seen noticed how closely he resembled Kyam. Same face shape, same nose, same build. They could have been brothers.

"Have you made the arrests, Major Voorus?" Kyam asked.

"Yes, Colonel." Voorus obviously disliked reporting to Kyam; QuiTai wondered if it was personal, or a matter of jurisdiction. Soldiers and intelligence services could be jealous of their territory, or so she'd heard. She tried to keep away from both as much as possible.

"We picked up the werewolves in a tavern near the town square. They were slobbering drunk. We had no problem bringing them in."

QuiTai swallowed a gasp. The werewolves? So all this time, Kyam had really been after the Devil. He'd only stumbled on the Ravidian's plot because of her. If the Thampurians hung the werewolves on some trumped-up charge, Petrof would lose his enforcers – she was sure that's what Kyam planned. But the werewolves were only a small part of the Devil's syndicate. The true heart of it was her people, and Kyam couldn't begin to imagine the scope of the network she controlled.

She fought down her panic and fury. She had to stay in control of her emotions.

Did he have Petrof? That was the question. He'd hinted that he knew the Devil was a werewolf, but he couldn't know which one for sure. Maybe he was expecting her reaction to confirm his suspicions. She refused to give him that information. No matter what, she would show no curiosity about these wolves.

"Then it's time we headed to the harbor," Kyam told the soldiers. He pointed to QuiTai. "Until I say so, your prime directive is to protect her. But under the circumstances, consider her hostile. Extremely hostile." He half-bowed to her. "You weave a wonderful story from wisps of fact, Lady QuiTai. But it isn't proof."

Kyam led the way through town. QuiTai, surrounded by four rude soldiers, followed. If Kyam had any respect for her dignity, he would take quiet streets; instead, he marched her through the marketplace. Voorus kept trying to grab her arm. Every time she yanked away from his touch, the other soldiers laughed.

The usual loud clash of voices quieted as they walked past the stalls. People stared. Stubbornly, she lifted her chin and looked straight ahead. If the crowd thought she was in disgrace, they were wrong. Kyam was the one who had acted dishonorably. She'd given him exactly what he'd bargained for, and in return, he'd had her arrested: He called it protection, but she wasn't fooled.

Kyam and the soldiers paused at the road leading to the harbor. "Keep a sharp eye out, men. There are lots of places at the switchbacks to stage an ambush," Kyam said.

She wanted to know why they were heading to the harbor. It didn't make any sense. But she refused to speak to him. He'd only use her words against her.

He turned to her. "If you sense a growl, or anything that sets off your instincts, let us know immediately. From the way you reacted in the marketplace earlier, you're much more attuned to it than we are."

She'd be damned before she warned him about anything; but every nerve in her body went on alert. She tried to listen, but the soldiers were making too much noise. They had no idea how to move stealthily: typical Thampurian heavy-footedness. Kyam, however, moved with a slinky grace she never expected from such a big man, gliding from shadow to shadow down the hill ahead of them.

The sun hadn't set yet, but it was already below the hills of west Levapur. Cool orange tinged the sky, and hot pink glowed on the underside of puffy clouds. Night fliers rose and swarmed on the evening onshore ocean breezes. Bats gathered in the trees chattered restlessly as the group passed. One of the soldiers flinched when a large ring-tailed lizard ran across their path. She wasn't the only one who was tense. But the Ravidians were probably several miles away, and the soldiers said the werewolves had been captured. Why so much caution?

Near the bottom of the hill, they came upon the funicular wreck. QuiTai had to blink a few times before she could make sense of it. The car she and Kyam had been in was so crumbled that the sight made her stomach heave. Then she realized it was actually the last two cars, sandwiched together. The only car that wasn't ripped open or flattened sat atop the remains of the ticket booth. Huge splinters of wood and the contents of busted crates had been thrown far by the force of the explosion.

QuiTai glanced at Kyam. He looked a bit queasy too as he

nodded tersely and then headed for the wharf.

The Zul junk sat in the middle of the harbor with its bow now pointed to the sea. Sailors moved purposefully across the decks. Beyond the junk, the fortress loomed. A sense of dread sank into her stomach.

"Into the skiff, Lady QuiTai," Kyam said. He stepped onto a boat tied to the wharf and offered her his hand.

She shook her head.

"I'm afraid that I must insist."

The soldiers grabbed her arms and dragged her toward the boat. "You aren't taking me to the fortress, are you?" It made her blood run cold.

"Of course not. Calm down," Kyam said.

Voorus pushed in front of QuiTai. "That's not correct, Colonel Zul. I have orders to relieve you of the prisoner. This is now a matter for the colonial military."

Panic gave QuiTai strength. She used every trick she knew to escape from the hands that clenched her. One soldier fell back into the water. Voorus grasped his groin. She spun to face the other two.

Kyam leaped back onto the wharf, grabbed her, and covered her mouth with his hand. He whispered, "Be still. Keep your wits about you. My protection has limits. If you bare your fangs to these soldiers, they'll have cause to toss you into a cell and throw away the key."

The feel of his breath on her neck made her shiver. She swallowed. She vowed not to give up. She might possibly be able to talk her way out of the fortress.

When Kyam felt her relax, he let go of her. Spinning around, she told him, "I acted in good faith, Colonel Zul. I should have known that Thampurian justice would be my reward."

"You think you're under arrest?"

"I think I'm dead. That's the only reason to take me to that place." She pointed to the fortress. A body, illuminated by the last golden rays of the sun, hung from the western ramparts. "No Ponongese has ever left there alive."

The soldiers were pulling their comrade from the water.

They looked angry enough to attack her again. They probably wanted to see her quake. To see her plead or cry. She wouldn't give them the satisfaction. Head held high, she stepped into the skiff.

Kyam and the soldiers boarded after her. Kyam untied the ropes while the others sat at oars. He looked as angry as she felt.

"You'll be the first, then, I swear," he whispered.

She laughed bitterly as they cast off.

They disembarked onto the fortress's short wharf, tucked in the far end of the harbor near where the fishing fleet and small merchant skiffs anchored for the night. The soldiers, Kyam, and QuiTai stepped onto the landing.

"Come, Lady QuiTai," Kyam said as he touched her arm.

Her heart recoiled at the sight of the thick stone walls, massive iron door, and the red banners proudly displaying the Imperial chop as they furled and snapped in the wind like waves. Kyam was Thampurian. He couldn't know how it felt to be so close to the hated symbol of colonial power. He thought of it as a place of justice; her people knew it as death.

"I want to watch the sun set," she said.

"You're in no position to make demands," Voorus said.

"Is she under arrest?" Kyam asked.

"Not officially."

"Then there's no reason to rush her inside, is there? It's not as if she can escape."

It was possible to climb the huge boulders that formed the seawall between the fortress and the shore, but it would be a perilous trip. Waves from the Sea of Erykoli slammed against the north side and sent plumes of spray high in the air. Small crabs and water bugs scurried for shelter as the water crashed down. Anemones, sea urchins, barnacles, and slippery kelp strands clung tenaciously to the rocks. Anyone trying to climb could easily be swept off the rocks by one wave and then slammed against them by another.

No. Escape wasn't possible. Not that way. And she couldn't cast off the skiff before they got to her, even if she somehow convinced Kyam to help her.

"Fine. Watch your damn sunset." From the way Voorus said it, it struck her as granting a last wish to the condemned. He probably felt it was more than generous.

She turned to the harbor, but the fortress loomed in the corner of her vision.

Past the bow of the Zul junk, the light of the brilliant orange sun smeared across the endless waves. It seemed to flatten as the lower edge met the horizon. The sapphire sea turned to gold.

According to Thampurian legend, the sun and sea were the lovers Kiruse and Erykoli, reunited every evening after a day apart. Erykoli missed her lover terribly, and so the sea tasted of tears. When they came together, she smiled with radiant light.

The Ponongese explanation for sunrise and sunset was simply that the planet rotated. "I prefer the poetry sometimes," she said, even though Kyam had no way of knowing what she was thinking.

He leaned closer to hear her voice over the crash of waves. Voorus and his soldiers stood ready to stop her from running, as if she had anywhere to go.

"Wouldn't it be pretty if the myths were real?" she said.

"If there were ever a time for faith, QuiTai, it would be now," he said. "It may be impossible for a regular Ponongese to leave the fortress, but that doesn't mean that you can't do it. After all, you would never let me out of my end of our bargain. Not that easily."

If he was trying to calm her nerves, he failed. She knew it would take a miracle for her to walk out that iron door again. But Voorus would never have the satisfaction of seeing fear in her eyes. This was merely a grand scene, full of drama, and the only way to play it was with a dignified mask over her face.

"What happened to the werewolves who killed those people during the full moon massacre?" Kyam asked.

"Forgive me if I've missed something, but I fail to see how the immortal beauty of the sea brought that to mind."

"No one ever tells that part of the story. When I ask, the Ponongese become unusually silent."

"You can't let me enjoy the peace?"

"We need to talk, and I don't want the soldiers to overhear. Watch your sunset while you tell me about the werewolves."

Watching was more than simply seeing the sun set. She needed this moment to collect her thoughts, to reflect... and possibly, to plan. She'd lost what little edge she'd had over him. No longer steps ahead, all she could do now was try to outthink him and outmaneuver Voorus as events unfolded.

"I warned you not to bring in the colonial government, Mister Zul."

"I needed help bringing you safely to the harbor."

"They're the last people you should have trusted."

"And the Devil is the last one you should trust, but we both cling to our loyalties." He lightly touched her arm. "The story about the werewolves, please, Lady QuiTai. The part no one tells."

No more Jezereet, no more sunsets. Was there anything fate would let her hold onto?

She cast a glance at the soldiers. They were far enough away that they wouldn't hear. "What no one tells is that I hunted them down and poisoned them," she whispered. "But not enough to kill. Only to paralyze. When people came into the marketplace the following morning and saw the criminals placed there for them, they tore the werewolves limb from limb. The werewolves felt it all, but couldn't move. That's why no one speaks of it. No one likes to admit they were part of that mob. You think my people shun me because I'm the Devil's concubine? The truth is that every time they see me, they feel shame for themselves."

She didn't care if the truth disgusted him. But he didn't back away or lecture her. Instead, he seemed to concentrate on his thoughts. He slowly nodded, as if things he'd heard and seen suddenly made sense.

He gestured for her to continue.

"I'm not a nice woman, Mister Zul. I will do things that others fear to. When justice is in short supply, I will step in and fill the void. That day, I gave the names of the werewolves to these Thampurian soldiers, but since the victims were only Ponongese, and the werewolves were from the continent, Voorus planned to simply deport them. Articles of transport and a free ride home are hardly appropriate punishment for eating a little girl's kidneys while she screams in agony for her mother."

"That's a bit of melodramatic embellishment."

"QuiZhun was my daughter."

He flinched.

She meant to tell him that she hadn't simply let it happen, how she'd run downstairs and thrown herself at the blockaded doors. If her neighbor hadn't sunk his fangs into her arm and temporarily paralyzed her, she might have broken through – and let the werewolves inside. She wanted him to know that she'd tried to save her daughter, but emotion clenched her throat and wouldn't let the words pass.

"I'm so sorry," he said.

He flicked away the glinting tear at the corner of his eye.

Then I asked the Oracle for guidance. She only whispered a name. The Devil.

"How can you even stand the sight of werewolves after that?" Kyam said.

She sniffled and squared her shoulders before looking at him.

"Would you like me to make a speech? I could say that there are those who are guilty of crimes, and then there are those who merely look similar to the criminals. I could pretend that unlike Thampurian soldiers, I don't confuse the two. But the truth is that it's a struggle every day to remind myself of those higher ideas. The werewolves loathe me. They make it clear that if it weren't for the Devil, they'd feast on my entrails and throw my corpse into the Jupoli Gorge. It doesn't help that he uses me as a threat to keep them under his control."

"Are you sure you got the right ones? Can you tell a man

from his werewolf form? From all that horror below you, how were you able to remember who they were?"

The truth was that she couldn't. It was too dangerous to be near them when they shifted. Even if she knew, she couldn't positively identify them from the horror she'd witnessed. Even in her nightmares, they were blurs of fur and fury. The screams she would never forget; the blood was seared into her memory. But the werewolves were hazy. She'd only seen them from above.

Petrof had handed them over to her. She heard whispers from the rest of his pack that he gave her men who challenged his rule regardless of their guilt in the killings, but she'd dismissed those grumblings much as she ignored everything else they whispered around her. Now, looking back, Kyam's question planted a seed of doubt. She remembered Petrof laughing when she marched into the den and demanded justice. He could have killed her then; maybe she even hoped he would, because she could barely stand to live anymore. Instead, when he stopped laughing, he told her he admired her bravery, and then he gave her names. He even told her where to find them. After she'd extracted her revenge, her people shunned her, but Petrof wooed her. He could be so charming back then. He said he liked her style. He admired her ruthlessness. They were lovers before he asked her to eliminate his competition. It had seemed like such a small price to pay for justice.

But now she knew that it would be so like Petrof to put the wrong men at her mercy for his own gain.

Used. She'd been used. First by Petrof, and now by Kyam. And she kept letting it happen, so whose fault was it? She kept expecting there to be a clear line to cross between loyalty to Petrof and betrayal, but if there ever had been, it was too hazy to see anymore.

Kyam still waited for her answer.

"I had a vision," she said. "I saw every ugly incident building on another. The Ponongese wanted blood. If they couldn't get it from the werewolves, they would have turned on the Thampurians in reprisal for the lenient sentences. The Thampurian government would have sent troops to slaughter the Ponongese. So I did what was necessary. I did what no one else would do. I sated the mob's blood lust before it got out of hand."

"Are you sure you had the right wolves?"

"Quit asking me that." Guilt and uncertainty made her angry. "What does it matter now? The past is past. I'm done with it."

"It might not be done with you," Kyam said.

CHAPTER 11: THE FORTRESS

*B*ehind the fortress's iron doors was a stone foyer dimly lit by green jellylanterns. The walls were damp and smelled strongly of the sea. QuiTai tried not to flinch when the doors clanged shut behind her.

A soldier stationed in the foyer led them to a solid metal inner door. He put his palm to a biolock to open it. QuiTai saw a hallway beyond.

The solider saluted Voorus, turned on his heel, and returned to his post.

QuiTai stepped in.

A man with world-weary eyes sat behind a barred window several feet away. He barely looked up as he held a pen poised over a stack of papers. "Name?"

"Colonel Kyam Zul of His Majesty's Intelligence Services."

The man's sigh echoed against the stone walls. "The prisoner's name."

"She's not a prisoner."

The man peered through the bars. "She's Ponongese."

Voorus stepped to the window. "She's QuiTai, the Devil's whore. She's here for the execution."

They weren't even going to pretend to give her a trial? It didn't surprise her. Fear's icy fingers clutched her lungs and squeezed.

"What execution?" Kyam's voice echoed off the stone walls.

Voorus arched en eyebrow. "That werewolf you had us arrest earlier today for killing the harbor master's brother."

QuiTai couldn't stop her legs from trembling even though it was Ivitch who would hang. She had no friends here, but Kyam at least had a reason to help her escape, so she lifted her gaze to him. His brows drew tight together as he stared at the floor. She wished she knew what he was thinking.

"You better hurry if you want to see it," the guard said as his pen scratched across a sheet of paper. "The chief justice signed the order of execution already."

"Wait at the gate." Voorus pointed the end of the hallway, where floor to ceiling bars covered an arched opening in the wall. "You'll be able to see it from there."

Through the bars, she could see the bare grass yard in the center of the fortress. Her pulse pounded. She had a feeling that matters were about to take a turn for the worse.

With his hand on the small of her back, Kyam steered QuiTai to the bars.

"Mister Zul, if I may make a request, whatever you do, don't let them separate us."

"Wouldn't dream of it," Kyam whispered. "So with your permission..." He clamped his hand around her upper arm.

A soldier in a captain's uniform crossed the grass toward them. Voorus and his men surrounded QuiTai and Kyam.

The captain saluted Voorus. "If you would follow me, sir." He placed his hand on a biolock. QuiTai heard the lock click, but the gate didn't open until the admitting guard came out from behind his window and placed his hand on a copper plate on the wall beside them.

The amount of security was daunting. She could handle the individual guards at the inner and outer doors; however, with biolocks on both sides of the gate, and two guards needed to trigger them, there was no way she could open it. The uneasiness in the pit of her stomach grew stronger.

QuiTai forced her mind to focus on details. From the outside, the fortress appeared round, but inside it was hexagonal. Barracks for the soldiers were on the harbor side. Three sets of stairs led up to the ramparts. The hairs at the nape of her neck stood up when she saw a man in a black hood at the top of the center stairs. He held a noose in his hand.

The captain spoke to Voorus as he led them across the courtyard. "He's been a talker. Mostly about the whore."

QuiTai thought for a moment the captain meant Jezereet, but he jerked his thumb over his shoulder at her.

"Nothing about the Devil, even though our best men worked him over."

"Damn." Voorus punched his hand. "What about her?"

"Said she killed the dirt, not him."

Voorus stopped short. "Oh?" He turned toward QuiTai.

Kyam's grip on her arm tightened.

"Two of my men remember seeing him leave the dirt's skiff yesterday afternoon. They didn't see her," the captain said.

QuiTai shot a warning glance at Kyam as he drew in a breath. She was certain he was about to say something. Now wasn't the time to talk.

"Wolf-slayer!" Casmir's voice carried across the yard.

"Come this way." The captain led them to the north wall, where rows of thick metal bars stood under archways of stone.

The cell was full of werewolves, but in the shadowed cell, she could only make out a few faces. She couldn't take another step. "Get me out of here, Mister Zul," she whispered.

Ivitch paced along the bars. Chains trailed between his legs. "I'll get you for this, you bitch! The Devil should have killed you when he had a chance!" He grabbed a jellylantern tube from the wall holder and smashed it against the bars.

Medusozoa glowed like wet slime on the rock floor. Shards of glass reflected the sky.

Shards of glass. The image of a single bloody shard flashed

through QuiTai's mind as pain shot through her hand.

Several big soldiers drew nearer to the cell as the captain prepared to open it. "All right. That's enough. Back up, the lot of you, except Mister Ivitch. It's your time."

Casmir lunged at the bars. The other wolves joined him. They stretched their arms for QuiTai and shouted vile names at her.

"We can just as easily hang the rest of you too," the captain barked at the pack. "Back away, or it's the rope!"

Voorus shoved her toward the cell. If it hadn't been for Kyam's grip on her arm, QuiTai would have stumbled close enough to the bars for one of the werewolves to grab her. Ivitch's face pressed against the bar as he wildly jabbed the broken glass tube at her.

She could see them all now. Petrof was not among them. The werewolves' tawny eyes never left her face. They pulled back their lips in snarls and growled at her. The energy of the pack crackled over her skin.

"Moon-mad," a soldier muttered.

The soldiers used long metal poles to push the werewolves away from the bars. The captain put his hand on the biolock plate.

QuiTai's mouth went dry. "Don't open that!"

The captain laughed. "Don't worry, miss. We have them shackled."

She put her hand over Kyam's. "We have to get out of here. They can shift without the full moon. As soon as that door opens, they'll rush the soldiers!"

"Come on, get closer. It's safe," the captain said. As soon as he said it, though, she knew that it wasn't, and he knew it too. It felt as if she were laced up in her tightest corset.

"We have to go," she whispered to Kyam. "Right now."

Voorus gripped her wrist, and the captain put his hand to the biolock. The cell door clicked open.

The werewolves dropped to all fours inside the cell.

Casmir said, "Fuck the Devil. You're going to die now, bitch."

163

The wolves began to change.

Kyam's eye widened. He looked from her to the werewolves. Shackles were made for human wrists and ankles, not slender wolf legs. He yanked QuiTai away from Voorus and pushed her away from the cell.

"We dreamed about this, Zul," Voorus said. "All the Devil's minions rounded up and ripe for interrogation. We can finally break his syndicate. But not without her."

"The werewolves are shifting!" Kyam said. "Shut that cell, you idiots!"

But only Kyam and QuiTai sprinted across the grass, while the soldiers stupidly watched the werewolves shift.

"You, amazingly brilliant plan, right now," Kyam gasped.

The wolves howled. Fear spiked through her. A man screamed.

QuiTai ran up the stairs to the ramparts as soldiers dashed past them down to the yard. The executioner dropped his noose and reached for her, but she managed to dodge around him. Kyam's footsteps pounded behind her. She darted a look over the wall to the rocks and waves below.

Where? Here?

No place looked safer than anywhere else.

The wolves bounded up the stairs, headed straight for her. Like the night of the massacre, all she saw was fur and fury, and all those teeth were coming for her. Petrof had told her that he didn't think like a human while in his wolf form, but she knew from the wolves' eyes that they knew exactly who they were after. Another Petrof lie exposed.

"What are we doing?" Kyam called out.

"You're a sea dragon," she said. "You figure it out." She tucked her sarong into her waistband and climbed onto one of the crenellations in the wall.

The lead wolf sprang.

Praying that she didn't hit the rocks, QuiTai jumped feet first into the churning waves of the harbor.

Slamming into the water was like hitting a wall. Someone hit the water beside her with a loud splash. She hoped it was Kyam, but didn't waste time finding out. She struggled up to the surface and swam as hard as she could. Her wet blouse clung so tightly to her arms that she could barely lift them. The waves pushed her back toward the boulders at the base of the fortress.

There was another loud splash nearby. Her toes brushed against something but her vision was too clouded to see. She forced her inner eyelids to open. A welcoming path of warm gold led to the last arc of the hot orange sun on the far horizon.

A huge wave bore down on her. The silhouette of a long, dark shape that could have been Kyam or a wolf moved under the translucent water.

She gulped in another breath and dove deeper. Her toes brushed against wet fur. It was like the nightmares where she tried to run but her feet rooted to the ground. She screamed as pain shot through her ankle.

Red foam capped the wave that curled overhead. The sting of salt water on her ankle made her think the blood was hers. Summoning up her determination, she kept swimming.

Something scaly undulated past her. Water filled her mouth as she yelped in surprise. The water near her roiled. Red bloomed. Desperate, she swam for the fishing boats.

A shark fin sliced through the water between her and the small boats.

Then, thrown by a wave, a naked, headless body slammed against her. She gritted her teeth to hold back her scream. A shape moved quickly through the water, headed straight for her. She braced for the impact and the pain of the teeth.

A creature's head rose several feet in front of her. Its eyes were pits of darkness. Long barbs like whiskers sprouted above the nostrils at the end of a long, thin snout. Thick bloodied teeth the size of daggers curved from its upper jaw as the head rose higher above the waves on a strong, thick, snakelike neck.

QuiTai treaded water as she unwound the silk scarf around her neck. His talons gently gripped her waist and pulled her closer. She looped the scarf around his long, sinuous body above his arms and mounted his broad back. "He bit my ankle, Kyam," she said through chattering teeth. "It's bleeding. The sharks are coming."

As Kyam lurched forward, she slipped down his body. She tightened her grip on the scarf and hoped it didn't choke him. Waves threw her from side to side until she wrapped her legs around him. His scales were surprisingly smooth. She could feel the strong muscles beneath her as he surged across the harbor. They wove through long shadows cast by the towering monolith stones.

Men shouted, but she wasn't sure if their voices came from the fortress or the deck of the Zul junk, the *Golden Barracuda*. She glanced behind them. The fins of more sharks sliced the tranquil harbor water. The headless werewolf body jerked, then disappeared under the waves.

QuiTai gripped the side of the wharf. Weak with exhaustion, she didn't have enough strength to pull herself out of the water. Kyam boosted her. Gasping and panting, she climbed onto dock. Splinters tore her clothes.

She rolled onto her back. Above her, the cloudless lilac sky deepened to indigo infinity.

She felt the heat of Kyam's body along her side as he slithered onto the deck, and then the energy of a shift surging over him. She didn't watch the change.

Then his bare human skin spooned against her. He brushed water drops from her face Okay?" he asked.

"I'll survive."

"That's my girl."

Her eyes narrowed as she turned her head. "Say that one more time, Mister Zul, and I'll teach you what it means to be my boy."

"You assume I wouldn't like that." He stood and offered her his hand.

His thigh muscles were thicker than she'd imagined. All that swimming must have sculpted them. Her estimation of his chest hadn't been too far from wrong, though.

There was no need to stare at the rivulets of water that trailed down his chest to a damp line of dark hair under his navel. But she took her time lifting her hand to his.

Kyam pulled her to her feet. "I told you that you'd get out alive."

"You plotted with Voorus. Ouch!" She winced and balanced on her good leg. Her ankle wasn't as mangled as she'd feared, but it bled freely. She turned to look at the harbor. Sharks thrashed in a feeding frenzy that sent sprays of bloodied water flying. Beyond was the fortress. She knew she was safe, but her body still wanted to run. She shook. In a day filled with brushes with death, she knew this was the one that would leave her with the most nightmares.

Kyam wrapped his arm around her waist. "Months ago. Idle talk over drinks. We both want to see the Devil in chains. But you – no, you're not part of the deal."

"Until you have your Ravidians."

He shook his head slowly.

He bent down close enough to kiss her, but stopped a breath away of her lips. His gaze dropped to her mouth but rose to meet hers again. "Please trust me." And then he gave her no time to answer before kissing her.

"Kyam!" a man called out. Kyam groaned. The hand pressed to the small of her back dropped away.

"Danger?" QuiTai hobbled into a defensive stance to face the new onslaught.

"Worse," he said. "Family."

CHAPTER 12: THE GOLDEN BARRACUDA

What have you got yourself into now, Ky-Ky?" A Thampurian with a weathered face clambered out of a boat onto the wharf. He was a bit shorter than Kyam, with an unmistakable air of authority. His hair was more silver than black. The gold epaulets on the shoulders of his dark blue wool shewani jacket were tastefully restrained, unlike the fussy loops of braid she'd seen on the shoulders of other captains.

"Ky-Ky?" QuiTai's lips curved.

"Not a word," Kyam growled.

While his sailors secured the ropes to the cleats on the dock, the new arrival clapped a hand on Kyam's shoulder. The men embraced. Then the captain looked QuiTai over. When he saw the blood streaming from her ankle, his smile faded. "The lady is injured! Why didn't you bind that?"

"I was a little busy," Kyam said through gritted teeth.

"Yes. I saw your idea of busy." The man bowed. "Captain Hadre Zul. From the civilized branch of the family."

QuiTai pressed her hands together and bowed. "It's a pleasure to meet you, Captain. I'm QuiTai of the QuiYalin Provence."

The Captain startled. "You're – But of course. Who else would Ky-Ky drag into one of his crazy exploits?"

"He doesn't hate anyone else enough."

Laugh lines radiated from the Captain's eyes as he chuckled. "I'll have to salvage the family's reputation then." He swept QuiTai into his arms and carried her with no more effort than if she'd been a child.

"She doesn't like to be touched," Kyam said hastily, and reached out as if to take her from his cousin's arms; then a sailor coughed discreetly and handed him a pair of trousers. He yanked them on.

"We got your message. We're ready to sail," Captain Hadre told Kyam as he gently handed QuiTai to the waiting arms of sailors on the boat.

"Sail? Oh no." QuiTai tried to climb off the boat.

"Have you forgotten about the werewolves?" Kyam asked.

"They can cause all kinds of mayhem inside the fortress, but you know as well as I do that the only way out is over the wall, and I'm sure after they saw the sharks eat Ivitch – at least, I think that was Ivitch, it's hard to tell without his head… At any rate, I'm sure they'll stay put and hope for the Devil to save them at the last second."

Kyam slammed his hand down on his thigh. "He wasn't one of the prisoners? Damn it."

"Kyam! Language," Hadre scolded. "Now, Lady QuiTai, I understand your desire to return to the familiar comforts of your home, but it would reflect poorly on our hospitality if we allowed you to leave without first tending your ankle. And maybe a little bite to eat? A glass of wine? I must insist."

While his tone was gentler than Kyam's, it still brooked little argument. He was a ship's captain, after all, and from his confident bearing, used to being obeyed. Reluctantly, QuiTai sank onto the wood bench in the boat. The terrible thing about excruciatingly good manners was that there was absolutely no defense against them. She used that ploy against others often enough to know she'd been outmaneuvered by a master.

Smiling again, Kyam boarded and put his arm over Hadre's shoulders. "I owe you for this, cousin."

Hadre sighed. "Saving your neck seems to be my job. At least this time you brought pleasant company."

QuiTai sat on Hadre's bed aboard the *Golden Barracuda*. His cabin wasn't big, but it was a marvel of efficiency, with cabinets that opened to reveal all sorts of fascinating things that she wished she had time to explore.

Her ankle had been cleaned and bandaged by the ship's doctor, who tsked and tutted over every bruise and the scar on her hand. Her ruined clothes had been whisked away with a promise to return with something dry soon. Their definition of 'soon' didn't match hers: every time she asked to get dressed, someone brought her food or more pillows instead. Trapped under the sheets wearing nothing but the chain around her neck that held the vial of black lotus, all she could do was wait.

"My dear lady!" Hadre sat back as QuiTai finished relating most of the events of day. "My cousin has behaved abominably."

"I'm glad to find some courtesy in your family," QuiTai said. Then she said in Kyam's direction, "Unlike him." Kyam glowered and then returned to reading a message that scrolled out of the captain's farwriter.

"Ky-Ky, would you put on a shirt? You look positively barbaric running around clad only in trousers. QuiTai had to agree, but she didn't have any objections.

"I saved her from the funicular wreck," Kyam said. "That's hardly treating her poorly."

Wincing, she touched the purple bruise on her shoulder. "He shoved me out of the window of a moving funicular. But yes, in fairness, it saved me."

"And a good thing too! The other passengers were killed,

you know. And the engineer and ticket seller in the harbor station. We rushed to the scene, and our ship's doctor did what he could, but..."

"I didn't know," QuiTai said. She plucked at the sheet as she frowned. "We were the only two in our car. I didn't realize there were others on board." She felt sick. Petrof could be vicious and wild, but she'd never known him to attack innocents.

Then again, could she be sure that he wasn't one of the werewolves that night two years ago? For so long, she'd been sure that he'd given her the guilty ones... The more she looked back, the uglier the vision in her mind. Thampurian justice wasn't true justice, but hers had been no better. Was that Petrof's fault, or hers?

It was hard to accept that in her fury to make someone pay for that massacre, she'd lashed out at the first target she found. But she had. That made her worse than any Thampurian.

Kyam said, "Before you condemn me, Hadre, there's a little something you should know about Lady QuiTai."

Her fists clenched. Would Kyam tell his cousin that she was a black lotus user? That she was the concubine of Levapur's notorious crime lord? How about that she owned the Red Happiness? Or that she'd given possibly innocent men to a mob? Did she feel guilty about any of that?

No. Nor ashamed. She did what had to be done. No one's opinion of her mattered, even Kyam's.

Kyam pointed an accusing finger at her and said to Hadre, "She enjoyed every minute of this adventure." It wasn't clear whether he was exasperated by her or bragging.

She replied, "That's not true. I remember objecting vociferously to our visit to the fortress."

He grimaced. "The soldiers were only supposed to escort us to the harbor, not take us to the fortress."

"Really, Mister Zul? I'm shocked, simply shocked, to hear you say that."

A merry twinkle gleamed in Hadre's eyes.

Kyam said, "You must be feeling better. You sound like your old self again."

Hadre rose from his chair and reached over to pat her hand. "Don't you give it another thought. Nothing you could have done. At least those savage werewolves who sabotaged the line will suffer for their crime."

"While the mastermind goes free," Kyam said.

Hadre turned. "You know who planned it? I hope you've given his name to the authorities."

"It will be handled, cousin." Kyam shot a look at QuiTai.

The junk creaked. Through the windows at the stern, she heard the sailors shouting. Deep thrumming vibrated through the hull. Alarmed, she sat up.

Kyam pulled the window shutters closed. "Wouldn't want you to get a chill."

"A chill? Even the lizards are hiding in the shade today. As you said, Mister Zul, I am quite my old self again. Captain Hadre, I thank you warmly for your hospitality. Perhaps we'll meet again under better circumstances. For now I must return your generosity and do what any thoughtful guest does when the hour grows late: go home." She pulled the upper sheet off the bed, wrapped it around herself in a make-shift sarong, swung her legs over the side of the bed, and carefully came to her feet.

The junk rocked. She staggered a few steps and winced as she put weight on her bad ankle.

Kyam and Hadre both rushed to her side; as Kyam grunted at him, Hadre withdrew his proffered hand and said, "Dear lady, you're in no condition to walk up that hill to town. Your ankle will start bleeding again."

"And yet that's exactly what I intend to do. Walk all the way to my own bed. It's lovely. The mattress is firm, and the sheets smell of spice berries. The pillows are beyond count, and each one cradles my head like a lover's lap. But the best thing about it is that it's hidden far away from every other living being on this island, and I can sleep for hours, maybe even days, undisturbed."

"You don't live with the Devil?" Kyam asked.

"Heavens, no. What an absurd idea."

"You're his concubine. It's not that farfetched," Kyam

grumbled. "Although... female werewolves don't live with their males..."

"Take your time mulling that over. Days, if you must. I can wait for you to reach some wrong conclusion, just not here."

His face lit up. "Ah, I haven't delivered my end of our bargain! Would you risk everyone knowing that I got the best of you in a business deal?"

"Mister Zul, if I'd known I'd be nearly killed in a funicular accident, humiliated in front of the entire marketplace, marched into the fortress, attacked by a werewolf, almost eaten by sharks in a feeding frenzy, insulted by your egg-thieving landlady, and forced to eat your cooking, I would have solved Jezereet's murder my own way."

Hadre's eyebrows rose.

"Aren't you going to blame the sea wasp sting on me too?"

"That I'm saving for the Devil. He might take pity on me when he sees that I was hurt." She doubted it, but she could always try.

"You're going back to him?" Kyam bellowed. "After everything that's happened?"

There were so many mistakes she'd made, and only she could set them right. That meant she would have to face Petrof eventually. She'd expected Kyam to understand that, but he seemed to think she could simply walk away from everything. That was the thing about living on an island, though: there was nowhere to run. Nor would she hide if she could. They were her mistakes, and she had to face the consequences, no matter how painful.

It was almost impossible to have any dignity while wrapped in a sheet. Drawing herself up to her full height was futile when it only brought her head as high as Kyam's chest, but she did it anyway. "No need to shout. You seem to have forgotten that the Devil's work is my living."

Kyam said in a clipped voice, "Don't take that icy formal tone with me!"

"We'll never agree on the subject of the Devil, so let's discuss a matter of current relevance. You handed me over to

173

the colonial military. They were about to throw me in that cell with the werewolves!"

"I already explained about that! Believe me, I'm going to protest their interference in my operation all the way up the line if I have to."

"I'll bet you fill out a vicious form, Mister Zul. Emphatic verbs and terse sentences. I can picture the Thampurian government quaking as they read it."

Rage twisted his face as he pointed at her. He gave her a warning look and spun on his heel. "Cousin, a word." Kyam stomped out of the cabin.

Hadre said, "He cooked for you?"

"Rice-and-eggs. Rather crunchy."

He hid a smile behind his hand as he bowed. "I'll see about finding some appropriate clothes for you, Lady QuiTai." He started to follow Kyam out of the cabin, but paused at the door. "We've just been introduced, so this might be a bit forward of me, but it's a rare pleasure to meet someone who lives up to her legend. Although you're quite more petite than I imagined."

She was left alone to puzzle out what that might have meant.

QuiTai took another sip of the heady wine they'd drunk with dinner. Her glass was nearly empty. The junk rocked rhythmically now and the steady mechanical thrumming had a hypnotic effect on her; the stuffy air in the cabin muddled her thoughts. She wanted to open the window shutters to allow the breeze in, but her strength ebbed. She sank onto the bed.

Kyam and Hadre thought they were being crafty, but she'd sailed before and knew the sound of an anchor being weighed. The increased rocking of the junk meat that they had cleared the harbor and now were at sea, but that didn't explain the mechanical noise that reminded her of the funicular's engine. While the junks she'd traveled on before had sailed at night, none had dared the risky maneuvers of a harbor in the dark: There were dangers in Ponong's waters beyond the harbor that made even daytime sailing treacherous.

The Thampurians were sea dragons, though, so they must know what they were doing. She wouldn't worry about the ship. She wasn't even worried about being abducted by a Thampurian spy and his charming cousin. What bothered her most was that she wasn't alarmed or enraged, even though she should be.

Did she actually trust Kyam Zul?

Almost unwillingly, she admitted that she liked him. And she found him dangerously attractive. But trust was a rare coin, one she didn't spend freely.

Her eyes felt heavy. She blinked and forced them open.

There was a quiet knock at the door, and then Kyam ducked beneath the low entrance and shut the door behind him. Hadre wasn't with him. Before he could speak, QuiTai said, "I am curious about... well, many things, but first things first. Isn't it dangerous to sail at night?"

Rubbing the back of his neck, Kyam had the grace to look embarrassed. "Figured that out, did you?"

"As you mentioned before, I'm the brains of this partnership."

Kyam sat on the edge of the mattress. "Partnership? I like the sound of that. So, if you're the brains, that makes me... "

"The brawn, I expect." Without a shirt, it was hard to ignore that he was definitely brawny.

In a way, it was a relief being trapped on board. She didn't have to face Petrof yet. The world could go on very well without her help for a night, and there were worse ways to spend that time. She looked Kyam over. Much worse, indeed.

Grinning, he filled her wine glass and handed it to her.

"Stop trying to distract me, Mister Zul. I asked if it's safe to sail at night." It wasn't his fault that her imagination kept wandering into embraces with him. She would take responsibility for those wicked thoughts.

"I wouldn't dream of distracting you." He reclined at the end of the bed and massaged her good foot. Tension melted from her as his thumbs pressed soothing circles into her arch.

She sipped the wine. It only seemed to make her thirstier.

"Is this entirely personal, or do you have a professional interest in me? Do be honest. I deserve that. Your cousin recognized my name. That makes me wonder if your government knows it too."

Kyam looked sheepishly guilty. "I might have mentioned you in passing last time I went drinking with Hadre. The past few times, perhaps." He carefully rubbed her other foot. "And it's always been an entirely personal interest."

Sleepily, she grinned. "People are going to be terribly disappointed if we start being nice to each other in public."

Kyam commented rather crudely on what the people could do with their disappointment.

QuiTai covered her mouth as she yawned. Her hand trailed down her neck and stopped at the vial of black lotus hanging from the chain.

Kyam frowned.

"I keep it to remind me why I'm mixed up in all this. If you don't approve, that's too bad. I don't care what you think of me."

He made a face.

"I don't care what you think of Jezereet either. She was an addict. The past year, that's who she was, not just a problem she had. Everyone else abandoned her, but I couldn't, because it was my fault." QuiTai's lips trembled. "The Devil can be so charming when he wants to be. He has presence. She was so used to being worshipped by her admirers that she didn't suspect his plans when he shared the vapor with her. And she thought I was simply jealous. Then it was too late."

"I'm sorry about that. But that's not why I didn't like her. Still, you loved her, so I won't say anything unkind right now. Eventually you'll ask for the truth, and I'll tell you."

Rolling the vial between her fingers, QuiTai tried to explain. "Guilt isn't love, but since she became addicted, I pretended it was for her sake. Any love I had for her died long ago with the real Jezereet. It's terrible of me, I know, but that's the ugly truth. So when I ask, go ahead and let me know the worst."

"You can bet I will. Plenty of meat to go with that rice, so to speak." Kyam rubbed his forehead. His eyes were weary and his shoulders slumped. "I've seen too many vapor ghouls to trust black lotus, but if you need a little to help you rest, I might be able to find a pipe on board. You really do need to sleep. I'm surprised you're still conscious after the beating you've taken the past two days."

"You look beat too. Get some sleep, Kyam."

He nodded as he slowly came to his feet. He bent down and pressed his lips to her forehead.

Her eyes closed: this time, no matter how hard she fought, they wouldn't open again. One moment, she was awake; the next, she was in dreamless sleep.

CHAPTER 13: A VISION

*T*he murmur of men's voices brought QuiTai gently out of sleep. Hadre and Kyam spoke quietly across the cabin. Faint silvery light streamed through the cabin's open windows as if dawn hadn't broken the horizon yet.

"Awake already?" Kyam asked.

She held the sheet to her chest as she sat up. A blouse and sarong sat on the table beside the bed. They were old and a bit faded, but she didn't care. As she pulled on the blouse, she noticed that the movement of the ship felt different.

"Something changed since last night. When I sailed home from the continent, sea dragons swam alongside the hull, took guide ropes from the junk, and guided us into port. That wasn't the sound of sea dragons I heard, and the distinctive scent of juam nut oil lingers. You have an engine on board, a big one," she said.

Hadre set down the peculiar brass instrument in his hand. He pointedly didn't look at her. "Very perceptive. We raised the sails about an hour ago. Had to, now that the sun is about to come up."

"Told you she was sharp," Kyam said.

"If anyone asks, Lady QuiTai, I implore you to stick with our story that you fell asleep immediately after the ship's doctor tended to your wounds," Hadre said.

QuiTai wrapped the sarong around her waist. Hadre's face grew pinker. She'd forgotten how prudish Thampurians could be.

"Your secret propulsion device is safe with me. I'm much more interested in our route than sounds below the deck." She sat at the table and peered at the chart Hadre had spread out in a curious frame, but the wonderful smell of breakfast tore her from the puzzle. "Oh, food. Excellent idea. Does anyone mind if I... " Before the men could answer, she dropped a piece of fish on top of the rice, draped seaweed over it, and quickly formed a roll that she popped into her mouth. The seaweed was slick on her tongue. The fish had been liberally doused in tart citrus juice that puckered her mouth. Cuisine at sea was never to her liking, but complaining to her host was beyond rude. Even food she didn't like was better than none, after all.

Now that she'd eaten something, she could concentrate better on the machine before her. She pointed to the chart past the rendering of the island to the dashed lines that surrounded it. "I see you know about the sand bars off the leeward side of the island. In some places, you can walk a mile from shore and the water will only be up to your chin. I know that junks have shallower drafts than, say, Ravidian ships, but you'd still run aground long before we reached the leeward plantations. At least, I assume we're off to confront the Ravidians."

Resting his elbow on the back of his chair, Kyam grinned at her. "The adventure continues."

"You're in a cheerful mood this morning. Did I miss something?" She made another seaweed roll.

"Nothing we can't continue at a more convenient time. It's a pity we were both so tired last night."

"Kyam! Really!" Hadre sputtered.

QuiTai and Kyam exchanged an amused glance. "We've scandalized your cousin, Mister Zul."

"He's spent his life at sea, so that's saying something, Lady QuiTai."

"It's good to know that our ability to entertain and astound hasn't diminished. Tea?" She lifted the pot.

Kyam handed her his cup. "Please."

"Captain Hadre?" Dazed, he pushed his cup toward her. She filled it. "What was that instrument you held earlier?" she asked Hadre.

Obviously relieved at the turn from scandalous topics, Hadre picked up the brass contraption. "First I set the chart number into this bit by the frame, then set in our current longitude and latitude. I touch this end of the instrument to our present position on the chart and the other one to our destination. This wire connects the instrument to the frame, so it can read what I've touched. Then a series of numbers appear here, along the frame, that our navigator uses to calculate all sorts of wondrous information. Don't know if I trust it yet, but I'm under orders to use it and report back."

"Interesting." From the look on his face, her curiosity alarmed him. If it was such a big secret, he shouldn't have told her. As repayment for his kindness, she'd pretend to ignore it. "Now, about our approach to the leeward side of the island: How do you propose to avoid the shallow water? We're not going to sail all the way to the end of the archipelago, round the islands, and come back at the windward side. That would take weeks. So can I assume that you intend to sail through the Ponong Fangs?"

Hadre nodded. "Precisely."

She stood to get a better look at that end of the chart. Her ankle barely twinged when she put weight on that foot. "The tide pool plantations are clustered here, here, and here, but the one I'd take over if I were a Ravidian hoping for privacy is this one." She pointed to Cay Rhi, a small island about a mile southwest of Ponong. "The owners are notoriously private. They hardly even socialize with the other plantation owners. A monthly skiff brings their supplies and takes their harvest back to the harbor, and I'd be willing to bet that the harbor master and his brother were the ones who made that run. It might have been months, maybe years, before anyone realized they'd gone missing."

Kyam and Hadre studied the chart.

"That is why you brought me on board, wasn't it? To show you the exact location of the Ravidians? As I said, I've sailed on many junks before, and none raised anchor in ten minutes. The *Golden Barracuda* was ready to sail before the soldiers brought us to the harbor."

"Frightening, isn't she?" Kyam asked his cousin.

"Formidable. No wonder the Devil was able to consolidate his power in less than two years." Hadre bowed to QuiTai.

"That idiot doesn't seem to appreciate what he's got," Kyam said. QuiTai popped another fish roll into her mouth.

"The family that lives across the landing from my apartment is from Cay Rhi," Kyam said. "They wanted their daughters to get a better education and wanted their sons to marry up, so they moved to Levapur. They often talk about their village on the edge of the lagoon."

QuiTai pointed to the lagoon on the map. "That's where the skiff docks. Most of the Ponongese from that village work on the plantation." And then a horrible vision swept over her. She gripped the arm of her chair and collapsed into it.

"QuiTai," Kyam said, "What is it?"

Hopeless in the face of what she envisioned, she raised her gaze to his. "The villagers would know, Kyam. The Ravidians would have to silence them too. They have several days head start on us. We might be too late."

Kyam reached for Hadre's arm. "Cousin, you heard her. Lives are in the balance."

"I can't use the engine. As it is, I'm going to catch hell for using them last night. Enemy spies might be watching from Ponong, and our speed and wake would give them vital information I'm not allowed to disclose. I'm sorry, Lady QuiTai, but it would endanger the neck of every person on board."

Disgusted, Kyam tossed his pile of farwriter messages across the desk. "It will take hours to sail around the east end of the island, and longer still to negotiate the Fangs, even with your charts. Damn the rules, Hadre. People may be dying."

"This is precisely the kind of thinking that got you exiled, Kyam. And as Lady QuiTai pointed out, they already may be dead."

"Turn around," QuiTai said. Her throat hurt. The spark of energy she'd had when she woke sapped out into a fog of despair. If only she hadn't dismissed the Ravidians as simply a Thampurian problem.

"What?" Hadre asked.

"Turn your ship around, Captain. Sail west for the leeward side. We can be there in half the time."

"But the sand bars!"

Her chair tipped over as she jumped to her feet. She pointed to a section of the map with no markings. "You can anchor here, where the water is deep. We'll lower the lifeboats and row the rest of the way. Or Kyam can shift and I'll hang onto him. Or damn it, I'll swim the rest of the way myself!"

A moment... and then Hadre dashed out of the cabin, and QuiTai heard him shouting orders to change course. "I knew I liked him," she said.

Kyam said, "I think he likes you too."

CHAPTER 14: RACE TO CAY RHI

With the change of course, the activity on board took on new urgency. QuiTai withdrew from Hadre's cabin as his navigator and several other uniformed members of the crew gathered around his desk. She stood on deck, at a loss as to what she could do to help.

"Excuse me, miss," a sailor said as he rushed past her.

She headed for another part of the deck.

"Pardon me, I need to tie off these ropes."

She retreated to the bow, which seemed to be the only place on deck where no one was working. Sea spray misted her face as she leaned against the rail. Even with the wind favoring them, it would take two hours to come within sight of Levapur again. From the shadows on the deck, noon was still several hours away. It would be late afternoon before they reached Cay Rhi.

The crimson sails of the *Golden Barracuda* were like partially unfolded fans, with thin strips of timbergrass that ran through the sailcloth and bowed in the wind. High atop the masts, the banners bearing the Zul chop undulated like a sea dragon through water. At the far end of the junk, over Captain Hadre's cabin, a gang of muscle-bound sailors manned the rudder.

Kyam came out of Hadre's cabin and headed toward her. He moved with natural ease across the deck, unlike her awkward attempts to stay out of the sailors' way. She would have never called him clumsy on land, but she could see that he was much more at home at sea. His permanent scowl had been replaced by buoyant anticipation.

"I received a message on the farwriter from the fortress. We lost a few soldiers, but the rebellion was put down within an hour after we fled, and the werewolves were hanged at sunrise. Unfortunately, one wolf still seems to be at large."

She ignored his hint. She'd already accepted that Petrof was trying to kill her, even if she still didn't understand why.

The verdant smell of the island came to her on shifts of wind. It had been several years since she'd stood on a ship and seen her home from a distance. Long streaks of white cataracts cut through the deep green of the mountains. Mist shrouded some of the high peaks: Up there it rained every day, sometimes all day long. At the lower elevations, the plantation terraces made the mountainsides look like banded malachite. The land came to an abrupt stop at the edge of cliffs where few plants clung to the red clay soil. Below the cliffs, the water was shades of turquoise. The beauty of her island made her ache. When she'd returned home from the continent, she'd wanted to rush ahead of the ship to touch the land as soon as she could. Now the same urge overwhelmed her.

Kyam said, "I've sent messages to everyone in Thampur, protesting the actions of the colonial military last night. It's a mess. Intelligence is fighting to keep me in charge. Not for my sake, but because it's a matter of jurisdictional jealousy. The colonial government is calling in every favor they can to maintain their sovereignty. I shouldn't be telling you this, but you should know that I have the least influence of anyone in this fight. You keep believing in me for some reason, so I'm doing my best to be worthy of your faith."

"Fight for yourself, Mister Zul, not for my esteem."

He leaned against the railing. "At least Hadre didn't run the engines at full throttle last night. If he had, we would have been through the Ponong Fangs already."

"Thank goodness he didn't throw caution to the wind, so to speak?" It was the sort of flippant remark he'd expect her to make, even though her heart wasn't in it.

She cradled her head in her hands. "I keep thinking that if I'd convinced the Devil sooner to let me hire you to paint my portrait, we would be already be there. But then I remind myself that I didn't even know what the Ravidians smuggled onto the island until yesterday. Or was that two days ago? I'm losing track."

"You can't be serious. You blame yourself for this?"

"I should have seen it." The vial of black lotus nestled between her breasts. If only she could consult the Oracle. Who could she talk into taking the vapor, though? Kyam?

He gently pulled her hands from her face. "Even your vision has limits."

He couldn't have known how that tempted her. The Oracle was never wrong, but would she give the answers QuiTai desperately needed?

"As you've been pointing out with boring regularity, I can be selectively blind. That isn't what concerns me, though. I sense a pattern. Something is coming together, but I can't think fast enough to stay ahead of it, or to see what it's leading to. Selective blindness can be fixed. This… " She shook her head. "It's like trying to grasp wraiths in a vapor dream. Smoke through my fingers. It's as if I catch glimpses out of the corner of my eye, but when I try to look directly at it, nothing is there. Like the glass shards and the sea wasp stinger in that puddle on the skiff. That's the image that keeps coming back to me. Bloody glass. If only I could find the right angle… "

There was a glint of dark humor in his eyes. "Is this a daily thing? Do you get contemplative and morose every morning, or is there something about me that turns your thoughts to doom and gloom?"

Wryly smiling, she laughed at herself. "It's you, of course. Normally, I'm a little rainbow of joy and happiness."

"Of course you are."

Kyam leaned against the railing and looked at the coastline. "When I was five, or six at the most, my father and grandfather took me on my first voyage. I think we went to Rantuum. It was the longest and shortest week of my life. Longest because it was the first time I'd ever been away from home. Shortest because it flew by so fast. Every school break after that, I hopped on board whatever junk was headed to sea and worked as a common sailor. My grandfather believed in learning the business from the bottom up. Being land bound is the worst part of my banishment. Every time I see one of our ships in the harbor, I get that itch to go to sea."

She joined him at the railing. "Then go."

"I can't."

"I don't believe you. But even if it were true, there are far worse places than Ponong to live in exile."

"Once you get used to coming home to an apartment infested with monkeys because you left your window screen open, and checking your boots every morning for those little lizards, or those hot chilies they hide in your food in the marketplace, or being robbed ten minutes after you first set foot on the island." He turned to her. "What was that about?"

"I foresaw your future here, and objected to it. Now I see that I was wrong."

He clutched his chest. "You were wrong? Amazing. I'll remember this moment forever."

"Oh, do be quiet."

"Are you going to tell me this future?"

"No need to. It'll unfold as it unfolds." Serious again, she gazed down at her hands. "But as surely as the future begins, some things reach their end."

"That sounds ominous."

"I swear that you now know everything I do about the Ravidians. Do you agree that I've kept my end of our bargain?"

"Yes."

"Then tell me now who killed Jezereet. I think I know, but after the things you've shown me the past few days, I want to be very sure that I have the right culprit."

"I don't think this is the time."

"We won't reach Cay Rhi for hours. When else but now?"

"The whole truth?"

"You know how we Ponongese like our stories," she said. "Make it a good story, Kyam."

Hands clasped, Kyam thought for a while before speaking.

"We were down at the harbor doing the preliminary sketches for your portrait. When the funicular took me to the top of the hill, I decided to stick around and follow you to find out if I could get any leverage to force your hand. I got it, but believe me, not the way I would have chosen."

"You're getting ahead of yourself."

"Ivitch came up on the next funicular after me and took off running upslope. I would have followed him, but I knew that he was a werewolf and it was full moon. Besides, it was you I wanted. So I waited. And waited. Then the last cars came up and you still didn't show. The sun was setting. That's when I really started to worry about you. I almost headed down to the harbor when you finally staggered up the hill, looking like walking death. My first thought was that Ivitch was the Devil and he'd beaten you. It was hard to watch you, wracked with pain, fighting on the way you do. And then seeing you begging in that alleyway for vinegar!"

"Those men were quite helpful."

"They treated you like a pariah. They knew it was full moon and saw how hurt you were and still let you walk away." He shook his head. "Unbelievably, you kept going. The look on your face when you stood in front of that vine at the Red Happiness. Such utter exhaustion. Anyone else would have broken down in tears. Not you. Grim determination is more your style. It wasn't easy to stand back and let you climb up to the second story veranda, but I did, because I was sure you were near your breaking point."

That's what she would have done. It was good to know that he was willing to do what he had to. That was the kind of person she could count on.

"I already knew you had some sort of relationship with Jezereet, so I went into that voyeur's room between her room and the one next to it."

"There weren't any viewing holes through her wall. We plastered over them a long time ago."

Kyam cleared his throat. "There are now."

"Ah. Very resourceful." QuiTai wondered if he'd watched them together more than the one time, and if he would have turned away if she and Jezereet had been intimate. Not that there was much of a chance of that; at the end, Jezereet only had one appetite, and it wasn't for heated kisses.

"It was frustrating, watching that look on your face, as if you knew something was wrong about the way Jezereet acted, but seeing that you were too tired to put it together. I didn't have a chance of figuring it out. Until you took the vapor. Then it all became too clear."

Little flashes of QuiTai's memory were like puzzle pieces that fit together in a surreal picture. Too many pieces were still missing, although she suspected she knew what fit into the spaces. She braced herself. "Did I kill her?"

"What? No!"

She hadn't thought so, but she couldn't rule it out. The vapor stole a slice of time from her that would always be blank.

"Was I the intended victim?"

Kyam nodded. "At least, you were the first one he headed to, and he only stopped because he was interrupted."

"Was Jezereet working with him?"

Kyam flinched. That was enough of an answer.

He licked his lips, and then spoke carefully as if he weighed each word. "She fought him when he put his hands around your throat. I ran out into the hallway, so I missed part of what happened, but when I kicked in the door, he'd already broken her neck and was headed back to finish you off. I don't know why he didn't attack me, but he went out the window onto the veranda and leapt down to the street. That's why I had to get you out of there. He could have come back."

Revenge seemed like a moot point now, especially since Jezereet had invited the murderer in, but the name was what she'd bargained for, not a happy ending to a sad story.

"What is his name?"

Kyam shrugged. "I know I promised to give that to you, but all I know is what he looks like. He's a werewolf with reddish hair, and a medium build for one of his kind. He wasn't captured with the others that were taken to the fortress."

There was no way she could deceive herself anymore. Petrof.

She'd made him the Devil. She'd solidified his power and run his organization. Instead of anger, though, all she felt was vast disappointment and a strangely calm acceptance. She'd known for a while that it was Petrof who tried to strangle her. Even without Kyam's broad hints and accusations, she'd known. It seemed inevitable.

She squinted, as if trying to focus on something far away. "His name is Petrof."

"Is he the Devil?"

"He's the leader of the wolf pack." That wasn't a direct lie, she told herself. Besides, what exactly did she owe Kyam? Not a word about the Devil. Their deal only included the Ravidians. That mess with the colonial military proved that she had good cause to keep her secrets.

"Damn it! I hoped – "

"I know what you hoped, Mister Zul. But never fear. I will see that he pays for Jezereet's death."

"Will you let me help you?"

Sadly, she shook her head. Then, with a small smile, she caressed his cheek. "This is the Devil's business."

Color flooded his face. "What has he done except let a mad dog killer come after you again and again? How does he hold your loyalty? I'd love to know why you set aside your safety for his convenience, when as far as I can tell he's never done a damn thing for you!" He pointed to her throat. "Do you think this is the first time I've seen bruises on your neck?"

She pointed to the wrapping around her ankle, and pulled down the shoulder of her blouse to show him the purple and yellow bruise on her upper arm. "These past few days with you haven't been restful."

"Don't you try to pin the blame for any of that on me! That's Petrof's doing, not mine."

"And he will pay. I assure you."

"The risks you're taking aren't worth it."

"Don't you dare try to take the satisfaction of revenge from me."

"You'll enjoy it, won't you?"

"You knew what I was when we set out on this little adventure. Don't try to change me now."

He snarled with frustration as his hands twitched at his sides. "Damn it! I'm not trying to change you. I'm just trying to make you see that the Devil doesn't love you."

She snorted. "Of course he doesn't."

That gave him pause, but he'd worked up indignation and he had to vent it. "Yet another person you love who doesn't love you in return."

She laughed. "What makes you think that I love the Devil? Do I strike you as the lovesick type? Believe me, when I bed a man, it's not because I'm picturing some romantic future. I got over that a long time ago. The pleasure of the moment is my only concern."

"Then why are you with him?"

"I told you that I always pay my debts."

"But you said that he addicted Jezereet to the black lotus out of jealousy. How could you forgive him for that?"

It was like being slapped by Jezereet's ghost. "I am not responsible for her foolishness."

But even as she said it, she knew it was a lie. Could it be that Petrof was her addiction? And that she was coming out of it as if freed from vapor dream? The lure of his body, his dangerous streak, his skill in bed, all of it seemed distant now. It shamed her to admit how she'd let him use her. She was supposed to be smarter than that.

"Did you ever love him?"

How Kyam's questions pricked her conscious and stung her pride! If she were willing to rip away the veil of self-protection, she'd have to admit the most squalid, ugliest truth there ever was – that for once, a lover chose her over Jezereet, and for that, she'd forgiven the unforgiveable. "It's purely business. The Devil's business."

"So it had nothing to do with pleasure."

That wasn't true either, although in light of her discoveries the past few days, she'd never touch Petrof again. Given a choice between humiliating herself by admitting she'd been duped or pretending she'd endured sex she hadn't enjoyed, she chose not to say anything. It was a bitter enough potion to swallow without a public confession.

Kyam lifted his hands to the sky. "You're driving me insane."

"You should be used to that." She looked out to sea again. What she needed was a purifying bath to scrub away her past. Maybe Kyam Zul was like the priestesses of the Qui, able to conjure accusing ghosts from the dark places she thought she'd banished them.

She took a deep breath. "Did Hadre say how long before we reach Cay Rhi?"

"Hours."

Rationally, she knew that there was some element of revenge against Petrof in the little scenario forming in her mind, but she didn't care. After what she'd said, Kyam would be a fool to think she meant more than a pleasant way to spend a few hours. The desire from the night before lingered in her blood. Maybe she could exorcise Petrof's grip on her soul with pleasure at Kyam's hands. And if it didn't work, she would hardly count it as time wasted.

"Hmm. I wonder how we should amuse ourselves," she said.

His eyebrow rose.

"Do you play tiles?" she asked. To her amusement, his nose wrinkled.

"Only if I have to."

"Bores me too. But I've never was good at waiting patiently."

The light came back to Kyam's eyes.

"And it seems we have some unfinished business between us."

QuiTai sauntered away from the bow. Half way across the deck, she paused only long enough to look over her shoulder at him. Then she headed down the carpeted stairs to the passenger cabins. Blue light jellylanterns lit the short hallway. Only two cabin doors stood on either side. Evidently, the *Golden Barracuda* was primarily for trade, not passengers.

Kyam took his time following her. "Just like that?"

"We've been flirting for over a year. You made it clear you want more, and I've decided I do too. People like us don't need to make it complicated. But I can amuse myself perfectly well without you, so run along if you're insulted."

QuiTai barely had time to reach for the knob of a cabin door before he was next to her, cradling her face between his hands and stooping to kiss her. He fumbled for the door latch: when it opened, he dragged her into the room. For a passenger cabin, it was of a respectable size, meaning little bigger than a jail cell and as sparsely furnished. A wardrobe and small desk were built into one wall, a bed into the other.

Kyam pulled her away from the door and slammed it shut. The narrow passage between the bed and the walls wasn't wide enough for two people to stand face to face unless they were exceptionally well acquainted and rather fond of each other. His hands pressed to the wall on either side of her. There was no escape, not that she wanted to get away. His eyes already had that bedroom look, focused on pleasure and little else. As he leaned down, he grasped her head and pulled her mouth to his. With deft fingers, he unbuttoned her blouse and dropped it on the floor without breaking their kiss. He kicked off his trousers and slid his hand down to the small of her bared back.

QuiTai stepped back from his embrace. His shoulders rose and fell with each deep breath. He took a menacing step toward her. Waves of anticipation moved through her body. Her lips curved as she shoved him back onto the bed. The slight confusion that furrowed his brow eased as she straddled his hips.

"Wait!"

If he was going to be like Petrof, she would leave.

He pointed to the table beside his bed. "Top drawer."

She leaned over to pull open the drawer. As she drew out the sheaths, she nodded her approval. "I like a man who plans ahead." Then she leaned down and bit his bottom lip.

Kyam's head dropped to the pillow as he released a long groan. Grinning, he stretched his arm over his head. It was almost adorable how smug he looked, as if he'd conquered her.

"I've wanted to that with you longer than I've wanted to kiss you."

"How delightfully debauched of you. I approve." QuiTai climbed off his lap and stretched beside him. As her fingernails rasped lightly over his ribs, he laughed and grabbed her hand. Between kisses pressed to each of her fingers, his dark eyes gazed at hers. "I never should have let you find that ticklish spot."

There was a knock on the cabin door. Kyam got up and pulled on his trousers. He rubbed his chest as he looked down at her with possessive satisfaction.

There was another knock. "Just a moment," he called. He limped the few steps to the door and turned back to look at her. "You play rough, don't you, my dear?"

"I warned you." QuiTai pulled the sheets up to her chest in case the person at the door could see around him into the cabin.

He smirked. "Would you like some food? I'll ask them to send up a plate from the galley."

She leaned over the mattress to the small table near the

bed and opened Kyam's silver kur case. "And something to drink. Where's your lighter?"

Kyam opened the door. Hadre glanced at QuiTai as she lit a kur and exhaled a plume of smoke with leisurely contentment. His cheeks went pink. "Kyam, I received orders on the farwriter, and so did you. You must come to my cabin and read them," he said.

Kyam picked his shirt up from the floor. He sniffed it before he pulled it on. "Of course." He sucked a deep breath between his teeth as he walked stiffly out of the cabin.

Hadre looked toward QuiTai but couldn't seem to meet her eyes. "I'm so terribly sorry about this, Lady QuiTai. Orders." He winced as he pulled the door closed.

She heard the turn of a key. Kyam's voice eventually faded, so she guessed he must have followed Hadre to his cabin. She fluffed the pillows behind her and inhaled the stimulating kur smoke.

This was an interesting turn of events.

Who would Captain Hadre take orders from? Only the Zul family or the government. She could guess which one told him to take her prisoner. So why would the Thampurian government care enough about her to lock her in a cabin on a junk when she had no means of escape? She was no sea dragon. It wasn't as if she could dive from the deck, hit the water, shift, and swim away. Although that's almost what she'd done at the fortress.

She climbed out of bed and opened the window screen. They'd already sailed past DiaHoun Rock, a high, domed monolith almost big enough to be an island in its own right, if it hadn't been only thirty yards off Ponong's western shore. If she'd been anxious to escape, she would have wriggled through the window and dropped into the sea. She wasn't desperate, yet. Still, she looked down at the water to gauge the drop.

Long, sinuous shapes undulated alongside the junk. The sun gleamed off their scales.

Sea dragons.

Kyam once said that she could add one and one and come up with five. She added secret orders and being locked in the cabin with a platoon of sea dragons, and slowly sank back onto the bed. She didn't need the Oracle for this vision. Every step unfolded before her with horrible clarity. The things she'd sensed on the edge of her perception came roaring out of the darkness like a waterspout spun off a typhoon.

The *Golden Barracuda* had been ready to sail when they got to the harbor. Kyam had planned to board and then demand to know exactly where she thought the Ravidians were. He'd get his proof and then triumphantly report back to his superiors. Only something had gone wrong, and someone found out that he was on the trail of the Ravidians. They hadn't been exactly secretive about their investigation, after all. He'd told too many people, despite her warning.

Back at the fortress, Voorus tried to get her close to the cell that held the werewolves. The captain's hand had been on the cell's biolock. The military was after her. Not Kyam. *Her.* Voorus wanted to use her against the Devil, but they wouldn't have sent so many sea dragons to follow the *Golden Barracuda* just to bring her back to the fortress. There was a bigger reason behind that decision, and it went higher up than Voorus, she was sure. The only question in her mind was if it was the colonial government or the Thampurian government itself that wanted her dead.

She looked out the window again and counted sea dragons. Maybe twenty: a huge landing party, considering that there were only three Ravidians.

The bigger picture was clear, and it made her blood run cold.

Maybe Kyam hadn't meant to hand her over to the military, but his motives didn't concern her any more. Nor did his future: That would happen anyway, no matter what either of them did. The Oracle hadn't spoken about her future, though. Perhaps she didn't have one. Perhaps it would end on the cay. But she wasn't going down without a fight, no matter who got hurt. Even him.

A search of Kyam's cabin revealed nothing QuiTai could use as a weapon. The silk scarf he'd given her was crumpled under his pillow. She left it.

She sat on the bed and unwrapped the gauze around her ankle. Ivitch's teeth had scraped off some skin. There were only a couple of punctures, but the skin surrounding them was inflamed and warm to the touch, a sure sign that an infection had set in. At least it didn't hurt to walk.

After she rewrapped the gauze and dressed, there was little to do but wait. Eventually, someone would come for her. Until then, she should prepare as best she could for all the possible futures.

She unscrewed the cap from the vial of black lotus and carefully squeezed a few drops of her venom into it. After replacing the cap, she shook it hard to mix the resinous tar with the pale green neurotoxin. She wasn't sure that the combination would work the same as vapor, but summoning the Oracle wasn't her main objective. A person would recover from such a small amount of her venom – Petrof always did – but they'd be incapacitated for a while.

She peered through the porthole. In the far distance, haze wreathed the peaks of Ponong. They had to be near the cay by now. She heard footsteps on the stairs outside the cabin.

It was time.

CHAPTER 15: ENTER THE MILITARY

Kyam opened the cabin door. He wore a Thampurian military uniform and stood stiffly as he looked slightly over her head. "You've been summoned to the Captain's cabin."

She stepped into the hallway. Two soldiers in uniforms that matched Kyam's waited on the stairs; she recognized them from their march through the marketplace.

The soldiers led her upstairs. Kyam followed them to Hadre's cabin.

Voorus' boots rested on Hadre's desk as he leaned back in a chair. Hadre stood to the side, quietly fuming. Twenty Thampurian soldiers packed into the small space. Kyam pressed against her back as he closed the cabin door.

Voorus swung his feet off the table and leaned over the map. "Very good. Now that we're assembled, we can begin our operation. Captain Zul, your sailors will row us to the cay. The snake will accompany us as our native guide."

"I've never been on Cay Rhi before," QuiTai said.

His gaze rose to meet hers. It wasn't hatred that she saw,

just smug superiority. "I didn't give you permission to speak. I'm also not giving you a choice. Come willingly, or come in shackles."

QuiTai could feel the crackling energy of a shift spread through Kyam. She always thought sea dragons had to be in the ocean to shift, but every type of shifter was unique, and it had taken her almost two years to learn that everything she thought about werewolves was wrong.

"She told you that she doesn't know the cay. What use would she be?" Kyam asked.

"May I remind you, Zul, that you're an observer. This is my operation."

Sensing that it might be best to pretend that was a surprise to her, QuiTai looked over her shoulder at Kyam. "Colonel Zul?"

Voorus laughed. "Certainly he used to be a colonel, but he's nothing more now than a remittance man. Stripped of rank and sent away where he couldn't embarrass his family anymore. Did you actually believe he was in charge? I thought that you were supposed to be smart." His laughter was poorly faked.

Something didn't strike her as right about the scene. It might have been true that Kyam was currently in disgrace. He might have been stripped of rank: That explained why his government wouldn't listen to him, and why he'd tried to bribe her with family money. Could the Oracle have been wrong? No. It wasn't possible. Kyam Zul was much more than a remittance man, even if he and Voorus didn't know it yet.

"Tell her, Zul."

His eyes pleaded with her for understanding. "You think I'm a spy. I'm not. I still have my rank, despite what Major Voorus says, and technically I have duties on Ponong, but my real job is to fade into obscurity. Here's irony for you: As awful as you've been to me, you're the only person on this island who's treated me as if I still mattered."

A man like him with nothing to do all day but paint flowers while serving a life sentence on a beautiful island prison. A sea dragon forever banned from setting foot on a boat home. No wonder he simmered with frustrated anger all the time. She should have seen it. The entire plan to follow the Ravidians had been his desperate attempt to win back his place in Thampurian society.

Although Kyam couldn't know it, the real irony was that she could see the future unfolding; and that she, of all people, would be the one to make the Oracle's vision come true after fighting so hard to stop it. Kyam Zul would become the governor of Ponong. She didn't know how, but it would come to pass, probably because he'd eventually get credit for bringing the Ravidian plot to the attention of his superiors. And he'd always know that she was the only reason he had figured it out. Colonial governor Zul would be in her debt. The possibilities were delicious. It was a pity she couldn't let him in on the cosmic joke: Kyam could probably use the laugh.

"You've been made the fool," Voorus told QuiTai. "I'm curious though. What could possibly tempt the Devil's whore into helping a man she clearly hates?"

The question was, what would Voorus believe? He didn't need the truth.

She lifted her chin. "They promised me that they'd get me into the new kinescoptic motion pictures in Rantuum. I've had enough of living on this boring island. I'm an actress. I belong on the stage."

That time, Voorus' ugly laughter was real. "A promise he won't keep, I assure you."

QuiTai spun around and slapped Kyam. "You!"

Voorus found that even funnier. "Get the little viper under control, Zul. We have work to do."

Kyam grasped her wrists. She put up a token struggle while Voorus ordered them to board the lifeboats.

Chapter 16: The Tide Pools

None of the soldiers or sailors spoke as they rowed toward the cay. The skiffs rode the crests of waves and dropped down into the troughs in the choppy water. The sun wouldn't set for several hours, but the edge of a tropical storm darkened the southern sky. Even over the sea, the air was sticky and thick with humidity.

QuiTai bailed water from the bottom of the boat until she realized it was useless. Without something to keep her occupied though, all she could do was watch their progress toward land and fret about what they might find there. Kyam didn't ask what she foresaw; they were surrounded by Thampurian soldiers now, and every word, every gesture, might have ramifications later on. For now, it was best to keep their public conversations hostile.

While Cay Rhi's lagoon was a safer harbor, Voorus decided it would be better to row to a smaller beach further from the tide pool plantation so that the Ravidians wouldn't see them coming. But the narrow, rocky beach was perilous landing.

Kyam jumped out of the skiff in the surf with the sailors, and shook his head when QuiTai slipped overboard and grabbed hold of one of the guide ropes. She saw him stifle a chuckle. If he could still laugh, he hadn't put together the pieces of the puzzle as she had. Or maybe he knew exactly what the soldiers planned to do.

No matter. Their business was concluded. They owed each other nothing now. It wasn't betrayal if he sided with the Thampurians, any more than if she chose her people over him.

When it became clear that the skiffs couldn't be dragged over the rocks to the narrow band of soft white sand, the soldiers reluctantly waded to shore.

The cay, like many of the small archipelago islands, was little more than a giant dune pushed out of the sea by the relentless waves. Even the monolith stones along its southern shore were worn to stumps that barely rose above the water. The cay was covered with coconut palms and stands of tall grass. Further from the beach, the jungle clung to the sandy soil with tenacious roots.

Voorus tossed an equipment pack at QuiTai. She staggered backward as the heavy pack hit her chest. He snapped his fingers at her and strode toward the jungle. Before she could drop the pack, Kyam took it from her, briefly touching her arm, pleading with his eyes for her to hold her tongue.

The sailors quickly pushed the skiffs off the rocks and rowed back to the junk. That made the little plan forming in QuiTai's mind a bit harder to carry out, but she was sure that she'd find a way around it. She had to.

The soldiers under Voorus' command quickly secured the beach and gathered by the trunk of a slim coconut palm that bowed toward the water. Rivulets of sweat already poured down the major's temples, even though he hadn't manned an oar on the skiff. He opened the equipment pack Kyam held and pulled out a machete. "Make sure that she only uses it on plants," he warned Kyam.

Clouds of mosquitoes and night spirit moths rose as QuiTai and the soldiers hacked two parallel paths through the jungle.

Kyam took the lead on the line of men to QuiTai's left. Even though the canopy overhead shielded them from the sun, the hot, humid air scorched their lungs. Ten minutes later, soaked in sweat, they yielded the lead to the men behind them and fell to the back of the line.

QuiTai joined Kyam as he paused to consult his compass. She was glad he had it; she knew her way around Ponong, but she had only a vague idea of where they were headed on the cay. The entire island wasn't more than half a mile wide and maybe two miles long, so it was impossible to get too lost, but she was in no mood to waste time.

"Let the soldiers do most of the work. Don't exhaust yourself. You need to stay alert," Kyam said in a quiet voice as he kept his focus on the compass.

Using her forearm, she wiped sweat from her forehead.

"And don't give me that look. You saw what the Ravidians did to the harbor master's neck. Not to mention that Petrof could be lurking anywhere."

QuiTai unhinged her fangs and ran her tongue down one with such relish that Kyam shuddered. Then he clamped his sweaty hand over her mouth. "That's not a good idea."

Her hand went on her hip as she gave him a look that she was sure he couldn't misinterpret. Then she turned and followed the line of soldiers who had moved ahead without them.

The lead soldier on Kyam's column stopped abruptly, motioned for silence, and ducked. QuiTai and Kyam carefully picked their own path through the undergrowth without using their machetes. They squatted shoulder to shoulder and pushed aside glossy, dark green leaf that blocked their view.

Gentle waves lapped a crescent of white sand beach around the lagoon; several small outrigger fishing boats bobbed in the pale blue-green water beyond. Jungle fowl clucked as if muttering to themselves as they scratched at the ground around quiet huts. But no people. No children laughing. No grandmothers on the rickety, modest verandas of the palm leaf covered huts. No men singing as they hung their fishing nets to dry.

The bad feeling in the pit of QuiTai's stomach wrenched

into pangs of fear. There: a bowl overturned yards from the water. There: a splatter of blood on the wall of a hut.

She tried to guess how many people lived in the village and how many could fit in the fishing boats. It would be tight, but if the series of events she expected came to pass, any Ponongese left behind would never leave the island alive.

QuiTai unscrewed the top from the vial of black lotus and spread a few drops of the murky mixture of her venom and the tar around her wrists.

The eerie stillness in the village seemed to affect the Thampurian soldiers too. They crouched and made their way through the underbrush without a word, skirting the village as if it were ground too sacred to touch.

As the soldiers paused to get their bearings, she stayed within sight, but at a distance. "Where's our guide?" Voorus asked. His dark eyes sought QuiTai. "Bring her to me."

A soldier gripped her sleeved forearm. She wanted him to touch her skin, so she pulled away. In the brief struggle, his fingers clamped around her wrist. Only then did she allow him to drag her toward the major.

"We wouldn't want you to get lost," Voorus said.

"I have no idea where we're going, so you could say that I already am."

"We're going to the plantation. That's where you promised the Ravidians would be."

"I said that's where I thought they might be, Major, but I made no promises. However, if you want to get from this village to the plantation, I suggest you take the established path rather than spend your energy cutting a new one."

"What path?"

"If the villagers work on the plantation, they probably walk there. If they walk there every day, there's probably a path. It shouldn't be too hard to find. Look for the place where the plants aren't growing."

Several feet away, Kyam covered his face and slowly shook his head.

"Men, look for a path," Voorus said.

The soldier who'd gripped QuiTai's wrist staggered a few steps and then stared at his hand. He giggled. QuiTai fought the urge to giggle with him as she felt the black lotus seep into his blood. Even from here, she could see that his pupils were contracted.

"Soldier!" Voorus' face flushed with heat and anger.

The man tried to come to attention, but collapsed in another fit of laughter. "My hands are floating."

Kyam shot QuiTai a piercing look and rushed to the soldier to unbutton the soldier's jacket and try to persuade him to sip water from a canteen. "He's overcome from the heat. Someone should take him back to the *Golden Barracuda*."

Interesting. Kyam suspected that she had something to do with the soldier's condition, but wasn't telling anyone.

"Leave him here. We'll deal with him later." Voorus ran his finger under his collar. Rings of sweat darkened his uniform under his arms. "Have you found the path yet?" he called out.

"Over here, sir," a soldier said.

"Come on." Voorus stomped off.

Kyam shook a warning finger at her. QuiTai barely suppressed a wicked grin and followed the major.

A flock of small gold, green, and red parrots rose from the upper limbs of a mango tree beside the path. The soldiers flinched as the loud voices of the parrots racketed through the jungle. When Voorus was convinced it was safe, he motioned his men to follow.

They were almost at the plantation wall before they saw it. The original compound hadn't been built as a fortress, but it was one now. Blue tiles that had once capped the wall lay in shards on the ground. Damp plaster, still smelling of wet clay, covered the top four feet of the wall. Strands of a slick gel draped over wires strung tight above the new bricks.

A single guard tower rose from the center of the compound. The Ravidian standing in it held something long and metal in his hands as he leaned against the railing and looked toward the sea.

The soldiers darted back into the jungle before the Ravidian could turn and see them, but QuiTai rushed to the wall and pressed her back to it. There was no way the guard could see her from that angle if she couldn't see him. As Voorus hissed for her to join them, she tucked her machete into the waistband of her sarong and moved along the wall toward the back of the compound, where the path widened into a large patch of cleared dirt in front of a walled-up gate.

She startled when she saw a body at the far edge of the clearing. Every detail came to her in quick flashes. The plants and dirt around him seemed to be covered with the same gel that hung from the wires; even his clothes looked wet. Flies buzzed around his bloated body but didn't land.

So this is how they use the sea wasps as a weapon.

She wasn't surprised. It was how she envisioned using them if LiHoun was successful.

How did they throw so many?

"Get over here now!" Voorus sounded remarkably like Kyam when he was about to start shouting, although she doubted he would raise his voice over his terse whisper.

I'll give you your native, *Voorus, and I'll play my role to the back of the house.*

QuiTai lurched toward the corpse with one hand before her face and the other stretched out. Her halting walk, perfected on stage, gave her a chance to pick a path through the nearly clear remains of shredded sea wasps. Sobbing, she dropped to her knees in a spot clear of the stingers. After choosing the safest place to touch him, she turned him over.

She gasped. "PhaNyan!" It really was him. The fool had gotten himself killed. His rascal's smile was a frozen grimace now.

Two soldiers rushed her. Kyam tried to hold the second one back, but he wrested free. In the scuffle to drag her back to cover, both brushed against plants coated with sea wasps. The stung soldiers muffled their cries of agony as they staggered back into hiding, but they didn't let go of her until they were well into the trees. Their friends doused their faces and hands with vinegar.

Damn Kyam for telling them how to combat the sea wasps' stings! She'd warned him not to tell them anything, and now they'd taken over the mission that could have saved his name and brought him out of disgrace.

Serves you right.

From the way Kyam seemed to hold his breath as his eyes fixed on a point far above the compound wall, she assumed that the Ravidian guard had turned in their direction. The soldiers, Kyam, and she held their collective breath. On an invisible signal, perhaps, the Ravidian in the guard tower turned away, and the men relaxed.

It was too bad she'd only been able to take out the two soldiers. That still left seventeen to neutralize, and then there was Kyam to consider.

Voorus' fingers dug into her arm as he yanked her deeper into the trees. "You know that Ponongese?"

QuiTai nodded. She continued to cry, although not as loudly as before.

Voorus beckoned Kyam over. "If she's never been on this cay before, how does she know him?" He pointed to the clearing. "Or is that one of the Devil's men?"

"I've seen her speaking with him before in Levapur, so he could be one of the Devil's men, but I swear that she hasn't left my side since we spoke at the Red Happiness." Kyam's mouth snapped shut as his eyes narrowed.

Voorus shook her so hard that her head swam. "How did you get a message to your operatives? Tell me. I swear I'll strip you and roll you in those sea wasp stingers if you don't tell me now."

"I sent him to keep an eye on the Ravidians, back before we knew what they were doing. He must have followed them here." She wiped tears from her eyes. "I haven't spoken to him since before Jezereet was murdered."

Voorus gripped her hand and forced it open. He pointed to her scar. "One wonders where you got that, since you claim you've never been on this island before."

"Two of my friends have died in the past two days, and all you care about is a red mark on my hand? Heartless Thampurian bastard." QuiTai let her knees buckle as she forced more tears to roll down her cheeks. She bit her knuckles, but her sobs grew louder.

Voorus pushed her into Kyam's arms. "Beat her if you have to; just get her to stop that unseemly wailing. The Ravidians might hear. I have to see to my men."

Kyam's eyes were dark with fury as he pulled her in the opposite direction. "You can cut the act now. Remember, I've seen real grief on your face."

QuiTai immediately stopped wailing and batted her eyelashes.

"How did you do it?" Kyam asked.

"Do what?"

He jerked her hard against his body. "Quit playing the innocent. How did you get a message to him? Was it that woman at the tavern?"

She wasn't about to let him know.

"This is going to stop, Lady QuiTai, and it's going to stop now. I won't let you hurt any more soldiers."

"Ah, you've found the mosquito in the dark room."

"What did you do to that one back at the lagoon? Did you..." With two fingers, he made a gesture like fangs in front of his mouth.

"Heavens no. Just a touch of black lotus. He'll have nice dreams and a wicked headache tomorrow."

Kyam exhaled as he ran his hand over his hair. "Okay. But no more. Letting those men touch the sea wasp stingers was cruel."

"Those men rushed into a trap without thinking while on a raid. That sort of carelessness could get them killed in any number of ways. And do I have to remind you that they tried to throw me into a cell with werewolves last night?"

"Voorus may be slow, but eventually he'll figure out what you're doing."

She smoothed her sarong and pushed her braid over her shoulder. "Just as I figured out what he's doing."

"He's securing the compound."

"No, Mister Zul. He's securing the production of sea wasps."

"You and your words. I swear I'm going to start calling you Princess Pedantic. What's the difference?"

"The Ponongese slaves working the tide pools."

Kyam all but rolled his eyes. "There are no Ponongese slaves, Lady QuiTai."

She didn't care to be spoken to like a dim child. "I assure you there are, Mister Zul. Otherwise, the village would be littered with dead. Remember when you told me the Ravidians treat the natives of their colonies worse than Thampurians do? So trust me when I say that there are enslaved Ponongese working the tide pools of this plantation, and after the colonial military secures the compound, they will still be slaves and no one will ever know."

From his suspicious look, she thought he didn't believe her, but she could see understanding dawning behind his anger.

Kyam ground his teeth. "The government in Surrayya will put a stop to that."

"You've been read the Secrecy Act, I assume. Tell anyone back in Surrayya what happened here, including your handlers in the intelligence service, and the colonial government will execute you. I'll be surprised if you still have a farwriter in your apartment when you return, and good luck boarding a Zul ship without an armed escort in the future. Ask your cousin Hadre to send a message, and they'll kill him. So no, I don't think your government will put a stop to anything."

"You could – "

"You really don't see it, do you? I'm Ponongese."

"I'm well aware of that."

"They'll never let me off this island alive. I know too much about the sea wasps, about the harbor master, about the slaves. You may appreciate my special talents, but to them I'm just another snake." She strolled a few steps away from him. Her gaze flicked to his groin then back up to his eyes as the corner of her mouth curved. "At least I'll be safe from Petrof here. Isn't that what you wanted?"

Shaking his head, he mouthed the word 'no.'

Exploiting his weakness for her was no way to treat a lover, but it wasn't the time to play nice or fair. One of them had to be the villain to play out the rest of this script the way it was meant to unfold. And that was a role she was born to play, especially for a Thampurian audience.

She circled him. "Would you like that, Colonel Zul? Me held captive here, pried away from the Devil's bed, at your mercy, in chains?"

Kyam clenched his jaw as he drew in a ragged breath. His fists clenched. She stood on her tiptoes to whisper into his ear. "Tempting vision, isn't it?"

"You have no conscience, do you?"

"Don't be ashamed of how it stirs you, Kyam. Many people fantasize about such things. I would relish binding your hands to your headboard with that silk scarf you bought me." He closed his eyes and swallowed hard as her fingernails rasped across the nape of his neck. "I know that right now, you would very much like to control me. Maybe even make me beg... "

"QuiTai... " Her name was a plea on his lips. The fight for control passed over his face like a shadow. He dropped his voice into a harsh whisper. "Not another one of my men, QuiTai. I'm warning you."

A mocking smile played across her mouth as she bowed. Against his better judgment, he would still protect her, because that was the type of man he was.

"And don't you dare think of siding with the Ravidians. Even the king couldn't save you then."

"I will never show mercy to anyone who enslaves my people." He could interpret that as he wished. "I'll make you a new deal. From now on, you concentrate on your people, and I'll focus on mine. No more shared rice."

At that moment, he clearly hated her. "Agreed."

A couple of soldiers drew near them. "Major Voorus says to move out, in case the Ravidians come to investigate."

QuiTai studied the guard tower in the center of the compound. It looked as if it had been hastily constructed, but ugly aesthetics didn't change its effectiveness. From that height, the Ravidian in the tower could send pain and death raining down in a wide circle, and he obviously had the weapon to do it.

For three men defending such a large position with no cover and no geographical advantage, they had an effective set up. She'd assumed they were scientists, but now she suspected they were military.

"They won't bother to come here," QuiTai said as they returned the main group of soldiers.

"What does that mean?" Kyam asked.

"The Ravidians don't ever have to leave that guard tower," QuiTai said.

She daubed the last fake tears from around her eyes. "Take another look at PhaNyan's body. The area surrounding him is covered in sea wasps, but closer to the wall, there are none."

Kyam's eyes opened wide. "They have some way of propelling the sea wasp stingers all the way from the tower?"

"Nonsense," Voorus snorted.

"Go stand in that clearing and catch the Ravidian's attention. You'll find out soon enough." She hoped he would.

"How?" Kyam asked.

"I think the Ravidian in the guard tower is carrying some sort of propulsion device for a load of stingers. We guessed that they'd weaponized them. Now we know how," QuiTai said.

She was speaking to Kyam, but she looked at the soldiers who gathered around her.

"Listen, I know weapons, and I can tell you that there's no way that splatter came from that guard tower. They must have surprised your spy while they walked the perimeter," Voorus argued.

She squatted and searched across the ground for stones. As the soldiers watched, she formed a short stack and a tall one. She squinted as she compared the heights. "The tall stack represents the tower. The short stack is the compound wall." She stripped a twig of leaves and rested the stick on the two piles of stones. Where the twig touched the ground, she drew an arc. She pointed to the inside of the arc. "No spray." Then she pointed outside the line. "Spray."

The soldiers looked from her model to the clearing.

"That's ridiculous. No one can send something flying that far without a catapult of some type, and there's barely enough room for a man to stand up there," Voorus said. But he squatted beside QuiTai to look at her stacks of stones. "Unless they've developed a weapon we've never seen before." He looked at QuiTai with a measure of respect she hadn't expected.

"We have to rethink the plan for this raid," Kyam said. He uncapped a flask and drank from it. The other soldiers leaned against trees and took out their flasks. One started to hand his to QuiTai, but Kyam pushed it away. "Don't take anything she hands you. And from now on, be very careful about touching her. She's poison."

She smiled and shrugged. They would have tasted the black lotus if she'd added it to their water anyway.

QuiTai wandered away from them and squatted in the shade. Her inner eyelid slid down to protect her from the swarm of gnats trying to drink from the corners of her eyes. Ivitch's bite on her ankle itched under the gauze wrappings. She tried to scratch it through the bandage. Blood-tinged pus had seeped from the infected punctures and hardened on the gauze.

Watching the soldiers gulp down water made her mouth dry. She searched through the plants with thick stems until she found one with reservoirs of rain water trapped in its crevices. After picking out the drowned insects and plant debris, she pressed her face to the stem and sucked as much of the water as she could reach.

She could see Kyam's face as he addressed Voorus. His gaze met hers. She listened as he said, "Assume that it is possible that the Ravidians have such a weapon. What are our options? I need a good plan, and I need it now."

"You need? I think you've forgotten your place, Zul. You're an observer," Voorus said.

When he wasn't using his height and rumbling voice to intimidate her, QuiTai had to admit that Kyam's glowering was quite effective. There was no humor in his eyes now as he faced the major. "Fine. Then you come up with a plan."

"Can we go over the wall?" a soldier asked.

"I think those are sea wasp stingers hanging from the wires. We could clear a section, but if we're seen, we'll lose any advantage we had. Besides, we'd risk one of the men touching a stinger, and we can't waste vinegar," Kyam said.

"We could build a battering ram and smash the wall, sir."

Voorus shook his head. "Focus on the Ravidians, not on destroying the compound."

Kyam's eyebrow rose. Maybe now he believed her that the soldiers had been sent to secure the plantation, not to destroy it. That didn't mean he would betray his people though. They were each taking care of their own now: That was the deal.

The new plan was to scout the front of the compound for a way in. It wasn't QuiTai's plan, but she approved of it. What else could they do? With the back gate bricked over and the walls turned into death traps, there was only one way in.

The jungle thinned as they drew closer to the beach. The soldiers moved farther from the compound wall to keep under cover. Now instead of simply hacking through the growth blocking their way, they selectively cut leaves and branches and affixed them to their uniforms with tightly cinched belts. Up close they looked a bit ridiculous, like the odd crabs that stuck bits of kelp and sea anemones to their shells, but from a distance, it would be harder for the Ravidians to see a human shape.

"We need to get a closer look at the compound. Voorus, QuiTai," Kyam gestured for them to follow. Despite Voorus' fuming, Kyam couldn't seem to overcome his natural leadership. How he'd controlled that instinct around her was a mystery to QuiTai.

"She doesn't need to come along," Voorus said.

"She's Ponongese."

QuiTai guessed what Kyam was thinking and nodded. It was refreshing to work with a smart man.

Unfortunately, Voorus needed it spelled out for him. "So?"

Kyam explained in a patient tone, even though she saw his jaw muscles clench from the effort. "If the Ravidians see us and come to investigate, we'll sacrifice her so that they won't know Thampurians are on the island."

"Oh. Well. Yes. Of course."

While QuiTai tried to stop her eye roll and loud sigh, Kyam glanced at her and raised his eyebrows. Even when they were at odds, they were still in agreement.

Kyam dropped to his hands and knees and crawled forward. The sandy soil clung to QuiTai's hands as she followed him. The machete in her sarong's waistband clapped against her thigh. By the time she, Kyam, and Voorus reached the last low growing plants, they were using their elbows to slither along.

In the water at the end of a small, rocky beach, a small fishing boat bobbed on the waves.

Two Ravidians stood near the ocean. They held odd contraptions similar to the one their countryman wielded in the guard tower. The Ravidians watched thirty or so Ponongese: some children and the rest adults. Guessing from the size of the village, there were many more she couldn't see. They were probably inside the compound.

Anyone inside will have to be left behind.

It pained her to accept that, but she could only do what was possible.

The Ponongese and Ravidians were on a massive stone outcropping that rose about twenty feet above the ocean. Slick, rusty algae clung tenaciously to the rocks. Big waves slammed into the rocks and sent plumes of spray high into the air.

Eons before the plantation existed, waves eroded the pitted rock to form deep tide pools where crabs, anemones, and barnacles gathered. During high tide, the water level rose fifteen or twenty feet in the dark crevices and spilled over the rock. Bigger fish and squid followed silvery schools of smaller fish into the tide pools as the water rose. They had been fertile fishing grounds for her people. Similar plantations on Ponong dammed the natural tide pools so that the briny water – and the blue medusozoa they bred in the pools – couldn't escape into the sea.

The tide pools reflected the blue sky and puffy gray clouds, but even in daylight, they should have glowed with faint blue light emitted from the medusozoa. There was no sign of it. The pools had to be full of sea wasps.

Two Ponongese women walked toward each other on a narrow path between pools, both with their attention focused down. They didn't see each other coming as they tossed small fish into the water. QuiTai held her breath as one slipped, and then caught herself.

When the two women met, there was little room to turn around. QuiTai often heard plantation workers laugh about 'swimming in the green,' their term for falling into a pool of medusozoa. Since the green light medusozoa had no stingers, it wasn't dangerous. On hot days, even though they weren't supposed to, many plantation workers took quick dips in the terrace pools. Blue light medusozoa had stingers, so no one willingly went into their pools.

One woman rested her basket of fish on her hip and balanced carefully as she turned with little steps. From that distance, QuiTai could see the terror on her face. Every Ponongese was still as if they held their collective breath.

A huge wave broke over the edge of the pool, flinging water high overhead and knocking the first woman sideways into the pool. As she screamed, the Ponongese rushed forward. The woman who had been turning dropped her basket and wailed. She fell to her knees and tried to grab the fallen woman. Other Ponongese hurried to her side.

QuiTai forced her attention from the Ponongese to the two Ravidians guarding them. When one turned toward the commotion, QuiTai saw that he wore a backpack with a glass tank full of small medusozoa below his boney neck frill. The creatures were mesmerizing as they floated placidly. Long, bright orange threadlike stingers, four and five times the length of their white translucent bodies, trailed below them.

"Get back to work." The sunburned Ravidian QuiTai had seen in the Red Happiness used the butt of his contraption to hit the Ponongese man who stood watching the scene.

As the others pulled the woman out of the pool, a proud, broad-hipped Ponongese woman stared him down. The Ravidian lifted his gun and pumped something along the side: The woman backed away with her hand held out before her, as if it could protect her. She looked over her shoulder the woman they'd pulled out of the pool. A man shook his head.

QuiTai closed her eyes for a moment. Maybe PhaNyan had died that quickly too. It would have been a blessing.

"Did she drown?" Voorus asked.

"Sea wasps," Kyam said.

At least her people weren't chained. As the death of the woman who fell into the tide pool proved, the Ravidians didn't need to resort to that. It would make the plan she was forming a little easier, but it was still going to be nearly impossible to pull off.

Voorus turned to QuiTai. "And you say they can hit us with them from inside the compound too?"

The gate to the compound was shut. Even if it had been open, there was still the guard in the tower to consider. She noticed he had no tank on his back, but a thick black coil ran from the side of his gun. She envisioned a large tank full of sea wasps in the center of the tower, which would explain why he walked so close to the sides as he made his rounds.

Her eyes narrowed as she returned her gaze to the compound. A long, gently sloping lawn, bare of any ornamental plants, stretched from the compound wall to the tide pools. Without anything to use as cover, the Ravidian in the tower would have a clear shot at the Thampurians if they tried to rush the compound. They'd be safe from him they drew close enough to the walls, though.

She stared at the lawn.

What's his range from that tower?

Could the Thampurians get within thirty feet before they were in danger? Twenty? She tried to picture how far from PhaNyan's body had been from the back wall of the compound.

She shook her head. The Ravidians near the tide pools could shoot the Thampurians from behind even if the one in the tower couldn't hit them.

Something about the scene made QuiTai's forehead furrow. The two Ravidian guards could be seen by anyone on a passing skiff. It didn't make sense that they would stand so near the Ponongese, who could theoretically rush them en masse. That meant something.

The one in the tower can't shoot as far as the tide pools! That's why they have to risk being seen!

All she had to do was convince the Thampurians to draw the Ravidian guards away from the tide pools.

The corner of her mouth curved.

"I take it you've seen enough," Kyam whispered. Voorus answered, but she knew the question was for her. She gave a brief nod that she knew he saw.

CHAPTER 17: ESCAPE FROM THE ISLAND

They crawled back to the waiting soldiers. "We will wait for nightfall," Voorus said.

QuiTai stepped forward "No. Attack now." At nightfall, the Ponongese would probably be herded into the compound. She wanted them as close to the beach as possible.

"What? Who are you to – ?"

Kyam said, "Despite our differences, I'll admit Lady QuiTai has proven insightful today. At least listen to her suggestion." He would pay for supporting her later, but he had to know the consequences already.

Voorus folded his arms across his chest. "Then go ahead, snake. Tell me your plan."

"Take your men back to the compound wall. The Ravidian in the tower can't see this side of it, and the ones on the beach can't see around the side. Move quickly to the compound's front gate and get inside."

He seemed to seriously consider her idea. "The Ravidians on the beach will see us and give out a warning."

"Yes, but the wall will protect you from the guard in the

tower, and the two along the beach can't shoot that far upslope." At least, she hoped they couldn't. "That will give you cover until you're inside the compound. You'll be most vulnerable then, so attack the tower." Voorus frowned. QuiTai went on, urgently, "Look at the way it's designed. The Ravidian there will have a hard time shooting straight down, so you'll be somewhat safe once you get directly below him. Cover your faces: he'll aim for them as you come up the ladder."

"That's a suicide mission," he said softly. He stared at the compound. Then his eyebrows rose as if he'd seen the wisdom of her plan and was astonished to find himself in agreement.

"I heard that Thampurian soldiers were brave. For king and country and so on." She reined in her sarcasm. "Once you have the tower, you'll have a weapon to use against the other two Ravidians, and you'll have complete control of the compound. So you'll have to move quickly to secure it before the other two Ravidians reach the gate."

"But what about the Ponongese?"

She wasn't about to tell him that she planned to take care of them. "How thoughtful of you to worry about the safety of my people, major." He looked startled. "But I'm sure your primary focus here is to secure the compound and capture the Ravidians. After all, the Ponongese are your colonial citizens, but the Ravidians are the sworn enemies of Thampur."

Several of the soldiers murmured agreement. Even Voorus nodded emphatically. Kyam, however, seemed unconvinced.

"We can take out that tower, major," one of the soldiers said.

Now that they could see a plan of action, the younger soldiers were ready to go. QuiTai could feel the surge of their adrenaline around her. Where they had once been hot, tired men, now they were soldiers, infused with the will to fight.

"The Ravidians have spilled enough Thampurian blood," Kyam said.

Voorus drew back. "Are you suggesting we back away from this fight, Zul?"

"Caution – "

"How typical of the intelligence services. You cower in shadows while the army risks their lives."

"You wouldn't even know about this if it weren't for me," Kyam said.

At least he realized the mess was his fault.

Playing the peacekeeper, QuiTai coughed quietly. "Gentlemen. We risk discovery with every moment that passes. This situation calls for decisive action." She nodded respectfully at Voorus. "I believe that's your department, major?"

"Indeed it is." He spun around and gestured for his men to draw close.

While he discussed the plan with them, QuiTai and Kyam hung back.

Voorus motioned his men to follow him. "All right. Let's go!"

As Voorus led his men back toward the compound wall, Kyam cast one last glance over his shoulder at QuiTai. He looked concerned and angry.

"You don't owe anyone anything. Leave now, before it gets too dangerous," he said. "Run. Hide."

"I've never been fast enough to outrun my conscience."

She pressed her palms together and inclined her head in a slight bow.

He shook his head in resignation. Then he bowed, deeply respectful.

Under any other circumstances, she wouldn't have let the moment end like this.

When his gaze met hers, his eyes were full of pleas, but he spoke none of them as he suddenly turned and rushed to follow the soldiers.

They were both too fiercely patriotic to work together for long, and too jaded to be good for each other. Still, it would have been – no. She had no time for regrets right now. They were something to be meditated upon during the long hours of the night when there were no other distractions.

As soon as the Ravidian guards left the beach and headed for the compound, QuiTai would move. For now, all she had could do was wait for chaos. She squatted down, put the tip of her machete into the sand, and twirled it back and forth.

The Ponongese at the tide pools set aside their baskets of fish. They formed lines from the pools to the edge of the rock. Their guards drew together to talk. While they kept their devices aimed at the Ponongese, they clearly weren't concerned about anything.

It always seems to take longer when you're waiting.

She crept forward as far as she dared. She couldn't see the Thampurians.

The Ravidian in the tower walked a circuit.

The Ponongese at the front of the line drew ocean water in the bucket. He passed it down the line. Another group bailed water out of the pool. QuiTai knew little about raising medusozoa, but she had a bad feeling this might be their last chore before heading back into the compound.

Come on, Voorus. You should be there by now.

She shifted her weight to keep her feet from going to sleep.

Finally, she spied the blue of a Thampurian uniform jacket in the jungle near the compound wall. Their movements looked quick, but it seemed to take forever for the soldiers to reach the corner.

She glanced up at the Ravidian in the tower. He looked directly down at the compound's front gate. She chewed her bottom lip. The soldiers couldn't possibly see the guard in the tower from their hiding place. Thankfully, they hung back.

QuiTai checked the guards. One of them patted the other one on the shoulder as he laughed.

This is like waiting in the wings for my cue. I wish I knew what it was.

The Ravidian guard shouted something to the Ponongese and gestured with his weapon. The Ponongese started walking away from the tide pools in two lines. The Thampurians still hadn't moved.

"Remember me as a fool, Kyam Zul," she muttered as she tucked the machete into the back of her sarong.

She ambled out of the jungle onto the beach. The Ravidian in the guard tower shouted and pointed at her. With her hands spread before her, she continued her slow approach. The Ponongese muttered and exchanged glances.

The Ravidian guards turned toward her and started pumping their weapons. QuiTai braced herself for pain. She was going to die.

Come on Voorus! Go! Go! Go!

A bell rang.

The guards swung their weapons toward the compound.

"Intruders!" The sunburned guard ran for the compound. The other one cursed and followed.

QuiTai waved frantically to the Ponongese villagers. "Everyone follow me!" But the villagers seemed too stunned to move. QuiTai picked up a small boy and balanced him on her hip. "Now! Move!" She didn't wait to find out who would listen. She ran along the beach, headed for the lagoon. Secrecy wasn't important now, speed was.

She heard footsteps behind her on the rocky beach.

From behind her, a woman wailed, "But my family is still inside the compound."

Why were there never any good answers? She'd bragged to Kyam that she was willing to do the dirty work for the greater good, but where would she begin to pick whom to save and whom to sacrifice? Just as she had done with the werewolves... She could blame Petrof for misleading her, but the choice had been hers. It wasn't so much a case of damned if you do, damned if you don't, she decided. It was more like being so mired in hell that even your best intentions reeked of evil.

"If we go back for them, none of you will escape," QuiTai shouted.

"But this is our home," a gasping man said.

A deep woman's voice said, "Hold on, Wolf Slayer."

Shouts and screams carried to her from the compound. As much as she hated to, QuiTai stopped running. She turned.

The proud woman with broad hips and the gap between her front teeth squatted. So did many of the other villagers. At any moment, the Thampurian soldiers could come after them, but nothing would stop her people from telling a story. QuiTai stifled the groan of frustration rising inside her, put down the boy in her arms, and squatted too. Patience was key in the middle of chaos.

This is going to be a damn short story, so don't get too comfortable.

"We don't have much time. There are only three Ravidians. After the Thampurian soldiers kill them, they will come after you. We have to get moving again," QuiTai said.

The villagers asked, "Why will the Thampurians come after us?"

QuiTai cast a worried look back at the tide pools. No one was coming, yet, but she could hear a distant fight. "It's the sea wasps in the tide pool. They don't want anyone to know about them, even other Thampurians, and they'll stop at nothing to keep it a secret."

"What else am I going to do for a living but work a plantation?" a man said. "I'll keep their secret. Who am I going to tell?"

The gap-toothed woman gave the man a sour look as her eyebrow rose. "Are you an idiot, RhiFa? Do you want our children to fall into one of those pools and die like RhiNyan just did? Or is your memory that short? How about the Korours? Have you already forgotten their bodies tied to those stakes in the middle of the compound?"

"Who are the Korours?" QuiTai asked before she could stop herself.

So much for the short version.

She listened intently for sounds of the fight for the compound as the woman began her tale.

"The Korours were the plantation owners. The wife was Ponongese. That's why they didn't mix with the other Thampurians. They treated her like... well, you know how

Thampurians are. When those bastard Ravidians took over, they stuck those sea wasp stingers on her and the children, then washed them off with vinegar, and did it over and over again and made Mr. Korours watch. Us too. I don't think I'll ever forget those screams." She stopped to catch her breath. "I'm leaving this cay, and I don't care if I ever see it again. No child of mine is growing up on this cursed land." She spat in the sand.

QuiTai put her hand over her heart. "They will be mourned, auntie…"

"I'm RhiHanya." The woman rose. "Well? Are we escaping or not, grandmother QuiTai?"

QuiTai sent a brief prayer of thanks to the goddesses for sending her RhiHanya.

She came to her feet. "You know who I am."

"I called you Wolf Slayer, didn't I? Even out here, we know what happens on the big island. And I would follow you anywhere." RhiHanya swept past QuiTai and marched up the beach with the grandeur of a diva.

QuiTai cast thanks to her reputation. She smiled gently at the little boy she'd carried away from the tide pools. "Can you ride piggyback, little brother?"

He scrambled onto her back. His thin arms encircled her neck as he hooked his ankles around her waist. She jogged quickly after RhiHanya. To her relief, many of the others followed with quiet determination and haste. All it took was one person to have faith.

They reached the lagoon and piled into the outrigger fishing boats. QuiTai winced as the boats sank close to the waterline under the increasing weight. But no one who had followed her would be left behind.

Adults grabbed oars and stroked hard for the sea, while the children huddled together in the center. As soon as the boats were clear of the lagoon, the fishermen in the group stepped forward to set the sails.

QuiTai's feeling of impending doom didn't lift. Their escape had been too easy. How had Kyam fared? She shook her head: Now was not the time to worry about him. He had his own end of their new bargain to tend to, and she had hers.

"We're being followed!" someone shouted.

She looked to the sea and her chest tightened. A flat head with a barbed snout skimmed quickly at the surface of the water; a long, sinuous body stretched behind it. The sun glinted off the shimmering scales.

"Row for Ponong! We must reach land before the sea dragons reach us!" QuiTai gripped an oar and rowed hard.

The villagers threw themselves into rowing with co-ordinated speed as the fishermen called out a steady beat. As if they were riding to war with a neighboring cay, they put their all strength into flying across the water.

Another sea dragon's gleaming coils broke the surface. The fishermen sped up their tempo.

In the slow setting of the sun, the outriggers closed the distance between Cay Rhi and the island of Ponong, the sea dragons gaining. Sea water stung the palms of QuiTai's raw hands but she kept rowing. She couldn't bear to look at the land. She fixed her gaze on the steady movement of sea dragons, now seven of them, drawing ever closer.

The boat jolted. QuiTai wondered if a sea dragon had come underneath to tip them over, but when villagers began to clamber over the side of the boat and run through the shallow water, she realized they had made landfall. She pulled the boy once more onto her back and waded through the waves. The verdant mountains of Ponong rose before her. The sand ebbed under QuiTai's feet as waves broke around her ankles. Then the sand was hard and she knew they'd made it to shore.

"Into the jungle! Quick!" She didn't need to urge them; they were already running up the sand dunes for the cover of the jungle. As she followed, she heard the sea dragons beach themselves and begin to shift back into their human forms.

If they could evade the Thampurian soldiers until the sun

set, they would be okay. Ponongese eyes saw much better in the dark. If all else failed, they had their fangs. The Thampurian soldiers had to know their silly laws wouldn't protect them now.

QuiTai hacked a path with her machete until her lungs felt as if they would burst. She wasn't used to running with weight on her back. Her knees burned. She wasn't sure if the person crashing through the jungle behind her was Ponongese or Thampurian, so she ran as if the devil himself were on her heels.

The land sloped steeply upward. She pushed blindly through the plants. Then a hand grabbed her and yanked her back. Fangs drawn, she turned.

RhiHanya put her finger to her lips and pointed down. QuiTai's next step would have sent her tumbling into a small ravine. RhiHanya pointed inland. "You keep going. I'll grab any stragglers. You have to lead, grandmother."

Too exhausted to argue, QuiTai nodded and began to find her way along the rim of the ravine.

CHAPTER 18: PETROF

By nightfall, QuiTai's side ached. Her arms were numb from using the machete, her hands sore and blistered. The scab over the wolf bite on her ankle seeped pus onto the wet bandage around it.

She had to put the boy down. He didn't complain. No one did. They simply pushed forward. Their little group drew closer together, but it was too dark to tell if everyone was with them. She had no idea if anyone had been captured. To her relief, RhiHanya appeared, straggling behind the group. They exchanged weary, grim smiles.

The sounds of the pursuing soldiers grew fainter. She hoped they were good and lost in the jungle.

The sound of rushing water grew stronger as the Ponongese moved downslope. Even in the dark, QuiTai began to recognize their surroundings. She cursed herself: In her mental stupor, she'd led them straight to the Jupoli Gorge. The Devil's den.

She was tempted to redirect them upslope, back into the jungle, but they might cross paths with the Thampurian soldiers. And she couldn't ask them to keep marching without food or water.

She swore she felt a low growl down her spine. She stopped and listened with all her body. Then she squatted with her back to a tree trunk and motioned for the others to make a ring around her. She swallowed hard as the growl's vibrations grew stronger. The villagers glanced around as if they felt it too.

Petrof had found her.

QuiTai milked her fangs and spread her venom liberally over her wrists and throat. Several of the villagers noticed and did the same.

She spoke quickly: He could attack at any moment, and she had to make sure her people got all the information.

"I know you are tired, my aunties and uncles. You have been brave, and it's been an honor to be your guide. We have escaped much danger, but more lies ahead. Some is evil that I have brought on myself, and I must face it alone." She nodded at RhiHanya, silently appointing her as the leader. "If you follow this trail along the rim of the gorge, you will eventually hear an engine to your right. To your left, there will be a stone bridge over the gorge. Cross the bridge. On the other side, soon, you will see a big house. Cat people from the Lisudtan Islands live there. One is named LiHoun. Tell them I have sent you, and they will see that you have a place to sleep and food to eat. Talk to no one else; be seen by no others. Trust no Thampurian except the one called Kyam Zul. He distracted the Thampurian soldiers tonight so that I could help you to escape, and he will pay dearly for that from his own kind. Always remember and honor his sacrifice."

Slow clapping filled the air.

"Such a valiant speech, QuiTai," Petrof said as he stepped from behind a flowering tree. "Is it from one of your plays?"

He pushed the plunger on an instant jellylantern and shook it. "Ah, a little light thrown on the subject." Like the Thampurians, he couldn't see as well in the dark as she could. The jellylantern actually made it harder for her to see, something he probably knew.

QuiTai motioned the Ponongese to rise with her.

"Did you think I wouldn't smell you?" He lifted his nose to the air. "Especially when you're so fragrant with fear." Then he turned to the Ponongese. "Run away." He bared his teeth and snapped at them.

"Should we go?" RhiHanya asked QuiTai.

"Yes. Go to LiHoun. But tell him that I will need him."

"Tell LiHoun that she is already dead," Petrof said.

"What about him?" RhiHanya jutted her chin at Petrof.

A wry smile crossed QuiTai's lips. "I'm the Wolf Slayer," she said.

The Ponongese edged away uncertainly. QuiTai wished they would move faster; she didn't understand why they hung back. RhiHanya was the last to go, and she looked over her shoulder many times as she drew away.

QuiTai forced concern for them from her mind and focused on Petrof. The villagers would survive without her; the safety of the entire world did not rest on her shoulders. The deadliest threat was to her alone, and he stood before her.

"Tell me, my little bitch, what did the Ravidians smuggle onto this island? I'm sure you know, just as I'm sure that you decided to cheat me out of my take."

"Nothing you could sell. Not without bringing the entire colonial government and Thampurian military down on you with a vengeance."

Petrof circled. "You think you're so smart, but you don't know everything. I'm good friends with the colonial government right now, or at least a high-placed official. He paid quite handsomely to make sure you couldn't help Kyam Zul."

"Someone paid you to kill me? Is that what this is about? Then why take Jezereet?" Matters were more complicated than she had thought. Someone thought she was dangerous enough to want her dead. That someone also probably hoped she'd be enslaved with the other Ponongese on Cay Rhi. They wouldn't react well to her escape.

"That greedy whore sold you out for a vial of black lotus. She knew I would kill you. She opened the window so I'd know you were there. She's dead because she wouldn't let me finish strangling you until she was paid. That's all that whore wanted. And you thought she loved you." He sneered. "No one loves you, QuiTai. Not even your own people."

Get angry, she thought. His anger was the key to her survival. The thing she feared most was his wolf form. She'd seen what a wolf could do to a Ponongese. There was no way she could move fast enough to strike him with her fangs before he mortally wounded her. She had to provoke him into attacking her while still in his human form.

Get angry and grab my throat, and then we will talk of love.

"All your dumb dogs are hanging from the fortress ramparts, Petrof. Food for gulls until they rot and fall into the water. Then they're shark bait. That's hardly the heroic end werewolves sing about in your pathetic drinking songs."

"Shut up!"

"There's nothing sadder than a lone cur eating garbage from the gutter."

"I prefer the fresh, juicy liver of a young girl." Petrof held the instant jellylantern near his face so she could see him smack his lips. "Your daughter was tasty, QuiTai."

Rage washed over her with blistering heat. Old wounds ripped open in her soul. Harsher than the sea wasp's sting, the memory of her daughter's dying screams stabbed her heart. Tears poured down her cheeks.

She'd forgiven every betrayal. She'd handed him everything he'd ever asked for. She'd cared for him.

He hurt my QuiZhun.

She lunged at him with the machete.

His hand shot out and gripped her throat. Her machete fell to the ground as he lifted her from the ground and shook her.

Petrof's grin mocked her. "Oh, QuiTai, QuiTai, my favorite little snake." He put the instant jellylantern close to her face, nearly blinding her. "Your lips are turning blue. Soon your tongue will bloat. I'd eat it first, but then you wouldn't be able to beg.

The fearless hatred, so quickly roused, drained from her as she struggled for breath.

Emotion led me into this mess. Only thinking can save me.

She thought desperately for something to buy time while her venom sank into his skin. "The Oracle! I'll tell you – " Her voice was a harsh whisper.

QuiTai felt the charge in the air. His eyes went feral.

"I'm not falling for that anymore."

QuiTai gasped for air as his grip tightened. She sucked on her fangs, filling her mouth with venom. Black spots slid across her vision. She spat in his face.

"You stupid bitch!" He smeared her spit off his cheek with the back of the hand holding the jellylantern. She kicked as hard as she could: the jellylantern flew from his grasp and shattered on the ground. Her mind swam. Her lungs were ready to burst. She was going to pass out. Gathering her last reserve of clarity, she filled her mouth with more venom and spat at him again.

He screamed as he dropped her, and clapped his hands to his eye. "What did you do? It burns!"

QuiTai doubled over and gasped for air. Tears welled in her eyes as her venom connected to his nerves. He made a wild grab for her, but she stumbled away.

"I can't fucking see, and my face is going numb."

He didn't need to tell her. She could faintly feel everything he did, even his rising panic.

Petrof staggered like a drunk as he clutched his face. He tripped over a vine and fell to his knees.

QuiTai drew in deep breaths through her nose. She felt cruel and powerful as his fear overwhelmed his anger. "The Oracle is real, Petrof, and you're going to meet her. Of course, you have many times before, even if you don't remember." She kicked his shoulder as hard as she could. He slumped to his side. She punched his jaw, sending him sprawling. Then she dropped her full weight onto his chest and pinned his elbows to the ground with her knees. She could see every step. She knew exactly what needed to be done, and how it would all play out. The clarity was exhilarating.

"Never say I go back on my word, Petrof." She held up the vial of black lotus. "This is the Oracle. Can you see? Maybe if I put it in front of your good eye."

He tried to spit at her, but it dribbled down his chin.

She unscrewed the top of the vial. "One part vapor, another part venom. Although the black lotus I used isn't exactly vapor, so I'm not sure if it will work right. This could be extremely painful for you. Hmm." As if deep in thought, she put her finger to her chin. "I'll tell you what. You tell me who hired you to kill me, and I won't force this on you. Or you can refuse, and we'll find out how much pain the Oracle can put you through. I'll be sure to take note of every scream. Is that a deal?"

It was a lie, of course. Black lotus never brought pain, and her venom only paralyzed, but from the fear pumping through him, he didn't know that.

"Fuck you."

QuiTai gripped his jaw. He thrashed back and forth. She crawled up his chest and trapped his head between her knees. He punched her ribs and tried to throw her off him. Then he clenched his jaw. No matter how hard she tried, she couldn't pry it open.

Another punch knocked her off balance enough that she had to put a hand down to steady herself. Pain sliced through her palm. She lifted her hand: a glowing shard of the broken instant jellylantern glowed across the sea wasp scar. She gripped the slippery chunk and ripped it from her skin. Blood spilled from the wound.

Petrof's shifting energy gathered. He began to change.

QuiTai shoved the shard of glass into his throat.

As he howled in outrage, she poured the black lotus mixture into his open mouth and clamped her bleeding hand over it.

Petrof grabbed her neck again with both hands, but his fingers couldn't keep their grip. He looked at his hand as if he'd never seen anything so terrible before.

Forcing his mouth open was easier this time. She leaned close enough that her lips brushed his while she milked the last drops of her venom into his mouth.

"I tried to be exact about the dose, because you know how much I hate sloppy work, but it's pretty much a guess at this point how long it will take all this venom to work through your system. It could take hours. I, of course, would prefer it take days."

She tore strips from his shirt and bound each of his forearms tightly. Another strip bound her blood-soaked hand.

"What are you doing?" His voice broke.

"Making sure you don't bleed to death. I can't possibly carry your entire body back to the den by myself, after all."

Real fear opened his eyes. It quickly changed to anger.

"I kept you alive, you ungrateful bitch! The man from the colonial government paid us to kill the Qui clan. You were supposed to die too, but I protected you! And for that, they tortured me. They said they'd let me go if I killed you or gave them the secret of the Oracle. But you – oh no, you wouldn't tell me. They were going to torture me again, all because of you!"

The rising terror in his babbling voice would have been enough to convince her, but she felt the depth of his horror too. She wasn't about to bargain with him for the name of the man who set the wolves loose on her daughter and family. She would make it her life's work to find out who he was, but without Petrof's help.

QuiTai picked up the machete and slowly wove it back and forth in the hypnotizing dance of a snake charmer. She chose her words with great care, so she could relish them when she repeated this story to herself later.

"The paralysis will spread slowly. You'll feel everything, and you'll be conscious for most of it, but you won't be able to move."

"Please, don't." His voice slurred as the venom spread to his tongue.

He had interrupted her story. How very rude.

"You expect mercy from me?"

The fool had a faint glimmer of hope.

"I warned you who I was when we first met." Her face drew into an awful smile. "I am vengeance."

He whimpered as his eyes followed the machete's moving blade.

Now she could finish her story.

"The flies will find you first, and take little nips of your skin while they plant their eggs in you. Birds will peck out your eyes. The land crabs will find you, and when the wind spreads the stink of your blood and fear, the small predators will slink out of the darkness to dine on your flesh. This island will devour you over days, Petrof, and you'll feel every second of it. But before any of that happens, the ants will find you. Millions of them."

His memories crowded into her thoughts as a jumbled rush so violent she almost fell from his chest. Thampurian soldiers laughing as he struggled against a net. A small timbergrass cage at the edge of the jungle where he liked to hunt. Shifting into his human form to plead for mercy. A man Petrof didn't look at holding a bowl of water just beyond her reach. Her tongue felt thick and dry. She wanted that water more than she'd ever wanted anything.

"You promised me the Oracle, Petrof," the man with the water said.

"I need more time."

"Zul is making his move. Bring us the Oracle now, or kill your whore."

"Just a little longer!"

Petrof looked at his arm. It was black. The black moved. She gasped and drew back even though she knew it was his arm, not hers. Her skin prickled under tiny crawling feet. She wanted to tear off her clothes and run. She took deep breaths. It was his fear, not hers. She wasn't the one in danger. It wasn't real.

She brought the blade down on his forearm.

He screamed and screamed as she hacked through the bone. His pupils, once large, imploded to pinpoints. He convulsed and sputtered bloody foam.

When he spoke, it was in the voice of the Oracle. And it only confirmed what she already knew.

QuiTai stumbled toward the Devil's den with the hem of her sarong gripped in her hand. Blood dripped through the fabric onto her toes. Rivulets of sweat pasted her hair to her face. Petrof's rage and fear coursed through her. She wanted to cry from the exhaustion.

The Thampurian military would continue to hunt her down. If Kyam were still alive, he was probably in chains, because they had to blame someone for the Ponongese escape from Cay Rhi. Oh, and someone in the colonial government wanted her dead and a Zul was somehow involved; she mustn't forget that. Still, her heart was curiously light as she crossed the timbergrass bridge.

Despite the stink in the Devil's house, she drew in a deep breath and smiled with satisfaction. It was good to be alive.

She pushed back the sliding door that led to Petrof's room. She climbed onto his bed and balanced on the pillows as she faced the intricate puzzle on the headboard. She had all night to move the hundreds of pieces in the right combination to reveal Petrof's safe. The puzzle really was a marvel of craftsmanship. She'd enjoyed working out its secrets over the past year.

Piece by piece, the picture formed. Blonde and dark woods combined to form the Devil's chop. He was predictable.

The panel slid away to reveal the safe.

She took Petrof's dismembered hands from her sarong and pressed them to the biolock.

The lock opened.

Someday, I'll tell Kyam it worked... No. It's the Devil's business.

Gold and jewels spilled onto the blood-splattered pillows under her feet. She tossed aside his hands and gathered his fortune together: It wasn't enough to do everything she planned, but it was a good start. Petrof never had any vision; hers was as vast as the sea.

Chapter 19: The Devil

QuiTai sank into Petrof's ornately carved high-backed chair. It felt good to sit. She was so weary.

She heard the footsteps of a lone person on the timbergrass bridge. Relief spread through her. Still, she propped the machete handle-first into the corner of the chair with the point behind her heart, so she would only have to push against the blade if her visitor were a Thampurian soldier. She would not be taken prisoner.

LiHoun stepped into the room. His eyes widened when he saw her on Petrof's throne.

"Greetings, favored uncle. Have you eaten?" QuiTai asked.

His gaze darted around the room, pausing briefly on the discarded hands. No matter where he tried to look, though, his eyes seemed drawn to the blood smeared down her blouse and sarong. "I have, auntie. And you?"

She supposed it would be rude to mention how distracted he sounded. "Yes. Thank you for asking."

He seemed concerned. "Are you... well?"

"This blood is not mine."

LiHoun smiled, showing his few teeth. "I am greatly relieved to hear that."

Perhaps she wasn't as friendless as she'd thought.

"I take it that the Ponongese reached your home," she said.

"Yes. The woman RhiHanya" – he traced a curvaceous figure in the air – "led me to where they'd left you with the wolf." His catlike eyes slid back to the curled fingers of the dismembered hands on the floor. "I followed the blood trail here."

"Excellent work, as always. Forgive my terrible manners, uncle. I don't even have a kur to share with you. But I invite you to stick your finger into this rice bowl." She tossed a heavy bag of coins to him.

For such a bandy-legged old man, he caught it easily. "Rice, and meat."

"Tomorrow, before dawn, the Ponongese in your house must be spirited away where no one can find them. If they wish to live on one of the outer cays, so be it. Buy them anything they might need: fishing boats, food, clothes, cooking utensils, anything within reason. Or if they need more time to decide, take them to my estate. But do not let them stay on this island."

He bowed. "I understand."

"I have another request, but it has me in a bit of a personal quandary. The soldiers who tried to stop me and the other Ponongese from escaping Cay Rhi are still somewhere in the western jungle. As of this moment, the colonial government has no idea if they found us or not, and it is to my advantage to keep my enemies guessing for as long as possible."

"Do you want me to hunt down the soldiers and kill them?"

QuiTai grimaced. "I gave my word to Kyam Zul that I would harm no more Thampurian soldiers. An unfortunate promise given the current situation, but once word gets out that your word is no good, business suffers. No, I must honor that pact."

"So you want them taken alive?"

Her forefinger slowly tapped against the arm of the chair. "Keeping prisoners is too much trouble. They're always trying to escape. The soldiers are sea dragons, so we can't simply maroon them on a monolith stone fifty miles from shore. They'd make it back to Levapur before you did. And I have no desire to put you in greater peril, favored uncle."

He pressed his hands together and bowed.

"So they can't be killed, can't be allowed to report to the colonial government, can't be held prisoner... Well, you see my difficulty."

"It is a puzzle," LiHoun admitted. His tongue darted out to wet his lips as he squatted. "While you decide, perhaps you'd like to hear a story? This is a whole suckling pig for your bowl."

With a satisfied sigh, she moved the machete and settled back in the throne. "I do so enjoy your stories."

"Late last night, the Ravidians locked the gate of the compound on Cay Rhi and stayed inside the walls. We were able to sneak over to the tide pools and take the sea wasps without being seen. It was an elegant operation, to use one of your favorite phrases, auntie." He inclined his head toward her. She returned the gesture. "The people at your estate received two large glass containers of the sea wasps early this morning."

QuiTai nodded.

LiHoun hesitated before continuing. "I don't know if you're aware, but PhaNyan is dead. Since he didn't come with us, we chose to leave his body behind. We were afraid its disappearance would raise questions, and you said that speed was vital."

"Of course. I trust you to make wise decisions. Little brother PhaNyan was careless." She would miss PhaNyan, but there was no sense dwelling on his death. The soldiers were a more pressing concern, and she had to decide now what to do about them.

Her fingers curled over the arm of the chair. She could understand why Petrof had liked sitting in it. She felt positively regal in such a throne. Setting was so important for a scene.

Petrof. The Devil. She felt his rage and fear. He was still alive, and every sound and shadow of the jungle brought him closer to complete madness. She relished it.

How frightened they all were of the jungle – the werewolves and the Thampurians.

Her lips curved.

"I have decided how to deal with the soldiers, uncle LiHoun. Hire a dozen of the swiftest hunters to dress in the clothes of the escaped Ponongese and lure the soldiers deeper into the interior of the island along the game trails, keeping far away from any villages and the coastline. Warn the hunters that they'll be killed if they're caught. Offer them enough money to make it a merry chase that will ideally continue for several days. Once the soldiers are thoroughly lost, the hunters may leave them to their own devices. If they find their way back to Levapur, I'll have enough of a head start on them that their report won't matter. If the soldiers remain lost in the jungle forever, well, I might have promised Kyam Zul that I wouldn't harm any Thampurians by my actions." She steepled her fingers under her chin. "But the Devil made no such bargain about harm by inaction."

LiHoun glanced again at Petrof's hands. He seemed confused. "I thought the Devil was killed tonight. If I am wrong, grandmother QuiTai, forgive this old fool for telling a poor story."

In the jungle, after she had taken Petrof's hands, he had said in a voice not his own, *You are the Devil.* The goddess had spoken; the Oracle was never wrong.

QuiTai spread her bloodied hands and smiled at LiHoun.

"The Devil lives," she said.

THE END

THE STORY CONTINUES...

The Devil Incarnate picks up where *The Devil's Concubine* left off:

There's no rest for the wicked, especially for the Devil. While QuiTai recovers from her last adventure, Levapur is turning into a police state. The Pongonese are pushed to the brink of rebellion against their colonial masters, the Thampurians – but who is behind it, and why? As the new Devil, QuiTai must wield her power and use her brilliant mind to outsmart her mysterious nemesis before a bloody uprising erupts.

CHAPTER I: A PLAN

The morning QuiTai awoke completely sane, she knew Petrof was dead.

He'd killed her family. He'd eaten her daughter. And he'd tried to kill her too. Three days wasn't nearly long enough for him to suffer, but it would have to do.

Her arms, legs, stomach, and face were raw where she'd scratched at imaginary ants that crawled over her skin on millions of tiny, prickling feet. She hadn't been taught how to shield her mind from the empathic connection with Petrof through her venom. Some would call it sacrilege to try. The goddess Hunt decreed that the Ponongese should feel their prey's suffering, so they'd deliver a quick, merciful death, but QuiTai had enjoyed sharing every moment of Petrof's horror and descent into madness as the jungle consumed him.

Now that her mind was free of him, she had business to attend to. The first step was to get out of bed. Her thick, wavy black hair had come undone from its traditional braid, and every wrinkle in her sarong reminded her of how sour her skin was, but the steady drum of monsoon rain against the shack's tin roof made her want to pull the sheet over her head and drift back into sleep.

The inland shack she'd withdrawn to was smaller than Kyam Zul's apartment, too small to divide into rooms. The shack's only bed was a low, wide cot of woven leather strips. The thin bedroll she'd put on top of it hadn't done much to smooth out the lumps. Days before, she'd told Kyam that her bed had countless pillows, each as comfortable as a lover's lap. There was a bed like that waiting for her, but not on Ponong. She'd have to travel through the mouth of the underworld to reach her hidden estate on the tiny island of Quinong to reach it. The vision of soft sheets tempted her, but she knew there was far too much for her to do in Levapur to run away now.

She forced herself to sit up. Her first step on the bare dirt floor made her wince. The infected werewolf bite on her ankle oozed pus. If she'd been in her right mind the past few days, she would have gathered herbs and cleaned the wound properly. Now it was going to be much harder to heal. Although the weather was soul-sappingly hot, she suspected the dull ache in her bones was the start of a fever.

Each step sent sharp pains up her leg as she hobbled across the room. Three low stools sat around the cooking pit, but she forced herself to stand as she lifted the small iron teapot onto the hook and swung it over the remains of the fire. The fire looked as if it had died, but as she stirred it, bright orange embers glowed in the downy white ashes. She added a small log and a handful of dry leaves. The kindling flamed too quickly to light the log, but the embers she'd banked against it would eventually catch.

There were signs around the shack that hunters had used the remote shelter despite the green symbols painted around the doorway. They hadn't touched her emergency food and water, though. Taboos against violating the trust of communal shelters were stronger inland than they were near Levapur.

While she waited for the water to heat, she went to the doorway and leaned against the threshold. There were no wood screens over the windows. Rain blown inside by gusts of wind turned the dirt floor to mud in places. She combed through her hair knee-length hair and braided it, even though she planned to hobble to the nearby stream and bathe as soon as she had the strength. She didn't consider herself a beautiful woman – not even particularly alluring, despite the many lovers who spouted such nonsense words during their love-making – but she had her vanities. She'd never risk being seen with her hair down as if she were a child, even in this remote place. And she most certainly wouldn't let anyone see her in a wrinkled, filthy sarong.

The shack sat on the north face of Ponong's mother mountain. According to legend, at night the bioluminescent jellyfish floating in mountain's caldera lake cast green light to the stars, but she'd never seen it.

Curious birds with orange heads and bright green breasts watched her from nearby trees, their heads swiveling constantly. From the tracks in the mud and piles of little round black droppings, she guessed a herd of the diminutive island goats had passed this way only a few days before. Perhaps the hunters had been after them, but there was no sign of a kill.

Through a break in the trees, QuiTai looked down into the valley. The wide, shallow river winding between the steep mountain slopes was as gray as the sky. Sheets of rain pocked the surface of the water. She'd seen children play in the river before and knew of two small villages along its banks, but there wasn't a human to be seen there this morning.

Her gaze moved to the smaller mountain across the valley. Agricultural terraces like bands of malachite carved laboriously into the mountain's rock face reached all the way to the peak. The villagers working in the rice paddies would have blended into the scenery if it hadn't been for the pale yellow of their woven hats.

It was a good thing the Thampurians rarely set foot across the Jupoli Gorge Bridge, although they claimed to control the entire Ponong Archipelago. Some day, when they grew brave – or greedier – they might dare to explore the island and discover these and many other forbidden farms. If they thought Levapur was hot and humid, they'd melt in the interior valleys, but the Ponongese couldn't rely on that to keep the Thampurians from stealing the food from their mouths.

She wished nature had provided other deep water routes through the archipelago besides the Ponong Fangs, which separated the island of Ponong from a much smaller island. Or maybe if there hadn't been a natural harbor on the sheltered side of the island, the Thampurians would have left the Ponongese alone. She'd often heard her grandmother ask their gods, "Why us? Why not some other people?"

Gifts from the gods always came with a price.

The whistle of the tea kettle roused her from her thoughts. Although she knew she should drink tiuhon tea to help fight the fever rising in her blood, she chose pale leaves that smelled like fresh grass and sunlight. While it steeped, she went back to the doorway.

Could she be content now that Petrof was dead? Vengeance had robbed her of too much time already. It had made her do unforgivable things. She wanted to let it go, to find peace and move on with her life, but she knew she couldn't. Once people figured out that Petrof was dead and she was still alive, the men who'd hired him to kill her might seek another assassin. She would be foolish to give them the chance. Despite how weary she was of killing, it came down to them or her, and she definitely chose herself.

Taking inventory of her situation, she put into the negative column an ankle that had to be tended to and a colonial militia that would gladly hang her on sight. On the plus side, she was the Devil now. Better than that, she was QuiTai. If there was one thing she excelled at, it was gathering information and digging for the truth. The men who'd hired Petrof didn't stand a chance against her.

She blew a gentle breath over the surface of her tea. Before she tasted it, she glanced at the tin in which it had been stored.

"Maybe the people who stayed here were hunters. Maybe they were hunting me."

To her ears, her voice seemed to crack uncontrollably, like a teenage boy's.

With a flick of her wrist, the tea flew out of the cup and onto the ground outside the shelter. Several of the tiny birds flew down to see if she'd scattered food, then flew back to their perches and scolded her for fooling them.

"How should I find the men who paid Petrof to kill me?" she asked the birds. "Tell me that, and I'll give you crumbs."

Their trust, once lost, seemingly couldn't be restored. If they knew, they kept the answer to themselves. What she needed was some sage advice. A vision. She slumped against the doorway.

Across the valley, mist swirled over the higher mountain peaks like curls of smoke.

Or vapor.

The corners of her mouth curved.

A plan unfolded in her mind.